KING OF
Snowflakes
MICHELE FOGAL

Dreamspinner Press

Published by
DREAMSPINNER PRESS

5032 Capital Circle SW, Suite 2, PMB# 279, Tallahassee, FL 32305-7886 USA
http://www.dreamspinnerpress.com/

King of Snowflakes
© 2014 Michele Fogal.

Cover Art
© 2014 Aaron Anderson.
aaronbydesign55@gmail.com
Cover content is for illustrative purposes only and any person depicted on the cover is a model.

ISBN: 978-1-62798-959-6
Digital ISBN: 978-1-62798-960-2
Library of Congress Control Number: 2014943213
First Edition August 2014

Printed in the United States of America
(∞)
This paper meets the requirements of
ANSI/NISO Z39.48-1992 (Permanence of Paper).

To my first readers, Karen and Claire, for a combined fifty-plus years of reading, discussing, encouraging, and believing.

Acknowledgments

Writing novels can be lonely, but it cannot be done alone. I'm lucky enough to have friends and family who never say that my career choice is crazy or foolish. My grandmother wrote me a note to be delivered only after her death that said, "Please, please, please continue with your writing." She and my mother then funded my first novel writing year. Claire and Karen read everything, sometimes multiple times and without that, and their countless pep talks, I would have given up long ago. Other readers like Rene, Renee, Steph, Roz, Laura, Paulo, Dean, Elan, Kelly, and Patrick kept me going. Erin let me use a spare room for office space and Michael changed everything when he said this story was "still warming" him. Amber gave me music advice and Blanka gave me medical info. Many authors and gay men agreed to be interviewed and shared their wisdom and experiences with me, and Author Divas Rhys Ford and Amy Lane took me under their angelic wings. My husband hugged me countless times and said, "Follow your passion," even though he doesn't read fiction and my "Passion" consumes so many of our resources. My parents think what I'm doing is cool, and my kids laugh when I hide in the bathroom to read, and still think I'm normal. Without all of you I wouldn't have had the strength to open the door that I kept locked for a decade, breathe, and step through it. Your actions, words and belief have changed my life. Thank you so much.

AUTHOR'S NOTE ON SOUNDTRACKS

Music washes away from the soul the dust of everyday life.
~Berthold Auerbach

WHEN YOU'RE in love *and* when you're heartbroken, song lyrics seem like they're talking about your very own soul. The same was true for the West Coast Boys stories. The guys whispered their very strong opinions about what songs spoke to them and for them, and I've tried to listen and include as many as I can. The result is a soundtrack that goes with each story. I've made this as accessible as I know how to by creating a sharable playlist that you can access on my website, michelefogal.com. My hope is that you can listen as you read, and see what these great musicians have to offer to the ongoing story of your own life.

For me, story sweeps up the dust of our lives, moistens it with breath, and grows food for the soul. If this can happen with music, well then, the soul is both washed and fed. Amen to that.

KING OF SNOWFLAKES SOUNDTRACK

"Headphones" by the Mounties

"Somebody That I Used to Know" by Gotye

"Sleep Alone" by Two Door Cinema Club

"Shake It Out" by Florence and the Machine

"Steps on the Path with Summer Evening Ambience (Soothing)" by Music with Nature Sound

"James Bond Theme" by Moby

"Boredom and Joy" by Jets Overhead

"Moves Like Jagger" by Maroon 5

"Desafinado" by Stan Getz

"Fuck You" by CeeLo Green

"Firework" by Katy Perry

"Wide Awake" by Katy Perry

"Suddenly I See" by KT Tunstall

"Fight Test" by The Flaming Lips

"One More Robot/Sympathy 3000-21" by The Flaming Lips

"Yoshimi Battles the Pink Robot, Part 1" by The Flaming Lips

"Yoshimi Battles the Pink Robot, Part 2" by The Flaming Lips

"In the Morning of the Magicians" by The Flaming Lips

"Ego Tripping at the Gates of Hell" by The Flaming Lips

"Are You a Hypnotist??" by The Flaming Lips

"It's Summertime" by The Flaming Lips

"Do You Realize??" by The Flaming Lips

"All We Have Is Now" by The Flaming Lips

"Approaching Pavonis Moon by Balloon (Utopia Planitia)" by The Flaming Lips

CHAPTER 1—SKYLER

SKYLER RESTED his forehead against the cold steel of his locker, closed his eyes for a moment, and then tried again. *Left all the way around, then to fourteen. Right all the way around, then to twenty-four. No, wait... shit.* His combination lock was not normally a problem, but today he just couldn't think straight. He shrugged his backpack back up onto his shoulder, and his recently pierced nipples rubbed on the inside of his stiff button-up shirt. Just one more reminder of Christmas break that made the permalump in his throat swell up again.

As the hallway filled in around him, Skyler could hear the guys all laughing and shouting as they grabbed each other. Was it the team that made it okay for them to touch each other all the time? *Nah, it's not just that.* There were plenty of guys that acted like that that weren't on a team. *Maybe it's just that they feel so comfortable with each other.* There were always gay jokes flying between them, but the playful ass-slapping and groping were in complete contrast to the bubble of space they kept around anyone who actually called themselves gay.

"Hey, Skyler!" The teasing sound of that voice set his teeth into clampdown mode, and his palms started to sweat. "How's your BOYfriend?" There was some chuckling as the school's soccer team moved in around him. It was lunch hour, so they probably weren't going anywhere. *God, not today. Left all the way around to fourteen, right all the way around to twenty-eight.*

"What's the matter? Don't you like me anymore?" Ryan was leaning against the next locker over and grinning at him. Skyler glanced at him. Ryan's shoulder-length hair hung in curving locks around his face and seemed to be full of natural sunny highlights despite the fact that it had been raining in North Vancouver for three months straight. *Nice dye job, asshole.* Sure he was good-looking, but his grin was pure wickedness. Christmas had more than fulfilled any attraction to that sort of guy. The sparkle in his eyes just lit a spark of rage in Skyler's stomach.

"Just because I'm gay doesn't mean I'm into YOU." The guys around them oohed loudly and Ryan clutched his chest.

"Oh baby, I'm crushed! Don't I measure up to your older guy?" The guys laughed and finally the damn lock gave way and slid open.

For some stupid reason the words "We broke up" were out of his mouth before he could stop them. Heat burned up his neck and into his cheeks.

"Now's your chance, Ryan!" somebody shouted, shoving Ryan from behind. They collided hard, but he grabbed the back of Skyler's head before it hit the lockers behind him, and the resulting crush of bodies and Skyler's armful of books was oddly intimate. He watched as Ryan's white headphone fell out of his ear and hung over his shoulder between them. Ryan's face had gone from cheeky to surprised to something different now, but Skyler's rage spark was up to full blaze now, and he didn't care to try to decipher it. *If this were Jeremy, he'd be kissing me by now.* He put his free hand on Ryan's wide chest and shoved.

"As if I would ever date you," said Skyler. *How long will it be before a guy holds me like that again?*

"Why not?" said Ryan as Skyler rammed books into his locker with one hand, digging for his lunch bag with the other.

He slammed the locker shut, locked it, and then turned and made a show of looking Ryan up and down. A lot of the guys were staring at him now. "Well, you're good-looking enough until you open your mouth. I don't date people who go out of their way to bug the shit out of someone just because they're different. Who enjoy harassing people to make themselves feel bigger. Who think that being on a fucking team makes them better than everyone else. You think I like being gay at this fucking school? Well fuck you for making it harder than it already is!"

Skyler was stomping away to the oohs of the team behind him when Ryan caught up to him. "Hey, wait up." Skyler ignored him, and someone called "Drama Queen" after them. Skyler fingered the air and didn't deign to turn around, but Ryan shouted back. "Shut UP, Evan. Seriously!" They were halfway to the next wing of the school before Ryan grabbed Skyler's arm and stopped him.

"What?" Skyler was still shaking but the anger was starting to turn into something more dangerous, something that might involve bursting into tears, and that was something he could NOT afford to do.

"Hey, I mean, uh, I didn't mean to…. I just thought we were messing around, you know?"

"YOU were messing around. With ME."

"You're right. I'm a total dick. I'm really sorry. I just didn't think, okay? I'm not like that. I mean, I don't mean to be like that."

"What, like you don't have a choice?"

"It's just my sense of humor. It gets me into trouble."

"It's just your lack of empathy for other human beings! That's what gets you into trouble."

"You're right. Seriously. I had no idea."

"No, you don't. You have no idea how much it sucks to be avoided like the plague most of the time and then ganged up on the rest of the time. I'm not asking to be one of the guys, I know I'm not like you, but fuck, 100 percent ignoring would be better." Skyler swallowed hard. The throat lump was making it hard to talk.

"It would?"

"Yes! No! I don't know!" And suddenly the lump was too big and tears started leaking out of the corners of his eyes. Ryan grabbed his arm and pulled him into the empty chemistry classroom, shutting the door behind them.

"Just sit down for a minute." Ryan put his hand on Skyler's shoulder and pressed him down onto a stool. "Look, I'm an ass, okay? I know it." He squeezed Skyler's shoulder and that oh-so-rare human contact was just too much. The tears started popping out faster, and there wasn't anything he could do but clamp his jaw down on the sounds that were trying to claw their way up his throat. It was like the throat lump was hatching and the thing inside was going to get loud.

Ryan slid his hand around to his other shoulder in a one-armed hug. "Hey, do you wanna punch me? Seriously, you can. I know I've got it coming."

Skyler had been staring hard at the ceiling, but couldn't help but look up into Ryan's eyes. He looked serious and kind of lost and flushed, and suddenly a laugh huffed up out of Skyler's mouth. "What!" said Skyler.

"Well not in the face or anything, but if I know it's coming, I figure I can take your best shot in the gut."

"No! Are you crazy? No, I don't want to hit you, for godsake."

"You don't?"

"No. Does that EVER help?"

"Well…."

"Don't answer that. I don't want to know." Skyler rubbed his face with his hands.

"Yeah, I know. I'm not that smart sometimes."

Skyler looked at him again. There was something there in his eyes. Maybe it had been there before too. Something naked and… vulnerable.

"Look, I broke up with my asshole boyfriend over the break, okay, so I just can't take shit right now. I'm sorry I freaked out."

"You're sorry? You were all avenging angel on my ass! It was awesome! I mean, it would have been awesome if it had been someone else's skin you were waxing. Since it was mine, it was kinda terrifying."

Skyler laughed again and Ryan's smile was less wicked this time but no less bright.

"Hey, why don't you come hang out after school? We can play some vids or something."

"I don't need your pity, Ryan. Thanks but no thanks." Skyler stood up.

"Don't be a snob." Ryan finally let his hand slide off Skyler's back.

"I'm not a snob!"

"So you're not too good to hang out with boring straight knuckleheads?"

"Of course not! My best friend is straight." Lisa was probably wondering where he was by now.

"Well, then what? I'm not smart enough or… or arty enough or something?" Ryan's face was strange. It looked like he was trying hard to be snarky and funny, but there was that thing in his eyes, that thing that wondered what people thought of him and wasn't sure he'd like to find out.

"Ryan, I just freaked out. I'm not a stray cat. You don't have to take me home. I'm fine."

"Good, then I'll drive you to my house after school." Ryan turned and walked toward the door.

"I have homework!"

"Okay. I'll do mine and you do yours. You can use my laptop if you want." Ryan put his hand on the doorknob and turned back. "I'll drive you home whenever. And it's not pity."

"Yeah, right."

"My friends can be jerks, okay? Maybe I wanna hang out with someone nice now and then." He smiled and it was shy and uncertain, and then he opened the door and was gone.

Lisa hardly believed him when he told her the story over lunch and insisted on racing over to his locker after the last bell to witness it for herself. Ryan showed up fast, too, and the two of them stared at each other amidst the afterschool crush of bodies.

"Hey, Lisa."

"Ryan."

"Permission to have Skyler over?"

"That depends on whether you're planning on being an asshat."

"No, ma'am."

"Well alright, then, but I'm warning you, Ryan. You upset him one more time and I will make you sorry you were ever born." She poked her finger into his broad chest. Lisa was about a foot shorter than Ryan, but her eyes were cold and her flat mouth left no doubt that she was entirely serious.

"God, can you guys make this day any weirder?" Skyler locked his locker and walked past them. He couldn't tell if the guys around them were listening in or just caught up in their own banter and not paying any attention at all. *Did Ryan talk to them and tell them to leave me alone? How mortifying.* Lisa caught up and stopped him.

"Call me later, okay?" She gave him her huge pleading eyes that he could never refuse, and he rolled his eyes and nodded. She smiled and kissed lip gloss onto his cheek. "Later!" she said, pointing at him and mock-scowling to threaten him with retribution if he forgot.

"Bye." He kept walking toward the doors, and then Ryan was pushing past him and holding the door wide. It was raining and cold outside.

"My car is right over there."

Skyler sighed. His mom wouldn't be home for dinner. She was going straight from teaching to rehearsal, and their silent basement suite didn't really hold that much appeal. *Am I really that hard up for human interaction?* He looked at Ryan's uncertain smile.

Yup. I guess I am.

Ryan walked like he had all the confidence in the world, striding along with one hand in his jeans pocket, but he kept looking over at Skyler. Waiting for him to bolt, probably. Ryan's car was an older Jetta. "It was my mom's, but it's a diesel so it never dies." He plugged his iPhone into a jack and fiddled with the tiny speakers balanced on the dash.

A song came on as he was backing out of the parking lot. Ryan said, "Do you know this song?" Skyler shook his head. "It's called 'Headphones'. Kinda my theme song right now. I love it."

It had a fun sound to it, and Ryan bobbed his head to the beat and smiled. Now that Skyler thought about it, Ryan did wear his headphones all the time. He was always bobbing and dancing around as he walked down the hallways. They had a few classes together this year, and Skyler had known him for ages, but they'd never hung out before. The song grooved along, kind of funny, very up and happy. It made sense that Ryan had picked it. He was always joking around.

They hardly spoke on the ride there, but Skyler was relieved to have his incredibly heavy bag at his feet instead of on his back for the mile-long walk home.

Ryan's house was huge and the front yard landscaped, and Skyler felt his shoulders creep a little higher as they pulled up. *Of course this is what Ryan's house looks like. Why in the hell did I agree to this?*

"It backs onto the canyon," said Ryan as he unlocked the door. "I hope you like dogs." A big shaggy dog wrestled out of the doorway, wagging its whole back end and whimpering with excitement. "This is Jesse."

Skyler held out a hand. Jesse licked it and seemed to grin up at him. Skyler couldn't help the big smile that came over his face. Jesse had this straggly beard and the softest ears, and she was somehow super strong and super hilarious at the same time. He'd always wanted a dog, but their landlord would never allow it. They'd settled for a cat and Siegfried was great, but it was apples and oranges.

"What kind of dog?"

"We say she's part German wirehaired pointer, part mutt, but we don't really know 'cuz she's a rescue dog. She likes you. Normally she's way more freaked out by new people. Come on in."

Ryan gave him a tour of the amazing, intimidating house and then offered him a beer.

"Homework," he answered, crossing his arms.

"Then beer?" Ryan's mischievous grin was back.

"Your parents don't mind?"

"Are you kidding? My dad's in the beer industry. There's always beer around."

"No wonder you have so many friends."

Ryan laughed, but the smile seemed to leave him after that. Skyler spread out his stuff on the kitchen table, and Ryan slowly followed suit. It wasn't long before he was sighing over his math textbook and Skyler was leaning over, trying to explain it.

It was almost five when Ryan groaned. "Enough. My brain hurts!"

"Alright, fine." It'd been nice, actually, having someone to work with other than Lisa. Skyler got up and stretched, feeling the rub of his shirt against his sore nipples again. One of them was still infected, thanks to Asshole.

"What?" Ryan was holding out a glass of beer to him, one hip leaning on the kitchen counter.

"Thanks. Just thinking about an asshole." Skyler looked up in time to see Ryan's eyes crinkle as he tried not to smile.

"You don't say."

Skyler blushed. "My ex, okay? Not his asshole." He took a quick sip, trying to hide his face. He hadn't wanted to admit that he didn't really like beer, but this one was like none he'd tried before, dark and rich but without any bitter aftertaste. It went down easily.

Ryan sipped his beer and sucked the foam from his top lip. "So what happened?" His face was serious now.

"You don't want to hear about that." He took a long drink of the beer. God, it was cold.

"Try me, Mr. Snobby." Ryan moved around the kitchen putting out corn chips and salsa. Skyler ate a few and drank some more beer.

"He cheated on me."

"What? That fucking prick!"

Skyler's eyes shot up as Ryan slammed the salsa down on the counter. *Is he serious?* Ryan did look genuinely pissed.

"Well, it was my own fault, I guess. He didn't seem to think it was a big deal."

"That little shitbag! How did you find out?"

Skyler shrugged. "He had marks on him. He tried to say they were from me, but I knew I.... Anyway, it shouldn't have been a big surprise. It was just my own stupidity."

"Skyler, you are the smartest guy I know and that asshole covered you in hickeys all fall."

Skyler blushed; god, that had been embarrassing. *I guess I shouldn't be surprised that he remembers that.* The soccer team guys that had their lockers next to his had found it hilarious. You could only wear a scarf for so long before someone grabbed it off you. "What has that got to do with anything?"

"If the guy is going to claim you like that when you're still in high school, he'd better treat you right and not make you feel stupid when he doesn't."

Skyler's mouth fell open for a moment. None of Lisa's outrage or his mom's care had cut to it like this did. It helped. It really helped to have someone big and athletic and... yeah, male, say it like that. He felt tears pulling at the back of his eyes and looked away. The rest of the beer somehow slid down his throat.

"I should go." He stood up and felt the rush of the beer along his arms and down his legs. *Man, I'm a lightweight.*

"You can stay for dinner if you want. My mom will love you. Anyone that helps me with math is like a saint around here."

Skyler shook his head and packed up his bag. "No thanks, I should get home." But when Ryan dropped him off and revved away in a cloud of stinky smoke, he turned the key in the lock and wondered why he'd come home.

The next day, it was like Ryan had decided they were friends now and that was the end of it. He grabbed Skyler in a headlock and rubbed his knuckles on Skyler's scalp during lunch hour and then teased him about his haircut, which was long in the front and short in the back and apparently he was too princess-y about styling it. Lisa's mouth hung open. Nobody, nobody, gave Skyler noogies in the hallway. It just didn't happen.

Skyler recovered enough to snark about how so-not-gay Ryan's shoulder-length hair was, and Ryan laughed and it was like some kind of spell had been broken. It was like if Ryan said it was okay to like Skyler, then it was okay. Within a week, guys were brushing shoulders with him at the lockers and not flinching away like he was dirty. Ryan dragged him over every day Skyler wasn't working and Lisa was busy, and finally Skyler relented and stayed for dinner one night. Ryan's parents and sister were really nice, and during dessert Ryan invited him to go to his family's cabin up at Big White with them.

"Come on, it'll be fun! We have a hot tub. You know how to ski, right?"

"Barely." Skyler's mom had insisted that he join the school ski club in grade eleven even when he knew they couldn't afford it.

"I'll teach you. Don't worry, I'm a really good teacher. And you'll only miss three days of school. Come on, you need some serious cheering up, dude. When was the last time you took a holiday?" The summer had been all about busting his ass at the restaurant to save for college this fall, and Skyler doubted that Ryan would count the weekends helping out at shows with his mom's theater friends.

Somehow he'd found himself loading bags and a cooler into Ryan's car four days later, getting driven to Ryan's, and then reloading everything into the back of Ryan's dad's monster Ford Expedition

SUV. His shifts at the restaurant hadn't been that hard to trade, and he'd done a stack of homework with Ryan so they wouldn't fall behind. Ryan's job at the local mountain was pretty casual, and he'd agreed to the homework to get Skyler to come.

"You brought a cooler? Dude, I told you we have lots of beer," said Ryan.

"No, I wanted to cook dinner at least once. You know, something nice."

"You realize my mom is going to disown me and adopt you. Thanks a lot. Here, give me the clothes bag. We need to make sure you have enough stuff." Ryan took it and him up to his room.

"Okay, show me your gear. The Coke is closed so we're going be delayed. Let's get you sorted out so I know what to bring for you."

"The highway is closed?"

"Yeah, Coquihalla's got avalanche warnings. But don't worry, it'll open up soon for sure. The good news is it's dumping up there!"

Skyler frowned. The Coquihalla was famous for crazy-assed eighteen-wheeler wrecks and whiteout blizzards. He'd never been up there in the winter.

Ryan shook his head at Skyler's sweat pant/rain pant combo and pulled out some old too-small snow pants that looked really expensive and told him to try them on. Skyler was a little shorter, but also much smaller boned and leaner.

"No, wait, not on top of jeans. Here, try this as an underlayer." He looked on without any hesitation as Skyler shucked down to his Calvin Klein form-fitting boxers (one gift from Jeremy that he HAD kept) and slid into the clothes. Then Ryan grabbed the waistbands, stretching them out and adjusting the elastic.

"Man, you need to eat more."

"I haven't been hungry much lately."

Ryan gave him a look but said nothing. Before he was finished, he'd packed an entirely new bag with the clothes he was either lending or giving to Skyler.

"What?" Ryan said, digging a knee into the bag and reefing on the zipper.

"You just kitted me out from head to toe. I feel bad."

"What? Whatever! I invited you. The least I can do is make sure you don't die of frostbite! Hey, can you check the website again?"

The highway was open, and there was a mad dash for the car and a rechecking of lists and then a rushing back in for sunglasses, and then they were off. Ryan's fourteen-year-old sister sat behind the passenger seat with headphones on and a portable DVD player with a mountain of gear packed next to her. Ryan and Skyler were in the third row of seats at the back. Skyler wasn't sure how that had gotten decided, but he was so relieved to not have to make conversation with the whole family that he relaxed back into the comfortable seat and watched North Vancouver slide by. He loved the window seat.

"Do you have an iPod? Or music on your phone?" asked Ryan.

"No. My cell phone's from 7-Eleven." He'd pulled his SIM card out of Jeremy's old iPhone and left it on the bed the day they broke up, and man was his regular crap phone hard to go back to. "That's okay, though. Go ahead."

"Here." Ryan handed him an earbud and ignored him when he tried to turn it down. Ryan shifted around, laid his head back against the seat, and closed his eyes. Ryan was in the center seat with a pile of gear bags next to him and his long leg splayed out, resting heavily against Skyler's thigh. Try as he might, Skyler couldn't get that thigh to relax, and it kept twitching away until Ryan opened his eyes and said, "What?"

"Nothing."

"What?"

Skyler glanced over at Ryan's sister Erika and then up front to where their parents were talking. He couldn't hear what they were saying. With the sound of the road, it was pretty private back here. "It's just.... You know guys are always acting like I have the plague, like if they bump into me I'm going to turn them to the dark side or something. But you're not, like, shy of me and the guys treat me a little different now. So, uh, thanks."

"Hey, my dad always says, 'a man can live without sex but not without snuggles.'"

Skyler laughed. Ryan's dad was a huge bear of a man. "Your dad did NOT say that," he said in a low voice.

"Whatever, man. He says it all the time."

"I don't think he was too, uh, impressed with your choice of invitees." Skyler had insisted Ryan tell his parents about the gayness before he would agree to come.

"Oh, he's fine. Don't worry, he doesn't hate gay people or anything."

"What did he say when you told him?" Skyler flicked his eyes to the front, deciding there was no way Ryan's parents could hear them.

"I think he assumed you were gay the minute he saw your earrings, but I told him anyway. He's a friendly guy. Seriously. Don't worry." Ryan's mom had, as predicted, loved Skyler almost on sight. She'd even admired his vintage rhinestone studs. He wasn't sure how the nipple piercings were going to go over, though. *Maybe I should just not go in the hot tub? Or wear a shirt?*

There was a bit of snow on the ground when they stopped for lunch at the White Spot in Hope. Ryan's dad insisted on paying, but Skyler passed on getting the combo anyway. Ryan slid his yam fries over. "I can't eat all of these, man. Help me out." The chipotle mayo was damn good and he'd eaten more of them than he felt was polite before he could help it. Ryan's leg was splayed out against his again under the table, and amidst the family banter, he felt this sudden rush of joy at having a friend. Someone who wasn't careful and guarded all the time. God, it was a relief.

As they stood up to leave, Ryan's dad muttered, "God, I'm not looking forward to all the rigs who've been sitting around all morning waiting for the road to open."

Sure enough, the highway was full of eighteen-wheelers. As they climbed higher into the mountains, it started snowing heavily. The windshield wipers were having a hard time keeping up, and whenever they passed a rig, the spray from its huge tires speckled the windows with mud.

"It's like mushroom soup," said Skyler. Ryan laughed and stretched, laying his arms out on the backs of the seats. They listened to music for a while, and gradually the SUV started to rumble and jiggle, despite the car's normally smooth ride. Skyler sat up and tried to see out the front.

"It's just lumps of ice stuck on the road. The plows can't get it all. There's still two lanes, though, and one is not all iced up. As we get higher, it'll probably go down to one lane."

"What do you mean? You come up here a lot, right?"

"Yeah, we rent it out mostly, but we come up a bunch of times a year. It's two lanes in both directions all the way, but see how that lane is getting really caked with ice? The plows can't keep up. When it gets bad, they end up only plowing down the middle."

"Oh."

"Hey, are you okay?" Ryan's hand slid off the back of the seat and pressed into his shoulder.

"Sure."

Right then Ryan's dad swore as a rig pulled out in front of him, coming awfully close to the rig in the next lane.

"Hey, man. Don't worry, okay? You're like a cat in a car. You look like you're going to climb under the seat."

Skyler tried to laugh but it came out really fake.

"Hey." Ryan put a finger on Skyler's chin and turned him away from the window. "What do you want to talk about?" He kneaded up and down Skyler's bicep and then pulled him in against his shoulder. Suddenly the friendliness of the touching felt too good. It went from comfortable to intense in a heartbeat, and Skyler's whole body went from stressed to taut. He could feel the denseness of Ryan's muscled body, and the firm grip of being held close like that made it hard to breathe. *Why couldn't Jeremy ever hold me like this?*

"Tell me about your boyfriend," said Ryan, and Skyler shivered. Ryan put his other hand on Skyler's thigh and rubbed it up and down. "It's good to talk about it, and besides, it'll distract you." Skyler wasn't sure what he needed distracting from more—the road or Ryan's hands.

"My mom thought it would help for me to meet some other gay guys." He tried to look out the window away from Ryan's up-close and suddenly amazing eyes. They looked brown, but when Skyler got this close, he could see they had other colors as well. Ryan turned his chin again.

"Uh-uh. Look at me. Okay, so, gay guys. How did she swing that?"

Skyler glanced up front. Ryan's dad's eyes seemed glued on the road ahead, thank god. Skyler looked down at his hands, rubbing his sweaty palms together. What would happen if Ryan clued in and saw the effect he was having on Skyler? "She let me get a fake ID. Me and Lisa went to Celebrities."

"I've never been there. How was it?"

It was a pretty well-known gay club, and it was nice that Ryan didn't just assume it was evil and the reason he was messed up or something. In fact, it was a haven. "It was amazing. To see all these guys dancing together, it changed...." Skyler risked a glance up into those eyes again. It was strange how serious Ryan looked right now when a couple weeks ago, Skyler would have sworn there wasn't a serious bone in the guy's body. He looked serious and older. God, sometimes Ryan really reminded him of Jeremy and right now that turnoff was a good thing.

"Changed what?"

"I don't know, just seeing all these guys so totally 'out' was like, inspiring and liberating and, I don't know, hot, I guess." Skyler blushed, but Ryan was nodding.

"I can see that. It's like, empowering. That they can be themselves." He shrugged. "Strength is hot."

"Yeah." It was nice that Ryan got it, but Skyler suddenly felt that sinking gym-class feeling: not strong enough, coordinated enough, beefy enough. Who was he kidding that a guy like Ryan, who was like the Leaning Tower of Muscle, would ever be interested in a willowy art boy? Even if he did like guys, which would be news to the string of girlfriends Ryan had had.

"What?"

"Nothing. So anyway, Jeremy was there. My ex. I met him there, or I guess he picked me up. I mean it wasn't that hard. I was so desperate I probably would have left with anyone that was brave enough to kiss me on the dance floor."

Ryan shifted beside him, turning his intent eyes away. "Sorry," said Skyler. "TMI?" *No shit that's too much information. God, why can't I shut up sometimes?*

"No, no, that doesn't bother me." Ryan glanced back at Skyler, and his smile was tight. "I just hate to hear you talk like it was your fault. I mean, god, you were seventeen in your first gay bar! Had you even had a boyfriend before that?"

"Not really. I mean no one that would call me that to their friends or their parents or anything."

"Huh, lame." Skyler couldn't tell if Ryan meant the guys were lame or if it was lame that he was seventeen and so obviously a virgin for Jeremy. *God, it is obvious, isn't it?* Suddenly it didn't seem like such a secret anymore. Or that part anyway.

"So he picked me up, I saw stars for about five hours, and then I got the bus home."

"He didn't even drive you?"

Skyler laughed. "You don't care that I gave my virginity to a stranger. You care that he didn't take me home?"

"Damn straight."

"Well, Jeremy didn't have a car, if that makes you feel any better."

"Not really, but go on. So then what?"

"Well, I gave him my phone number, and he called me a few days later to see if we could go out again on the weekend. And then I saw him most weekends after that. He'd take me to parties or bars or clubs."

"What was the best thing? You know, that kept you coming back?"

"I guess that he was so unashamed. He'd push me up against the bus shelter and kiss me in front of the world. He didn't give a damn if people thought it was gross."

"You guys weren't gross."

"How do you know? He never came to the school."

"I saw you downtown together one time. He was all wrapped around you and licking your cheekbones."

Skyler laughed. "And that's not gross?"

Ryan shrugged and Skyler felt it all along his body. "I just meant you were both young and hot and into each other. It might be, I dunno, inappropriate or something, but it's not gross." Ryan squirmed. "I mean it's not like he was some old creep and you were like 'get off me' or something."

Dear god, Ryan just said I was hot. Holy shit. Heat rose from his knees to his face in a wave, and he wondered if Ryan could feel the fever radiating off him. *He also said that Jeremy was hot. Get a grip. It's just an observation. God, say something! Anything.*

"Yeah, Jeremy was pretty good-looking."

"You miss him."

"Yes and no." Skyler was back on firmer ground here. He'd given this a lot of thought, and Lisa had helped a ton too. "I miss how he made me feel in the summer, but not how I felt in the fall. I don't miss being around someone I can't trust. Look, he's not a terrible person, he's just... he just wanted to play."

"And you didn't."

"God, I was trying to figure out how to commute to college from his place. Pathetic."

"That's not pathetic!"

"It's pathetic that I didn't... no, that I *wouldn't* see him for what he was. He liked to party. He liked to mess around. I just ignored all the signs and believed I was still 'it' for him."

"You mean he flirted with other guys in front of you?"

God. Understatement of the year. Skyler hesitated. Was there any way to explain that?

"Look, Skyler, I know how it is to get cheated on. My last girlfriend cheated on me for weeks before I found out."

"I'm sorry to hear that."

"Thanks. Anyway, I get it, okay? You feel like the biggest sucker and the worst loser and you wonder if all your friends knew and didn't tell you and if they really are your friends or what."

Skyler blinked. *Wow, that does pretty much sum it up.*

Ryan kept going. "But I've been that friend too, and that's a whole other kinda shitty. You wanna spill it, but it's... complicated."

"What do you mean?"

"Well, like you said, some people don't want to see the truth. It's too painful. So they won't believe you and then they'll hate you, and even when they find out that you were right, they still kind of hate you for seeing the shit go down. They should trust you more, but they trust you less for some damn reason."

"You were the guy that said something?"

"Yeah. It didn't go well. But my point is, people don't know what to do. They might be sick about it and mad as hell that they're being made a part of hurting you, but they just don't know what to do. Or they wonder if maybe you know and don't mind, or if maybe they didn't see what they think they saw and saying something would be just stirring the shit pot.... It's tricky."

"Thanks."

"For what?"

"For... understanding. For telling me stuff. For distracting me right before we all die in a car accident."

Ryan laughed and grabbed Skyler's head in some kind of weird wrestling hug, rubbing his fingertips hard over Skyler's scalp. "Don't mention it. And we are NOT going to die. YOU are going to die skiing, remember?" And then Ryan's arms were off him entirely and digging in a bag. "Want a granola bar? They're sweet and salty." He threw one at Skyler. "But seriously, don't worry about the skiing either. I'll watch out for ya."

Skyler bit into the soft bar and chewed. It was full of chocolate and no doubt preservatives and probably a zillion calories and was something his mom would never buy. It tasted fantastic. His brain did one of those jumps, and he could see how Ryan was like that too: something that looked like junk food on the outside, but was actually soft and rich and surprisingly filling.

CHAPTER 2—RYAN

SKYLER WAS just plain awesome. He was so fucking brave. Ryan looked over at him with his head back on the headrest and his eyes closed, one earbud in his ear, and sighed. *Like his earrings. What kind of guy wears earrings like that in high school?*

It had taken him a while to get it, but then, most things took their time sinking through his thick skull. He'd thought the guy was silly. Just gay and silly and flighty or something. Was that what he'd thought gay people were before? Sort of shallow and into drama or something? I mean, diamond studs? And these weren't single stones. Lots of guys had those. These were big rectangular-cut rhinestones surrounded by other tiny little ones. They were something a classy old lady would wear.

Last year, grade eleven? It had seemed ridiculous, but now he got it. How Skyler had outed himself in a way that left no room for doubt with anyone who walked past him in the hallway. The haircut, the funky clothes. Sometimes he wore this vintage suit vest over his button-up shirts with this old black-and-white movie kind of hat. The fact was that he not only stood out, but he… fit together. Somehow the earrings and the hair and the clothes and that open look on his face that said "Whatever, this is me, I'm so not tough and I don't care who knows it" fit together into this package that was galaxies more tough than any of the other guys.

Humbling. That's what Skyler was. He didn't try to laugh shit off or even have some snarky disinterested sense of gay superiority like a few of the other gay guys did. James was like that. He had a catty comment for everything, with his raised eyebrow and his fashionable clothes. James was out too, super-out, but he'd done it differently. He was part of this girl clique of all the prettiest, most popular girls and it was like he somehow made them even cooler just by being with them. He was like a trophy friend or something.

Skyler, on the other hand, looked shit in the face and gave it hellish honesty. God, that day at school… Ryan still cringed when he thought about it. That was the day the slowly warming halogen bulb in Ryan's brain had finally reached full wattage. Sure, Skyler could have whipped out some snappy comeback and put him in his place, and that would have been funny and brave, but he hadn't only done that. He hadn't put on any armor for the fight and had just stood there letting his anger and hurt SHOW. It was like he fought by taking his armor OFF. In front of everyone. It was crazy brave. It was so brave that no one even got how brave it was.

Skyler's eyelashes were long and dark against his face. He was too pale. Ryan wondered again if he was eating enough. He was pretty sure that bastard ex had something to do with Skyler dropping pounds, and it made him so angry to think about that he could hardly see straight sometimes. Sweet, lean little Sky-boy, all doe-eyed for that slick older guy, getting gobbled up and spat out by the person that was supposed to take him away from all the fucking rejection of high school. And even after that, Sky still showed up at school, still worked hard and got As. Skyler deserved to be taken care of properly, and it sure looked like his mom wasn't doing it. Sure, she was nice and everything, and she supported him, but she was so busy. Half the time it was Skyler making *her* dinner, not the other way around.

Every time Ryan saw Skyler, he felt his hands lift up of their own accord and reach out to touch him. Skyler had said he wasn't a stray cat, but nothing could be further from the truth. He was a tough-ass tom with a really deep purr, and Ryan just wanted to hold him still when he tried to struggle free, and stroke him until he made that sound again. God, what he'd give to see Skyler re-fucking-lax for once. To really smile or laugh? God, his shoulders felt like blocks of stone most of the time, held up around his ears. Even now, Ryan could tell Skyler wasn't really resting, and he felt bad. *Damn Coquihalla.* The highway did get pretty sketchy.

He half turned away and wiggled back against Skyler's body, nuzzling his head back into the curve of Skyler's collarbone. Skyler's earbud fell out, and Ryan craned his head around and stuck it back in Skyler's ear. "Okay?" he said.

"You're on my arm," Skyler whispered.

Ryan leaned forward and Skyler freed his arm, leaving it hovering in the air for a second, not sure where to let it land. Ryan took hold of his wrist and pulled the arm over his own shoulder, settling back against the curve of Skyler's body. *That's better.* He sighed and closed his eyes, his fingers still wrapped around Skyler's wrist where it rested on his stomach. There was something so reassuring about being in physical contact with Skyler. Everything seemed better... calmer. Like something in his head could stop worrying because he had proof in his hands that Skyler was right HERE and he was okay.

Ryan drifted and dozed, thinking about what he would do to Jeremy if he ever caught up to him. Skyler had asked if it ever helped to hit someone. Ryan was pretty sure that sometimes it did.

CHAPTER 3—SKYLER

WHY? WHY had he encouraged Ryan to touch him? Why had he ever confided that he missed human touch? *Because I am a fucking moron.* Ryan's body lying against him was torture. Sweet, amazing torture. Skyler's cock, which up until now had led him to believe that it could tolerate having a male friend, stood to attention and made it very clear to anyone who cared to look that this theory was flawed. Fatally fucking flawed. Okay, well maybe if the guy was super ugly or a crazy jackass like Ryan had seemed to be before, but now it just wasn't working. Ryan was far, far too… caring. And hot.

God, how had he missed that? It was like his brain had previously been doing an objective multiple-choice quiz on Ryan's looks. His hair was nice. His face was nice. His body was nice. Check, check, and check. And now suddenly there were no tick boxes to check off on some kind of cold assessment; there was only real-live Ryan snuggled up against him. Warm, comfortable, and terrifyingly hot.

What would happen if Ryan opened his eyes and turned just that little bit and saw how hard Skyler's cock was? Would he freak out? Would he make his dad pull the car over and kick Skyler out into the snow? He doubted it would come to that, but seriously. This was a major problem. A major problem that he himself had created. He clenched his teeth and squeezed his eyes shut, willing his molecules to not magnetize toward Ryan's and pull him around until he was wrapped around Ryan like a starfish and rubbing his face in Ryan's soft hair. Which was right up against his fucking cheek, for godsake.

And what could he say to Ryan? "I know I just thanked you for treating me like a normal guy, but now I'm totally turned on by you so please don't touch me"? Oh god. This whole week was going to be hell. He either 'fessed up and their new friendship became unbelievably awkward, or he had to pretend nothing had changed, and Skyler knew he was a total for-shit liar.

The heat that had filled his body before was now turning nuclear. He was sweating, and he never sweat. He was blushing scarlet for sure and kept his eyes closed. No way did he want to catch Ryan's parents' eye in the rearview mirror as they caught him gayifying their only son. The only thing he could do was pretend to be asleep. As if he could ever sleep next to Ryan. As if someone could blush this hard in their sleep.

The ride seemed to go on forever. The good news was that Ryan seemed to genuinely pass out. The bad news was he made this kind of humming noise, so soft Skyler wouldn't have even noticed if he hadn't felt it vibrate all along his side. And when the "mmm-mmm" sound stopped, his loose fingers would grip hard around Skyler's wrist for a moment, then relax again. The boner-from-hell would be just about gone, and then Ryan would do that again and wham, some kind of hard-on recharge shot would surge from Skyler's wrist, straight to his crotch.

As darkness fell, he tried to think about anything other than Ryan. The music would help sometimes, like when Goyte's "Somebody that I Used to Know" came on and he thought of Jeremy and how he hadn't heard a word from him since Skyler had cleaned all his stuff out of his apartment three weeks ago, and it was just like the song said. Skyler had told himself that Jeremy was right for him, but he HAD felt lonely when they were together. *Oh god.* The throat lump came back, but at least the boner went down.

But the music was also fickle. Two Door Cinema Club came on with "Sleep Alone," and he of course thought about how amazing it had been to sleep at Jeremy's apartment and how that was over now and he was so fucking lonely and would probably sleep alone forever. But before he knew it, his brain was producing flashes of Ryan propped up on his elbows on the bed in his bedroom, wearing that wicked smile and with his hair falling over his face when he looked down, only this time Skyler's fantasy hand was there tucking that silky lock behind his ear for him and their eyes were meeting and the light was going on in Ryan's eyes and....

"Mmm-mmmm." Ryan's fingers tightened again on his forearm, and this time a thumb rubbed a stripe back and forth on the inside of Skyler's captive wrist and Ryan's head rubbed that fine hair against Skyler's cheek so he couldn't help but inhale the lovely scent of Ryan's shampoo. Skyler wondered if he might just come in his pants.

Through slitted eyes he could see that they were going through a town and then over a bridge and through more town. He'd checked Google Maps while he packed so he wouldn't embarrass himself by having no idea where they were going, and he knew the only town with a bridge in the middle was Kelowna. Not far now. He wasn't sure which he dreaded more, Ryan sitting up and catching him aroused or Ryan sitting up and leaving him. Now that it was almost over, he tried to just enjoy it for a minute. Ryan's weight against him really was wonderful. He was so solid, so somehow... fully present. Jeremy had spoiled Skyler for human touch. Sure it had been rough and hot sometimes, but it had also been warm and casual, and walking away from Jeremy had meant losing that physical closeness entirely. It was like being addicted and quitting cold turkey, so this new dose was flooding his dried-up veins and making his heart pound like a junkie midrelapse.

His breath caught when they pulled into a gas station, but as they pulled to a stop and the lights went on, Ryan sat up and slid out from under his arm without even looking over. He scooted around all the gear bags, and Skyler dove forward to dig in the backpack at his feet, pulling out a long hoodie. He was struggling into it when Ryan turned back and said, "You want something?"

Skyler blinked and his mouth hung open. *Oh god, he saw!*

"From the store?" Ryan said.

"No. No thanks," muttered Skyler and Ryan was gone. Skyler zipped up the hoodie over the boner-from-hell and closed his eyes for a moment. *Holy shit, that was close.* Then he wriggled out of the car. The windows were seriously dirty, and any task that would take his mind off Ryan's firm flesh pressed against him was a godsend. The squeegee and the cold night air did him a world of good, and Ryan's mom smiled to see he was helping out.

When they turned onto the Big White Road about a half hour later, the two tire tracks in the snow where the road showed through disappeared entirely. They slowed down a bit on the all-snow terrain, and Skyler texted his mom and Lisa to say they had survived the highway. Ryan popped open a bag of nacho cheese Doritos and the smell filled the air. He tilted them toward Skyler. "Come on, I'll make myself sick eating all these."

They really were delicious and they seemed to distract him enough to keep the boner at bay. They turned off at a resort-type development filled with enormous mansions, and Skyler stopped eating and just stared out the window. The sign said "Snow Pine Estates."

Most of the places were three stories of stained wood with thick gingerbread-house cakes of snow loaded on their peaked roofs. Walls of glass hinted at great rooms with two-story ceilings, whole tree trunks acted as pillars for entranceways, and there were stone facades and cedar shingles. Each place had at least a two-car garage, and all of this was nestled in right next to a forest of snow-coated trees. It looked like some kind of Christmas movie set.

"Holy shit," whispered Skyler.

"You like it? It's pretty cool, eh? We're ski-in ski-out, so we can just get all our stuff on at the house and ski down to the lift."

"It's beautiful." And it was, but it was also entirely overwhelming. And it only got more overwhelming when they pulled up in front of Ryan's family "cabin," which turned out not to be a cabin at all. It was something that could only be called a "chalet."

The car stopped and Ryan's dad called, "Erika, can you go open the garage?"

"We'll go," said Ryan, and Skyler followed him as they maneuvered around the bags. As his Converse sank down into the snow, almost overwhelming the high tops, the cold air enveloped him. It was freezing! He looked up at the house and swallowed hard. The two-car carport in the middle was framed on either side by an enclosed garage, and above each of those were large decks on the second floor with whole tree pillars supporting the roof above. The house was four stories high, and the center was two giant two-story windows.

"It's a duplex. We own the left half and my dad's friend owns the right. Come on." Ryan ran into the left side of the carport and punched a code into the keypad on the door. "Six two six two, can you remember that?" At Skyler's blank look, Ryan waved his hand. "Don't worry, I'll write it on your arm or something if you want to go out on your own. I'll give you the Wi-Fi password too." He swung the door open into a small room. "This is the mud room and laundry. It's seriously too small when everyone is getting their crap on, but we have a bench in the garage, too, so that helps. I usually ski in and out of the back door, though, so my gear doesn't get mixed up with everyone else's." The room had two doors on the left, and Ryan went through the first one and pressed the garage door button and then kicked off his shoes. "Let me give you the tour before we unload." He pulled open the other door and leaped up the stairs two at a time.

They went up, turned, and went up again, coming up in the middle of an enormous room. On the right was a huge dining room table with a glass door to the deck behind it, and on the left was a gorgeous kitchen. If you walked in between them, you were in the living room looking out the huge window at the front of the house. There was an icicle that was more than a meter long hanging in front of that window, and a large stone fireplace monopolized the far corner of the room. The whole open-concept area was two stories high so it had an impressive wide-open feeling.

"We don't watch that TV much," said Ryan, waving a hand at the giant flat-screen above the fireplace. "We watch movies in here." He opened one of the three doors at the back of the house and there was a cozy den with another huge TV and a couch. The other two doors were a bathroom and a bedroom full of bunk beds, and then Ryan was dashing up the next flight to the third floor. There were three doors here as well.

"This is the master bedroom 'cuz it has an en suite, then there's this bathroom, and Erika's room. She likes being beside the bathroom, but up a bit from the living room. I'm up there at the top 'cuz it's bigger and I don't mind the stairs." Ryan raced through a large open area, past the back door, and up a more narrow flight. It opened onto a single room featuring a king-sized bed, a closet and two dressers, a high-peaked ceiling, and large windows looking out over the snowy forest. *Okay, good. I guess I'm in the bunk-bed room two floors away. Thank god for that.*

"My mom's friend might join us and she's got a bum knee, so we'll save the bunk-bed room on the main for her. You don't mind sharing, do you? Come on, let's go schlep some schtuff." Ryan was thumping down the stairs before Skyler could whirl around and cast a look of pure horror at the massive bed.

I'll sleep on the floor. It'll be fine. Or on the couch in the den. They probably have a foamy or something. I could drag one of the mattresses out of the room with all the bunks.

He followed after Ryan, refusing to think about it, and hauled coolers and bags up the stairs and up the stairs again. God, there were a lot of stairs. Ryan put both of their suitcases in the large top-floor bedroom, and Skyler just shut it out of his mind and poked through the kitchen, figuring out where everything was and unloading his cooler into the fridge. Ryan's mom was thrilled that he'd brought food but told him not to bother tonight. No one felt like cooking after everything was unloaded, so Ryan microwaved some pizza-pocket things and they washed them down with beer.

"You up for a hot tub?" asked Ryan as they put their dishes in the dishwasher.

"Uh, sure."

"I've got extra trunks if you forgot yours. Oh hey, do you wash them in the washing machine?"

"My trunks? Yeah, I guess."

"Oh. Sorry. The laundry soap messes with the hot tub chemicals. Don't worry, you can borrow some of mine."

Ryan's trunks were too big and hung low on Skyler's hips no matter how tight he tied the useless laces. He glanced up at himself in the bathroom mirror. *God, I've gotten skinny. Scrawny might be more like it.* The nipple rings stood out against his pale chest, and if he couldn't wear his own shorts, there was no hope of wearing a T-shirt or something to cover them up. He closed his eyes tight for a moment, wanting nothing more than to take them out right then and there and be done with it, but he couldn't shake the feeling that the shame of having them put in to please one boy was only doubled by removing them to please another. *It doesn't matter what you look like. He doesn't care. He doesn't like you for your looks.* But that only opened up the question, what DID Ryan like him for?

Clenching his teeth, he wrenched open the bathroom door and ran down the stairs. Erika was blasting the stereo, and it was Florence and the Machine's "Shake It Out." The beat steadied his stride and unhitched his shoulders as he walked through the living room, trying hard not to spin his head around to see where Ryan's parents were and fighting the desperate urge to slap his hands over his nipples. Erika looked up from the couch and smiled.

"I love this song," he shouted over the music. Florence was singing about how it was hard to dance with a devil on your back, and he shook out his arms. The song reminded him of Jeremy (as most songs did lately). Erika's smile got wider.

"Me too," she shouted back. "They're next door. My parents."

"Oh, okay, thanks."

Any composure Skyler had gained from the song was whipped away when he opened the door to the deck and stepped out into the cold. His nipples stood at attention, and he wondered for a moment if the rings might freeze and burn him. The deck was literally ice under his bare feet. Ryan was in the far corner of the hot tub, looking at him strangely, and Skyler blushed and tried for graceful as he climbed in. He lowered in fast and hissed as the heat engulfed him. Every hair on his body seemed to be standing up and electrocuting his skin like a million little antennas. There was an awkward silence where Skyler tried to look anywhere but at Ryan and to stop gasping. The view over the railing really was amazing. The house was at the end of the road, and the snowy hill beside them was steep and lumpy and bordered by forest. Everything lay under a heavy blanket of snow.

"Beer?" Ryan handed him a plastic glass.

"Thanks." It went down way too easily and tasted like burnt sugar.

"I didn't know you had your nipples pierced."

"Yeah, I haven't been in too much of a hurry to broadcast that at school."

"Yeah?"

Skyler laughed. "Yeah, it's just one more thing to make fun of, isn't it?" Ryan's face fell. "I didn't mean you," said Skyler.

"Well, you could have. I've been an asshole."

"I think letting me cry on your shoulder kinda covered that. We've been even for a while now."

"Thanks, but I doubt it."

"Okay, fine. If you want to do something for me, you can keep my nipple secret, okay?"

"No shit, man. You already said you didn't want people to know."

"Glad you were paying attention."

"Every now and then." Ryan knocked on his head and crossed his eyes. Skyler smiled, but furrowed his eyebrows.

"Why do you do that? Act like you're stupid?"

Ryan laughed. "I think you're qualified to know that the lights go on slowly upstairs. You'd think I'd at least realize when I was being a prick, but I don't until it's too late."

"Ryan, you don't owe me anything, okay? Seriously. You don't need to be so nice to me. You didn't need to invite me up here either." He took a long swig of beer.

"You think I feel sorry for you."

"Well don't you?"

"It's not like that."

"Then why am I here?"

"I thought you'd like it."

"Like it? Ryan, this place is a mansion! And look at this." Skyler stood up and waved at the view just as some snow blew off the roof, coating his skin. "OH!" He convulsed in a head-to-toe shiver and sank back down into the heat.

"It's freezing," said Ryan with his wicked smile.

"It's incredible. It's the most beautiful place I've ever been."

"Really?"

"Hell yeah."

"So why are you mad?"

"I'm not mad. I'm confused." *Dear god, am I confused.*

"About why I would want to be your friend?"

Skyler lifted a shoulder. "I guess."

"Okay, dumbass. Why wouldn't I want to be your friend? You're smart, you're funny, you've forgiven me for being an asshat, and you've helped me out with school like it was no big deal. Just because you're gay you think it's weird that I might happen to like you and want to hang out with you? Talk about snobs. Not all straight people are bigots, okay?"

Skyler blinked and stared at him. Ryan sipped his beer and stared back. "Shit," said Skyler softly. "I'm the asshat." He groaned and pressed the heels of his hands into his eyes. "Sorry."

"Don't be. I've got some earning back to do. I'm just doing it, that's all."

"What?"

"Well sometimes sorry isn't enough, is it? You've got to, you know, make it up to someone. Before they trust you not to do it again."

"That's why I'm here?"

"No, fuckwad, you're here because I like you. Jesus." Ryan swept his hand along the railing and then reached over and rubbed snow against the back of Skyler's neck. Beer sloshed as Skyler lurched and shrieked.

"Ha! You scream like a girl!"

Putting his beer glass down carefully on the corner of the tub, Skyler turned a serious face at Ryan. "No, I scream like a gay guy!" and with that he launched at Ryan, whose smile was uncertain now, and splashed him in the face with a wave of water. Ryan sputtered and Skyler's whoop of laughter echoed back from across the hill.

"Oh yeah?" Ryan's wicked grin was back, and he dove forward, not only swamping Skyler's corner of the tub, but completely submerging and grabbing Skyler around the waist. Skyler shrieked again and then couldn't stop as Ryan dug his fingers in for a frenzied tickle.

"My god, would you two keep it down?" Ryan's mom said as she winced over the deck in her bare feet. Her hair was up and she was in her bathing suit and carrying a wine glass. Luckily she was smiling.

"Sorry! Sorry! Ryan, stop!" Ryan was emerging from the water and growling like a bear, and Skyler was mortified but couldn't help one last giggle at Ryan's sea monster face.

"You boys better not splash me or I'm going to be really annoyed." She climbed in and sat beside Skyler. Her hair looked nice swirled up like that. It was light brown, maybe, but filled with stripy highlights of gold and blonde. "So what do you think of the place, Skyler?"

"It's amazing. I mean this view alone is breathtaking. And the house. God, it's beautiful."

"Well that's nice to hear, you sweet thing you! Are you sure you don't want to be adopted? All I hear is 'there's too many stairs' and 'there's no video games here.' Ungrateful wretches, my children, all three of them."

Ryan spoke up. "My older sister's at Concordia. Stephanie, but we call her Stevie."

"Oh." Skyler blushed. *I can't believe I didn't know he had another sister.*

"So what are your favorite subjects at school, Skyler?" said Ryan's mom. She'd said to call her Erin, but it seemed somehow too informal. His own mom was kind of hippy-ish and it felt totally unnatural to call someone Mrs. So-and-so, so he ducked it and just didn't call her anything.

"Well, I'm heading for business courses at Langara. The college is cheaper and the classes are smaller. I'm working hard in Math, but I really love my photography class, so I end up spending way too much time on that."

"What do you like to shoot?"

"Oh, everything. People, landscapes, interiors, and I love real macro stuff like insects and flowers and things. I like playing around with video, too, but I can't do too much with my laptop yet."

"What are you missing?"

"Hard drive space, processor speed, I think. Probably lots of things. My laptop's getting on."

"You can use mine if you want," Ryan said. "I got it for Christmas. It's pretty good."

"Maybe you could help Ryan with his helmet-cam videos. He's got a bunch of them now."

"Mom! He doesn't want to do that."

"No, no. I don't mind. Seriously, it would be fun to play around with. You don't mind if I download software?"

Ryan said, "Not at all. I think there's some video editing stuff on there, but I've been meaning to buy some better stuff."

"Oh, honey, your nipples!" said Erin. "Didn't that hurt?"

Why did everyone ask that? "Yes. Yes it did."

"Why did you do it?"

"My ex-boyfriend talked me into it." *Great, from nipple piercing to gayness. Why can't I just lie?*

"Well they're very pretty dear, but I can't imagine having that done." She shivered. Skyler was so relieved that she didn't flinch at the word "boyfriend" that he laughed and more words came tumbling out.

"It wasn't so bad until they got infected." Skyler's face turned red, and he wished he could just sink down under the water and drown. *Infected? God, could I just shut up?*

"Oh, you poor thing! That just sounds horrible! Were you tempted to just take them out?"

"Yeah, but it was… kind of a turning point. Like my earrings."

She nodded, surprising him again. "A statement about who you are. Well good for you. Those are hard to come by and more important at your age."

"It would be good if I hadn't kind of backed into it in the first place. That was pretty lame."

"Hmm, yeah, there's nothing like the aftereffects of peer pressure to make you feel shitty. I got talked into this bikini wax one time…."

"Mom!" Ryan was blushing, and Skyler laughed.

"Yeah?" said Skyler.

"Yeah, and dear god, was that a mistake! It was supposed to make you feel all hot and sexy, and instead it hurt like hell and I got this horrible rash!"

Skyler's laugh mixed with hers, and Ryan's scowl quirked up at the corner. "Oh, I get it now. You two are trouble!" he said.

She raised her wine glass, and Skyler got a glimpse of where Ryan's wicked smile might have come from. "To trouble," she said and clunked his beer glass. Her glass made a plastic-y sound.

"To trouble in plastic glasses," Skyler laughed.

Erin said, "Hey, don't knock it! I bet you haven't had broken glass in your hot tub!"

"I'm not knocking it! I'm just planning on limiting my trouble for a while."

"Aw, had enough of that from your guy?" She put her hand on his arm and frowned in sympathy. "How long ago did you guys break up?"

The laughter died in his throat. "A few weeks ago."

"Aw, honey. I'm sorry. God, you must still be in that horrible phase where you want to cry all the time and every song breaks your heart all over again."

He tried to laugh, but it came out more like a wheeze. "Yup, that kinda sums it up." He retrieved his beer and finished it, trying to swallow that throat lump again. Sympathy always undid him.

"Ryan will probably get you drunk and you can cry on his shoulder. You're welcome to drink whatever you like here, so long as no one drives and no one boils themselves in the hot tub alone and drowns and no one goes totally overboard and pukes in the house."

"You're not…." *Shut up. Don't say it.*

"What?"

"Weirded out that I'm gay?"

"Well, I don't have to worry about you hitting on my daughter, and as for my son's virtue?" She laughed. "No, dear, Ryan's a big boy and you don't seem like the pushy type. And no offense, but I think he could take you if you got crazy."

"Mom! Seriously!" Ryan's face was hilarious.

She smiled again with that devilish little curl at the corner, but there was a hard glint in her eye. "And aside from anyone getting pressured into anything or transmitting diseases or getting someone pregnant, I don't mind what Ryan wants to do in bed with his friends. I figure it's none of my business, and no, Ryan, don't get up. I know I've embarrassed you enough. I was just leaving." She flapped a hand at Ryan and turned back to Skyler. "I learned the hard way that my kids are going to fool around and experiment with drinking whether I'm ready for that or not, and I'd rather they did it somewhere safe where I can at least be there if they get into trouble." She climbed gingerly out of the tub. "Be careful here, honey, it gets really slippery. Good night, boys."

Skyler was the only one to answer "Night," as Ryan had his head in his hands and was moaning. "God. She. Is. So. Crazy!"

Skyler laughed. "I think I just got told the house rules by the coolest mom ever."

Ryan moaned again. "That's not coolness. That's evil. Pure evil." He looked up, his face still splotchy with the blush. "Or maybe mental illness. Something hard to diagnose. She loves you, though."

"Well, that would make her crazy."

"Seriously, she's never given anyone else permission to... oh god. That was like the most awkward mom moment ever. God! And she, like, has this way of just slicing right down to the bone, you know? She's like a scalpel." He heaved himself up and sat on the edge of the tub "Maybe she thinks your gayness makes you an honorary woman or something. I have no idea, man. I'm so sorry. It's not usually THAT bad."

Ryan's body was steaming in the cold air, and seeing that much of his skin was intense. Skyler swallowed hard and let his eyes roam while Ryan was too embarrassed to meet his gaze. His upper body was muscular but not cut into defined poster-boy sections. Comparing him to Jeremy was dangerous and yet inevitable, and so Skyler gave up fighting it and went there. By comparison, Jeremy's skin looked like shrink wrap over his gym-honed body. Ryan looked smoother and somehow strong in a more real way. Soft but firm. Skyler's brain did one of those psycho jumps again. *Like silly putty. Oh that's romantic.* He pushed the thought away. Ryan's wet hair hung in locks around his face, messy but somehow more appealing because of it.

Skyler swallowed and looked away. "I don't mind. Really. It's kind of refreshing to have someone speak their mind to me. I get a lot of weird energy from people." *God, did I just say energy? How flaky does that sound?* "I mean, I thought she was going to freak out that you were tickling me and get all awkward, like I was recruiting you or something."

"She'd probably like me to marry you."

"Finally a girl that measures up?" Skyler laughed.

"Something like that. You wanna go in?"

The deck was indeed slippery, and Skyler's wet hand stuck alarmingly to the metal doorknob. They grabbed rolled-up towels from a huge basket beside the door and started drying off. The music was lower now, and Erika was nowhere in sight.

"I've gotta shower. The chemicals make me itch if I don't," said Ryan, heading upstairs. Skyler followed and stripped off his wet trunks in the bedroom. He stood there naked for a moment, listening to the shower run downstairs. Ryan was naked one floor below him. Naked and soapy. The boner-from-hell was back with a vengeance. The hot tub had been seriously dangerous until Erin had shown up and shrunk things down to size for him. *Permission. She gave me permission.* His breath caught. *I have got to deal with this now or the rest of the night is going to be mortifying.* He fumbled with the room's sliding pocket door, trying to get it to lock. It was a flimsy little hook latch that didn't work very well. How long would Ryan be gone? Time was seriously short.

The lock held and he grabbed a handful of Kleenexes. Wrapping his hand around his cock, he yanked hard, almost to the point of pain. *This had better be fast, dammit.* He let go of his thoughts for the first time and thought about Ryan's hair, the shy look that would flash in his eyes only for a second now and then, his mischievous smile. Skyler thought about him sitting on the edge of the hot tub, steaming into the night air like a god, and the way the muscles curved down his arms.

The shower turned off downstairs. God, he was close. He dug for something more, something hotter to push him over the edge. He thought of pushing open the bathroom door where Ryan was toweling himself down right now, of sinking to his knees and taking him into his mouth. That hot silly-putty cock pumping in and out. *Oh god.*

He came into the Kleenex just as the bathroom door opened downstairs. He wiped up furiously with shaking hands, dropping the wad on the floor as he dug for his pajama bottoms. He had just pulled them up when Ryan thundered up the stairs and found the door locked. Skyler unlocked it before he could tug again and there was Ryan wearing only a white towel around his waist.

"Hey." Ryan smiled. "What?"

"Nothing."

"You're blushing."

Skyler busied himself looking for a T-shirt. Ryan came in. "It smells like... oh, man, were you just jacking off in here? That's hilarious. Do you want me to come back later?" Ryan laughed and

Skyler let his head bonk against the wall next to him. "Hey, whatever. We're guys, it's what we do. If you don't wank at least once a day at our age, you're probably not normal."

The truth was the sexual part of his brain seemed to have shut down since Jeremy. It had gone underground or something and touching himself just hadn't felt good. Until tonight.

"Hey." Ryan crouched down beside him. "I don't care, okay?"

"Okay." Skyler couldn't look at him.

"Look, what do you think I was doing in the shower? It's just natural." Images of Ryan sliding a soapy hand over himself burned themselves into Skyler's mind, and his blood seemed to pick up electric current from the air and zap down his arms. He closed his eyes and pressed his head into the wall.

"Now come on. Let's go have a snack before bed."

It turned into nachos and more beer, which Skyler drank more of than he meant to. The embarrassment just seemed to bring on this desire to drink he hadn't felt before, and before long his blushing awkward silences had turned into laughing at Ryan's goofing around. All too soon, Ryan was stretching that thick, dense body in a way that lifted his T-shirt up alarmingly and saying, "Come on, let's get to bed. We can't sleep in if we want to make the most of our passes tomorrow."

Ryan brushed his teeth with the upstairs bathroom door open and ushered him in, mumbling around his toothbrush and pointing at their toiletry kits on the counter. Skyler brushed his teeth, trying not to stare at Ryan's hip that was peeking out and pressed against the edge of the sink, and then went downstairs to pee in the other bathroom. His phone vibrated, and the text was from Lisa.

U ok?

He hated texting on his phone. There was no keyboard and the predictive thing was so annoyingly always wrong that he'd turned it off. And how could he explain how good and yet not okay he was feeling? He just texted back, **Yup thx!** and turned the phone off. It was past time to negotiate sleeping arrangements.

When he came back up the two flights, Ryan was already in bed.

CHAPTER 4—RYAN

SKYLER SAID, "I can, uh, sleep on the floor or, uh, the couch or...."

"Skyler, this bed could sleep an entire family. Don't sweat it. Shut the door, though. The heat gathers up here if it's open. What time do you want to get up, 7:30?" Ryan had compromised his usual nude sleep state to wear a T-shirt and boxers. Pajama pants were just too hot, especially in this bedroom.

"Yeah, sure. Uh, Ryan?"

"Yeah," he said, setting the alarm on his phone.

"You're sure you want to sleep in the same bed as me? I mean, I won't tell anyone but...."

Why does he always think I'm so uncomfortable with him? "Just because you're into guys doesn't mean you're into me. I get that, okay? Seriously. It's fine." The words brought back again that cold, burning look Skyler had given him that first day when he'd looked him up and down and told him the scathing truth. It was a look of pure loathing. *Wait, maybe he really finds me revolting and he can't stand to be this close to me.* "But if I give you the creeps or something, I can sleep on the couch."

"No, of course not." Skyler climbed into bed and turned off the light. Ryan's relief was like a surge through his body. It was so good to hear that Skyler didn't find him so horrible anymore.

"Wait 'til you see the mountain tomorrow. It's really nice. And don't worry about the skiing part. We'll stick to green runs and go really slow. I can give you some pointers if you want."

"Thanks. Yeah, I pretty much suck at it."

"No worries. It'll be fun to show you around." It made him smile to think about showing this place to Skyler. The mountain was special in a way that he couldn't seem to explain to the friends that had come up before, and it had felt so good when Skyler said it was beautiful up here. Ryan yawned and rolled onto his side facing Skyler. The bed felt heavenly, and the beer made Ryan's head swim a little as he tried to make out Skyler's facial expression. He had a mental flash of Skyler's face when he'd come out onto the deck earlier. He looked so shy and slender in those too-big shorts. The hair below his belly button was showing, and Ryan could suddenly see how handsome he was. He knew Skyler was good-looking, but that moment with his color high on those prominent cheekbones, his hair hanging over on the side, and then those big brown eyes flashing up…. It suddenly made sense to him in a different way, and he could tell that Skyler wasn't just good-looking. He was hot. And those piercings! *Damn.*

There was something about the whole package of Skyler that just made Ryan want to touch him. What did his skin feel like? It looked smooth. Ryan reached over and ran his index finger over Skyler's upper arm. "Have you ever thought about getting a tattoo? Like up here?" Ryan's fingertip slipped under the T-shirt sleeve and made a circle on Skyler's bicep. The skin was softer than he'd imagined it would be. Skyler shivered and Ryan smiled. "You're ticklish, aren't you?"

"I think we established that in the hot tub. And yeah, I was thinking about getting a tattoo actually. But then…."

"What?"

"Well, Jeremy wanted me to, and it was so hard to do something that permanent, you know? So I did the nipple thing instead."

Ryan was quiet. It was hard not to hate Jeremy. It was hard to think of anyone pressuring Skyler or making him feel like shit. He wanted to kill him.

"I know, it's weird, right?" Skyler sighed.

"No, I think it's cool. So your boyfriend, he was pretty pushy, eh?" He knew it wasn't good to just trash Jeremy all the time. That hadn't really helped when his friends did that about Chloe. Sure he wanted them to take his side, but oddly enough it hadn't really taken the sting out. In the end, it had been his sister Stevie who had really helped. She'd listened. And she'd been fair about it, fair to him and to Chloe.

"Yeah. I guess I liked that at first. He kinda took charge and swept me off my feet. I know that sounds pretty gay."

What is that? He keeps doing that, acting like gay is… what?

"I think everyone wants to feel that. You know, desired."

"Yeah, I guess he did. Desire me," said Skyler.

"Oh, I think that was pretty clear." He could see Jeremy wrapped around Skyler, his hand in Skyler's back pocket gripping his ass as he kissed his neck on the corner. Skyler's face had been flushed but bright and laughing. For some reason the image made Ryan hate Jeremy even more.

Skyler laughed. "Yeah, he wasn't very subtle. But I could never tell…."

"What?" Ryan wanted to sit up and turn on the light to be able to see Skyler's face. It was painful to not get the chance to read him.

"You want to know this gay stuff, really?"

"Yeah, sure. It's kinda new to me, but it's part of your life."

"And my life is really interesting."

"Yeah, exactly." He wanted to know everything, Ryan realized. Every thought and idea, every memory.

Skyler laughed. "I don't think devastated gay boys are all that compelling, Ryan."

"You're doing it again."

"What?"

"Acting like being gay is… lame or something. Or weak. You know I don't think that. Don't you?"

Skyler sighed. "Sometimes I wish I wasn't gay."

"Really? Why?"

"Well, it makes friendships hard, for one thing."

"It doesn't have to." Ryan scooted forward a bit and their legs brushed. Skyler moved away, but Ryan moved closer again. "You think it's weird between us, but it's not. I know you don't, you know, want me, and so it's just normal. I wish you could just chill out." Ryan put a hand on Skyler's shoulder and pressed his fingers in. "You're so wound up and jumpy. Dude, your muscles are like iron rods." He kneaded his fingertips in and followed the muscle knot up Skyler's shoulder to his neck. Skyler made a strange little noise. "Okay, that's it. You need some serious relaxation, buddy."

Ryan rolled to his side of the bed, clicked on the lamp, and rooted in his bag. He came back with his small iPhone dock and plugged it in on the bedside table. He slid his phone in and punched up some of his mom's yoga music, all trance-like songs with birds singing and stuff. Then he rooted around again and found his little kit and took out a rolled-up hand towel and a small bottle.

"What's that?" asked Skyler.

"Oh, this is my sex kit. I guess that makes me look like a slut or something, but it just lives in my suitcase. I don't sleep around a lot, but my dad says, 'a gentleman is always prepared.' Don't worry, that towel's been washed. Move your pillow and lay it on the mattress. I intend to make you drool."

"What?" Skyler's face looked completely freaked.

"Hey, don't look so worried. I give the best backrubs in the world. Take off your T-shirt." Ryan flipped open the massage oil and rubbed some between his hands. Skyler stared at him with his forehead all knitted up. "I promise it won't hurt. Lie on your front."

Skyler's hands were shaking as he pulled off his T-shirt and rolled over. "Wait, does it hurt to lie on your piercings?" Skyler face was turned away, but he shook his head.

Ryan started with Skyler's shoulders, working the oil in with slow, deep glides of his thumbs. He worked along the tops of the shoulders, and the music seemed to make time slow down and then hover. He'd always loved to give massages, and getting massage therapy for his sports injuries had taught him some great techniques. He'd done a ton of them with girls, but those had always been a come-on thing.

There was something so satisfying about having his hands on Skyler's skin. It felt right. But somehow that didn't stop the pull he'd been feeling more and more lately. The urge to touch him... more. To push all the tension out of his muscles, to press all the tightened-up sadness out of his face, that was what Ryan wanted. Skyler's muscles were loosening, but he wanted to dig deeper, to root it all out.

Ryan threw his leg over and climbed on top, sitting gently down on Skyler's ass. "Are you drooling yet?" he asked softly. Skyler moaned and Ryan laughed. "I'm going to crack your back, okay? Just breathe like this." Ryan took a long breath in and so did Skyler. As they let the breath slowly out at the same time, Ryan's large hands pressed down slowly and firmly on either side of the top of Skyler's spine until he was crushed down into the mattress. "Again." They both took a long breath in as Ryan released the pressure and exhaled together as he slowly pressed down again. This time his hands inched down lower on Skyler's spine. With each breath, Ryan moved his hands a little lower until, near the small of Skyler's back, there was a cracking sound.

"There it is." This was what he'd been wanting, oh yes. To feel the kinks pressed gently and firmly out of Skyler's system, to feel him give way. A smile spread over Ryan's face and he worked his way down, breath by breath, to Skyler's tailbone. When that was done, he spent a little time on Skyler's lower back, and then his shoulder blades. Skyler was too thin. He needed feeding. He needed to smile and laugh again. It had been so nice to hear him shriek when Ryan had tickled him. Ryan's smile fell. It had been nice until his mom had joined them. *God, what is with her?*

But the truth was he had a pretty good idea what she was up to. She'd seen something she wasn't meant to, and she'd just gotten it wrong. He'd sort of tried to explain, but it was so embarrassing. And she wasn't a guy. She didn't get it. He ran his hands from Skyler's shoulders, down his arms, and then dug the pads of his thumbs into Skyler's palms and rose up onto his knees. He lifted Skyler's arms gently and shook them until they hung heavy and loose, angled out behind Skyler like Superman in flight. Then Ryan leaned back and let his own weight pull slowly on Skyler's arms until gradually his shoulders lifted up off the mattress.

"Breathe like this," Ryan said, pulling in air really slowly and then holding it before letting it out. The sound of their breathing merged, matching up perfectly, and he held Skyler like that for four whole breaths before he could get himself to ease him down again. It just felt like exactly what Skyler needed, and somehow there was this urge to give him whatever that was. Ryan's cock was half-hard, but it had been doing that a lot lately. *It's probably just the satisfaction.*

Hormones. His old friend Logan had always gotten that guys' bodies had a mind of their own. He pushed the concern out of his mind. What his body did, it did.

Ryan ran his hands one more time over Skyler's shoulders and then went to work on his neck, using thumbs to push the cords of muscle along the sides and digging his fingers into Skyler's hair to massage his scalp. "Better?" he whispered.

Skyler grunted in response.

Ryan smiled. "Do I hear drool?"

"Mmmm."

Ryan had one hand holding Skyler's head in place and the other hand massaging up his neck and into his hair. Skyler's hair had something in it, some kind of product that was heavy and creamy without feeling greasy. He tugged on the hair a little as he reached the top of his stroke.

The massage could have ended a long time ago. But it was hard to stop touching Skyler now that he'd really started. When would he have the chance again?

"You might get sore from skiing. My mom loves my calf massages. I can give you one tomorrow." Did his voice sound hopeful? Was that weird? No, no it wasn't. This didn't feel weird at all. It felt fantastic. It was so nice to be able to be there for someone. He'd missed that. Not just the touch, although that was great too, but feeling... useful. It was nothing like the thing with Logan. He wondered if Gun had come up with his parents this time. Did he still have the attic room too? Maybe he was sleeping right on the other side of the wall. At least the walls were thick. They'd tested out what you could hear when they were younger, and it was only really loud sounds.

He laid Skyler's head down gently and ran his hands down his spine again. *Why am I thinking about Logan?* He shifted himself lower until he wasn't sitting on Skyler's ass anymore and just looked down at it. *Logan was never warm like Sky is.* Had it really been that long since he'd had a real friend? Not that Logan had turned out to be particularly loyal, but they'd been close, almost like cousins growing up together.

There was that muscle right in the middle of the ass cheek that could get so tight. He could just... no, that might make Skyler uncomfortable. He'd made his disgust with Ryan perfectly clear not that long ago. God, he thought about it every day since and wished he could fix it. Maybe this had repaired a little something. Better not to fuck that up.

Skyler stirred under him, and Ryan rolled off, pulling the blankets up over them both. "Here, here's your pillow," he whispered, easing Skyler up by sliding a hand down under him and lifting him gently. He pulled the towel out and slid the pillow in. He turned off the music and the light and then lay on his side. Skyler slowly turned toward him and flopped his hand out to land on Ryan's arm.

"Best. Backrub. Ever," whispered Skyler. He was slurring, and his hand tightened on Ryan's arm. Had he ever reached out and touched Ryan before? Ryan smiled for a long time in the dark and edged closer until their legs were touching again.

Ryan fell asleep after a while but kept waking up. It was like his body was tuned in to Skyler's, and if Skyler was restless, he couldn't ignore it. He was also sweating and thirsty. He sat up at about 4:00 a.m. and yanked off his T-shirt in frustration. He always slept well. It was probably the strange bed. And it was too hot. He got up and opened the window, but the rest of the night was fitful. When he was finally deep asleep, the alarm went off with its soft little chime. He'd been in the middle of a dream, and although it was slipping away, he fought to try to catch hold of it as it went. Chloe smelled funny. He rubbed his face in her neck, but her hair was short and that was strange. And then all of a sudden, he was fully awake and realizing that he was rubbing his lips on Skyler's neck and rubbing his morning erection into Skyler's butt crack. Not Chloe's. And he was wrapped around him, arms and legs both.

"Oh," Ryan said and began to loosen his grip. Skyler slid carefully, too carefully, out from his arms and sat on the edge of the bed. Ryan turned off the alarm. "I thought you were Chloe."

Skyler didn't say anything, just hung his head and crossed his arms over his lap. Seeing him like that caused a hard-to-breathe tightness in Ryan's chest. *Maybe that made him hard too, and now he feels completely grossed out. Shit.*

"Hey, man. Don't sweat it, okay?" He got up and sat down beside Skyler, wanting but afraid to throw an arm around him.

"It's just morning wood, right? It happens to every guy." He ventured the arm now, pulling Skyler's naked skin against his own. "We're guys, right? We have these dumb sticks that we can't really control." He looked down at his crotch and said, "Skyler, Mr. Stupid. Mr. Stupid, Skyler. You feel better now that you're formally introduced?" Skyler huffed a laugh. "Look, I'll go take care of Mr. Stupid so he passes out, and he won't bother you again. Okay?"

Skyler nodded, still not meeting his eye.

Maybe his hard-on is really disturbing to him, since it's not with someone he likes. I better not say anything. He rested his forehead against Skyler's temple for a moment, refusing to lose that feeling they'd had last night. "Hey, we're going to have a great day today. Laze around a bit and I'll help you with your gear after I shower."

CHAPTER 5—SKYLER

AN HOUR later, Skyler thought he might actually overheat and pass out before Ryan was done putting clothes on him in the downstairs entranceway. He was wearing fleece pants under snow pants, wool socks inside Ryan's old ski boots, a long sleeve T-shirt, a fleece zip-up hoodie, Ryan's old snowboarding jacket, lined ski gloves, a fleece tube scarf, and a helmet with ski goggles strapped on. He felt stiff and awkward and desperate to rip it all off. Somehow Ryan had put it all together for him while getting ready himself, and so they both stepped out the front door at the same time to clip into the skis Ryan had already pulled out of the garage.

"If I'd known how much work this was going to be for you, I wouldn't have come," Skyler said.

"Oh, don't worry. It's always like this before skiing. You wonder why the hell you go to all this trouble, but then it just gets better and better. Did you learn french fries and pizza?"

"Sorry?" said Skyler.

"Your skis side by side will pick up speed, so when I call 'french fries,' that means straighten out and go faster, and this"—he put the front tips of his skis together so they formed a point—"pizza shape will slow you down. I'll just shout 'pizza' if you get going too fast. Ready?" Ryan skied away from the chalet and down the road. A road. Like with cars. "We have to cut through the neighborhood a bit to get to the lift," Ryan shouted over his shoulder. All the roads were covered in snow so they could actually ski on them and the hills weren't too steep, but the trip was still stressful. *THIS is ski-in, ski-out?*

There were a few cars, but they were going slow so they didn't skid out. The hardest part was just remembering what to do with his body while sliding down a hill. It was embarrassing and slightly terrifying, but by the time they had gone down and around and then down a larger hill, he was starting to feel like he had some grip on it again, and he hadn't fallen on his ass, which was a major bonus. There was a long flat bit and then one last hill before they were under the chairlift poles.

"Got your ski legs back yet?" Ryan smiled at him.

"Maybe." Skyler smiled back and they shuffled over to the ticket window.

"My dad got us some free passes for the day so you don't need to pay. Some work thing."

"Really? That's awesome!" He'd brought all the cash he could from his work tips, but it was hard not to hoard that money for the fall when everything was going to cost him. Ryan bent down and put the little wire hanger through a toggle on the bottom of Skyler's jacket and said, "It's better not to put them on your zippers. Breaks the zipper sometimes and flaps in your face when you go fast. We'll put it here out of the way."

"Thanks." Skyler felt a wave of warmth flow through him at Ryan's generosity. Sure, he had a lot more stuff and money to throw around, but that wasn't the whole of it. *Like that day at school. He didn't have to come after me. He didn't have to put his arm around me.* Ryan just seemed to want to take care of everything. *He just seems to want to take care of ME. Maybe he can tell how broken I am and there's some kind of morbid fascination. I'm like a bad car accident or something.*

The line for the chairlift was tiny, and so they didn't have to share with anyone else. Before he knew it, the chair was swinging around and pushing on the backs of his knees. He sat down with a thump and his heart lurched a little as they lifted off the ground. The ski boots and skis made his legs feel dangerously heavy, as if they might pull him off the lift. They rose higher and he could picture sliding right off the seat and falling. The blood in his legs seemed to zing and his face got hot. "Do you want to put the bar down?" said Ryan, pulling down the safety bar, and Skyler didn't protest. "Are you afraid of heights?"

"Ah, I'm not in love with them."

They were full height now, ski runs stretching out on either side of them. The air was shockingly cold on his face, but everywhere else felt a little sweaty and hot from the trip. There was a long flat spot on the trek to the bottom of the lift, and while Ryan had glided over it in some kind of graceful skating motion, Skyler had shuffled along probably using about eight times the amount of exertion to go about an eighth of the speed. It would have been more discouraging if it hadn't been for Ryan's smiling face telling him all about the different runs he wanted to show him. The names had all run together in Skyler's mind while Ryan had skied circles around him.

The trees on either side of the chairlift towers were completely coated in snow. "They look like people, eh? They call them snow ghosts," said Ryan, and indeed, their blobby tops did look like heads or hats or something.

"Look, there's Gandalf!" Skyler pointed at one topped with a large pointed hat shape.

"I love those movies," said Ryan.

"Me too, but I prefer the books." Ryan's smile faltered and an awkward silence stretched out.

"Hey, sorry the room got so hot last night," said Ryan. "I should have opened the window earlier. I was so thirsty during the night I got a totally shitty sleep." Holding his gloves against his chest, he wiggled his hand free and pulled a Burt's Bees lip balm out of his pocket and put some on. "Want some?"

"No thanks." The thought of dropping something from this height was oddly terrifying.

"Your lips are all chapped from last night. That's just going to get worse in this cold. Here, I'll do it. You don't want to drop a glove from up here." He leaned in and rubbed some lip balm carefully and thoroughly onto Skyler's lips. Ryan stretched his own lips out in an unconscious demo, but Skyler just averted his eyes and kept his lips perfectly still. *Am I supposed to pucker? God, no.* It was hard having Ryan lean in so close to him, looking at his lips so intently. Their legs were touching from hip to knee despite his efforts to move away. The horribly vivid memory of Ryan's body wrapped around him this morning flashed through his mind again and heat rose through him.

"There." Ryan put the lip balm away and then set about tugging up Skyler's scarf to cover his face.

"Sometimes the wind picks up near the top of the lift and it gets really cold. Just keep this up and it'll be okay. You should put your goggles on now too." Skyler pulled those down and settled them on his face. Ryan had adjusted the straps before they left so they snugged down perfectly.

"You're taking pretty good care of me."

Ryan's smile was a little dazzling. "I'm trying." He swung around. "Look behind us."

The chair had been moving steadily up the slope, but Skyler was still shocked to see the view behind them. The mountain spread out below and fanned out into a snowy forest. The small village looked like a Christmas model train town, surrounded by the white carpets of the runs and the white-topped trees. On the left, several little white peaks poked up in the distance, and the sky was a vast and shocking shade of blue. There were few clouds, but somehow it was still snowing softly, and the sun shining through the falling snow created this glowing sheen to the air. Skyler's breath literally caught in his throat.

"It's nice, eh?" said Ryan.

"Nice?" Skyler's voice squeaked but he didn't care. "It's… holy shit, it's spectacular! Wow. Just… wow." They both stared at the view for a long quiet moment, drinking it in. There was a hush to the mountain, the heavy blanket of snow muffling things to the point where everything seemed to ring silently, crisp and still and sparkling.

Skyler turned away reluctantly, but his ski poles were dangling oddly, and he was scared he might somehow drop one. He looked down at the straps, making sure they weren't going to slide off, and noticed the scattered snowflakes gathered on his black ski pants. "Oh my god, look! The snowflakes are like… real snowflakes!" There on his legs were hundreds of perfect six-pointed stars in all their infinite tiny detail. "They're like the kind you would cut out of paper and stick on the window at Christmas! I've never seen that before!"

"I think it's the altitude." Ryan's voice sounded funny, but Skyler couldn't read his expression very well through the scarf and goggles. "Neat, huh?"

"God, wow. Do you really think each one is unique? Is that like an urban legend or something?"

"You'd need a microscope to tell, I guess. And even then, what are you going to do, capture each one and study it without letting it melt and make a huge database or something?"

"Yeah, maybe it's nicer to just believe that they are. I mean, even just the fact that they form themselves into these awesome symmetrical patterns is some kind of miracle. And hey, if it's possible for an entire mountain to be covered in a blanket of microscopic art, it's not that farfetched that each one's different. This place is like magic! I can't believe it. God, I wish I had my camera."

"You can use my phone." Ryan pulled off a glove again and dug in his coat.

"Oh no, what if I dropped it? No no, that's okay."

"Seriously, here. It'll save me from having to take pictures."

"Oh my god, you've got them in your hair! Okay, fine, this is too good to miss." He carefully arranged his pole straps and gloves so he could grip them in one hand and fiddled with the phone. His hand quickly turned pink, it was that cold. He tried the zoom on his legs to see if he could capture the stars but wasn't sure what kind of focus he was getting as the sun reflected on the view screen. He turned to Ryan. "Okay, look at me. Yeah, perfect."

Ryan's long hair was sticking out messily around his face, the threads turning gold in the sun. Somehow looking at him through the camera was easier. There was a distance there, and he could just study and enjoy Ryan's face as he took pictures, letting the background frame him in this way and that. His eyes were crinkled at the corners like he was smiling. That deserved a super close-up shot, with those snowflake stars adorning him like pixie dust. Skyler forgot himself for a moment and reached out, tugging Ryan's scarf down awkwardly with one hand, and managed to snap another picture just as Ryan smiled.

"Hey, your hand is going to freeze."

"I don't care. It's too beautiful," Skyler said, straining around to take some shots behind them. He couldn't even tell what he was getting.

Ryan laughed and said, "Here." He pulled the phone and Skyler's naked hand to his face and cupped them in his gloved hands. Leaning in, he breathed out his hot breath in a long slow *haaaa*. Skyler shivered.

It felt like new life being breathed over his stinging, freezing flesh. It was delicious.

"Thanks," he whispered.

"Here, put the phone in your pocket. Then you can take some more when we get off." The thought of getting off the chairlift soon distracted Skyler enough to make it not worth arguing over the phone just then. *I'll give it back at the top.* The trees were changing too, getting more and more coated with snow and more and more lifelike.

The chair had been steadily climbing, and now it crested the top of a large plateau. It was still sloped but not nearly as steep. The chairlift ended about a hundred meters ahead, but suddenly the wind was something serious to contend with, stinging the line of skin exposed between goggles and scarf. Skyler hunched down as far as he could, but it was still freezing. He was very glad his hand was back inside the glove again.

Skyler managed to get off the chair without falling down or crashing into anyone, which seemed a small miracle, but his heart was thudding with the dread of it. He shuffled over to Ryan, who was waiting for him.

"Let's ski around here so I can show you the map." Ryan took off, gliding away, and Skyler struggled to follow quickly enough to not lose sight of him. They skied around under the chairlift, and the enormous map looked like a whole mass of multicolored spaghetti draped over the mountain faces, with a jagged line of peaks at the top. Ryan pointed at the sign with his pole. "This is the green run I was telling you about: Serwa's. It's the one right behind our place, so we'll do it as the last run of the day when we're ready to ski out. It comes out here and we can get on the same chair again. Okay?"

"Sounds good."

"Take some pictures here if you want. It's... pretty."

Skyler looked around, forgetting his nervousness for a moment, and Jesus, pretty didn't do it justice. They were on the top of a rounded peak with other lumps and bowls next to them and the slopes unrolling far below. The blazingly blue sky seemed to stretch impossibly high. Skyler dug out the camera, dropping his glove, which Ryan retrieved and then held onto because Skyler couldn't stop taking pictures long enough to take it back. "Wow. Jesus. Wow," he muttered, trying to capture that shimmer in the air. "Can you stand over there? I want to get that thing behind you."

Ryan skied over to the spot, and Skyler took a moment to try and get it. The shimmering was so bright it was almost, but not quite blinding to look at. He edged forward a bit until the light of it surrounded Ryan like a brilliant halo and started taking shot after shot. He never knew which shot was going to turn out, so why not take a whole bunch? Besides, there was something so photographable about Ryan. He didn't hunch his shoulders or hang his head awkwardly, but he also didn't pose. He just stood there, as if he were so comfortable in his own skin that he didn't even think about it. The word *shameless* ran through Skyler's head, and he pushed it away and lowered the camera. *Of course he's shameless. What does he have to be ashamed of?*

He tried to give the phone back, but Ryan just shook his head. "Keep it for now. I always forget to take pictures. I think it holds a zillion or something, so take as many as you want." And then he was skiing away and the camera was getting stuffed into a zip-up pocket in Skyler's effort to catch up.

The wide run wasn't crowded or steep to start with, and after a few moments of snow plowing down the hill, Skyler remembered the slow rhythm of S-shaped turns. *Pole plant, turn, lift that ski a little to get them parallel, glide, pole plant, turn....* Ryan was ahead and going slow but not watching him, which helped, and Skyler could just concentrate on the movements. The run forked and narrowed a little, but there was still lots of space in between the trees on either side. The run had been groomed and they were early so the snow was still in tiny parallel ridges over most of the slope. Ryan stopped and waited for him to catch up.

"I'm glad we got up here early. See the corduroy?" Ryan waved his hand over the snow at their feet. The surface looked almost combed, small lines turning the whole run into a smooth blanket with tiny raised texture. "Freshly groomed. I love skiing on this."

It DOES look like corduroy! Skyler thought.

"What? Do you hate it or something?" Ryan asked.

"No! Just.... Do you mind if I take a picture?"

Ryan laughed, "Of course not. Especially if it's going to hurt you not to."

After a minute or two, Ryan shouted, "Hey, try following my line," and then skied ahead again, carving perfect long S-curves down the hill. Skyler focused in on that line, trying to stay aware of his own movements but never once losing track of Ryan out of the corner of his eye. As they got farther down the run, the hills started to roll in perfect roller-coaster waves. It was not so steep that it was too scary and not so long that you got going too fast. It was like the giant slide at Playland. Looking up now, he could see that Ryan was doing little jumps off the tops of the hills, lifting his feet off the ground in smooth, effortless motion. He felt a childish giddiness in the whoosh of the downhill and the whee of cresting the top of the next one.

The ski run leveled out after a while, and there was a series of smaller hills one after the other like an upside-down egg carton. Ryan shouted back, "Keep your speed up on the downs so you can make it up the ups." This quickly made sense when the momentum of the first downhill carried him uphill to the next rise. Down and then up, down and then up. There was that roller-coaster feeling again, and a sense of limitless power that you could glide up a hill with so little effort and so much speed. It was exhilarating!

"It flattens out, so…." Ryan's words were lost on the wind, but Skyler pointed his skis as straight down as he dared since the run took a few more rolling hills and ended in a fairly long flat spot. He got a ways along it, using his poles to urge himself forward, and then the momentum ran out and he was back to shuffling forward again and trying in vain to match Ryan's beautiful skating glide. Ryan skied back toward him after a minute or two.

"What did you think?" Ryan asked.

"It was awesome! Perfect! I wanna do that one again!" Ryan answered Skyler's enthusiasm with a sparkle-eyed grin. "I mean, whatever you want to do."

"No, that's fine. I love that run."

They got back on the chair and didn't have to share it with anyone this time either. Skyler lifted his goggles to look at the sky, positive that that blue must be somehow an illusion created by the tint in the lens. The color was different but just as insane.

"It's better to leave your goggles on," said Ryan.

"Why?"

"Well they tend to fog up if you're not careful, and that sucks, but there's a trick to it. It's like there's this little microclimate inside where the cold air comes in the bottom vents, and your face radiates heat and warms it up. If it gets warm enough inside, then the moisture turns to vapor and comes out the vents at the top and the lens itself is warm. Just like in a car when the heat blasts on the windshield. When the glass is warm, nothing condenses on it."

"That's a nice little science lesson," said Skyler.

Ryan shrugged and looked away. "Yeah, the science of goggles. That's going to take me really far."

"So what do you want to do after high school?"

"I don't know. My dad thinks I should travel for a year, but I haven't saved up nearly enough. I doubt my grades are going to be good enough to get me into much."

"But what do you love?" Skyler asked.

"Love?"

"Yeah. What makes you feel all... you know, excited. Like you wanna freak out it's so cool."

"Well, I love to ski. And I loved playing soccer. It's so weird that I've done both forever and now it just looks like everything I care about is going to end. I can't do those things for a living. I'm good, but I'm not pro material."

It had always looked like the guys that were talented athletes had it made. They were strong and competent—they performed and belonged in the worlds they lived in. How strange to see that Ryan wasn't feeling that brotherhood.

"But there's lots of sports-related careers, aren't there? Like... being a trainer or a physio or a coach or something. You could teach kids how to ski."

"Sure, but that doesn't pay well. I like my job at Cypress, but the lifties make shit money and there's hardly any better jobs on the mountain." Ryan had admitted that he'd mainly taken the ski-lift job for the free ski pass. "I've been thinking about a trade, like metalwork or something."

"Does that interest you?"

"Not really. I just don't know that I've got much going for me."

"What? What are you talking about? You've got lots of talents that people value."

Ryan laughed. "There are these people called Snow Hosts up here. They show people around the mountain, like tour guides."

"That sounds good. You're really friendly and...."

Ryan's smile twisted. "They're volunteers."

"Oh."

"See what I mean? I made the wrong choices. I focused on stuff no one pays for and neglected the stuff that really counts. I'm kinda fucked."

Skyler stared at him. Hadn't he said the very same thing to Lisa recently about all those athletic guys who just wanted to work out and party? It was getting really tough to get into a university. "It's not too late to rock your last report card, you know. I could help you."

"But the applications are already in. It's the GPA I have now that counts, and it's not good enough. I didn't do that great on my exams before Christmas."

"What about a sports scholarship?"

"They've cut a lot of those, so you have to be some kind of rock star. Downturn economy shit."

Skyler stared at him, at a loss for what to say.

"But hey, don't sweat it." Ryan bumped shoulders with him. "Let's have some fun this week, okay? I'll worry about that later." He turned away and pointed toward where he wanted to take Skyler next and talked about how they would spend the day, but Skyler wasn't really listening anymore. He was thinking about Ryan's future. *I have to help him. I can help him, can't I?*

They skied Serwa's again and the fun came back into the morning. It was hard to stay bummed on those whoop-de-do hills, especially with Ryan dekeing in and out of the trees doing little jumps. Skyler couldn't help but take pictures of a tree that was so curly at the top it was like a Dr. Seuss book, of the way the snow whooshed up in one spot, and of course of Ryan. They were halfway down when Ryan stopped and let him catch up. "You're doing good. You're rotating your body, but you need to bend your knees more and let the front of your calves rest on the boots instead of leaning forward. Just try noticing that for a while."

It was a helpful comment, and Skyler tried to weave it into his conscious movement stream. *Pole plant, bend, turn, lift ski, straighten out, glide, pole plant, bend, turn....* He felt like he should stick out his tongue with the effort of trying to make it all flow together. This time on the flat bit, Ryan skied slowly alongside him.

"What would you call that sound?" said Skyler. "You know the sound the snow makes as it crushes down under your skis? It's so unexpectedly... dry or something."

"Yeah I know, it kind of squeaks, doesn't it?"

"How about 'squink?' I think that's more like it."

Ryan smiled. "Or 'squidge.'"

"That sounds softer."

"Yeah, the local mountains squidge. It's wetter. This is squink terrain up here."

Skyler laughed, and then they were flying down the hill again and curving to a stop at the chairlift. "I want to take you down Sleepy Hollow next. We go up here and then ski over to Powder chair and it might get colder on the way up. Do you mind?"

"Sure. No problem." But by the top of the first chairlift, the wind was so strong that Skyler covered his face with his gloves in an effort not to freeze. They skied down a different run that ended up at another, smaller chairlift that looked old and a lot scarier. The seats reminded him of old lawn chairs, but at least he was getting better at getting on without feeling like the chair was going to knock him flat and then run him over. The trip up was really cold. They both hunched forward covering their faces as the wind really started to rage. Halfway up, Ryan transferred his poles to one hand and slung an arm around Skyler, pulling them closer together. Skyler stiffened, but the relief from the cold really did help, and he began to actually feel warmth along that side. Toward the end, as the wind whipped them, stinging even skin that wasn't exposed, Skyler relented enough to press his hunched-forward head into Ryan's chest. Ryan tucked him under his chin and held on tighter. It was both a relief and a regret when they reached the top and Skyler untangled himself.

And somehow at the top it wasn't that windy. "What the hell!" said Skyler. "NOW there's no wind?" Then he looked around and lost all words. The trees up here were different again. They were entirely white, but unlike the smooth globular shapes on the other mountain face, the snow's surface here was encrusted with intricate shapes. "It's like coral!" Skyler skied over to the trees and pulled out the phone. He'd given up trying to offer it back and had just started to enjoy it. "But not regular sticky-uppy coral. More like...." The crust had formed into rounded knobs, each one filled with tiny crystal formations. They sparkled like cut glass in the sun. "Brain coral. Have you ever seen that?" Skyler looked up from the camera, and Ryan shook his head. "I'll find a picture for you. It's super cool stuff."

As he turned from one tree to the next, Skyler looked out over the view and took a long, cold breath in. They were up above the clouds now, although there weren't many of them. "It's so crazy to look down on the clouds. Wow." He gave up trying to stay warm and tucked both gloves in his armpit so he could adjust the camera properly.

"Your hands must be freezing."

"Pretty much." They did feel bad.

"Here." Ryan pulled Skyler's hands up to his face again and pulled down his scarf. His hot breath felt wonderful, and Skyler groaned in appreciation. Ryan smiled up at him from under his lashes and then pulled off his own glove and put a hand on Skyler's numb cheek. "You're freezing!" He pulled off his other glove and put both his hands on Skyler's face.

"Mmmph," groaned Skyler, closing his eyes. It felt too amazing to try to fight. His skin was so cold it had started to really hurt. Ryan pulled back slowly and their eyes met and then slid apart. "Thanks," he muttered.

"Okay, let's get moving before we die." Ryan flashed a grin and then took off down the hill. Skyler raced to catch up and found that this run was completely different. It was way narrower and the crazy crusty trees crowded closer, making the whole thing dream-like and fantastical. It twisted right and left and the sides curled up like a bowl in places. They skied fast for a while, and Skyler could feel his blood pumping and warming him again. About the time he started to sweat, Ryan stopped and he caught up.

"Mind if we take a break?" said Ryan, lifting up his goggles.

"Sure."

Ryan popped his skis off with the end of his pole and then popped Skyler's as well.

"Come on, I'll show you a trick." He slid his skis over his shoulder in a smooth motion that Skyler was helpless to imitate and walked into the trees. It wasn't many steps before they were out of sight of the run and the snow was sinking alarmingly under their feet. Ryan slung his skis down in front of him and turned them upside down. He laid them side by side a little ways apart and then stomped down the snow in front of them. Then he turned and sat down on the skis, his legs hanging in the stomped out area. "It's a snow bench. Come and sit."

Skyler's mouth hung open. "Sweet!" Perhaps sweetest of all was an excuse to sit close to Ryan again.

Following Ryan's lead, Skyler lifted his own goggles up. *I thought we weren't supposed to do that.* But he didn't say anything. It was too nice to be able to see Ryan's face properly. The hair that had escaped from under Ryan's helmet was sticking out at odd angles, stiff with snow. The trees were so close it felt like they had been somehow instantly separated from the rest of the world once they lost sight of the run. The space around them felt charmed.

"Here," said Ryan, pulling off a glove and digging in his coat. He pulled out a little bottle. "You ever had Fireball?" Skyler shook his head. "It's cinnamon whiskey." Ryan cracked the cap, sipped it gingerly, and passed it over. Skyler took a tiny taste. It was sweet and burned all the way down his throat.

"Holy shit." He swallowed another sip. "It tastes like those… those Valentine's Day candies!" He passed it back.

"Yeah, cinnamon hearts." Ryan took another nip. "You like it?" He held it out to Skyler.

"I can't tell yet." Skyler sipped again. The burn was almost lovely. He shivered and Ryan moved closer so their legs were touching. "It really burns."

"Yeah. That's why I like it." Ryan's smile was so close to him, it felt like the heat was starting to move from his stomach down his arms and legs. Ryan pulled out some strips of fruit leather and handed one to Skyler. It was frozen and chewier than usual, but he let it melt in his mouth and it tasted somehow far more delicious than normal.

Ryan reached over and brushed Skyler's hair. "You've got crazy hair."

"What? You mean like yours?"

Ryan laughed and tried to look at his own hair. "It does that sometimes up here."

Skyler smiled. "Reminds me of those monkeys. You know the ones on nature shows that sit in the hot springs in the winter?"

Ryan laughed, "Snow-monkey hair. You're absolutely right. I'll have to keep you out in the hot tub long enough for our hair to freeze out there. It feels cool." He took another sip and sighed. It sounded like he was content.

"We've been coming up here for a long time. We bought the house a few years ago, but my parents have loved this place forever."

"I can see why. It's just... stunning how beautiful it is. It's like some kind of movie set or enchanted forest or something. Like Narnia."

"I love those movies."

"The books were better. Did your parents ever read them to you?"

"Nah. We were always going to and from practices and games. Three kids. There was a lot of rushing around."

"Do you read now? I mean for fun?"

"Not really. I'm not exactly the book type."

"Why do you think that? Did someone tell you that?"

"They didn't have to. It's obvious, isn't it? I'm fast and strong. It doesn't take me long to learn physical things. That's what I'm good at."

"There's lots of things you're good at. God, Ryan, you've helped me so much." Skyler bit his bottom lip. This was dangerous ground, but waking Ryan up was worth the risk.

"Yeah?"

"Totally. You have this way of just cutting right down to the heart of things, you know? Maybe it's that scalpel thing like your mom."

"That sounds sooo helpful." Ryan laughed.

"No, like when you said that Jeremy should have treated me better and not made me feel stupid about it. That really helped, you know? Maybe because you're a guy…. My mom and Lisa have been great, but… I don't know."

"They don't really get it?"

"Maybe. I guess I wonder if they do or if there's some kind of different code for guys. Like you shouldn't expect certain things."

"Like to be cared about?" said Ryan.

Skyler looked away. He could feel his eyes getting wetter, and that lump in his throat was starting again.

"Sky, that's bullshit," said Ryan. Skyler blinked. *He's never called me Sky before.* "Just because you're a guy, you don't need to feel loved? God, my mom would have a trip to Disneyland on that one. She's always talking about how guys need more than girls do from their… partner." He shrugged. "Something about how we don't have the same emotional support from our friends and we're not taught how to talk about stuff."

"See what I mean? I can't believe that you can just say that. I don't know any other guys that are comfortable talking about this kind of shit. And I thought Jeremy was…."

"What?"

"Well, it's stupid, but I thought because he was so completely 100 percent gay that he was going to… I don't know, like, fall for me I guess."

"Maybe he did."

"Oh, I don't think so."

"Why?" Ryan took out his little Fireball bottle and took a sip.

"It wasn't just him…. It's hard to explain."

"I'm a guy. Maybe I'll get it." Ryan passed the Fireball over and Skyler took a sip. That spicy heat burned down and his stomach felt warm.

"Okay, so Jeremy lives in the West End, right? And it's this amazing community of people who are all out, you know, like, out of the closet big time, and he has a lot of gay friends there."

"Loud and proud. What? I've been to Pride Day. The parade was awesome."

"Yeah it *is* awesome, right? I went this summer, and it was so great to be around people who didn't think I was weird or bad or sick. I was like the normal-looking guy for once, and it was really liberating. It was like I didn't know I was carrying this huge backpack around until I set it down, and then I just felt like I might lift off the ground I was so light. I really loved that."

"But?"

"But there's this sort of freedom in that group. Like sexual freedom." Skyler darted his eyes over to see if Ryan could handle this. Ryan shrugged.

"I can see that. You get out of your little high school where people make you feel like a freak, and then you find this big tribe of people like you and you feel like you can finally be yourself. I can see how that could lead to a lot of public make-out sessions."

"Yeah. And private ones. With more than two people."

"Oh." Ryan looked away.

"Yeah. And I wasn't sure how to handle that. I figured... god, I don't know."

"What?" Ryan was looking at him again but it was hard to meet his gaze.

Talking about this with anyone was like walking on thin ice, let alone talking about it to Ryan. But now that he'd ventured out onto this frozen lake, Skyler couldn't seem to turn back. It felt like racing forward was the only hope of getting across. "I think I thought that no matter what, I was HIS. That if he wanted another guy with us, it was just to be wild and free and not because he wanted to... cheat."

"I guess having other people involved makes it hard to tell when someone's cheating."

"Well, we had this agreement. It was his idea, actually, that we would never get into something unless the other one was there. Flirting was fine but taking off your clothes wasn't. That was a clear line."

"And he crossed it. And lied about it."

"Yup. But I can't help thinking that I left the door open, you know? If I'd just been stronger or not so naïve, I would have just laid down the law from the beginning. I mean, I was turned on and curious, but I didn't really want those other guys. I mean, I wanted them but not.... god." Skyler hung his head.

"It was just sex, right, not a relationship? The relationship came first in your mind, and that was only with Jeremy."

Skyler looked up and Ryan's eyes looked so steady. *Maybe he gets it?* "Yeah. Way first. The rest was just...."

"Playing," Ryan said.

"Yeah. Or like... performing? I wanted to impress Jeremy and it WAS really hot, but now I just feel gross about it."

"Like it was your fault that he cheated." Ryan nodded.

"Yeah. I guess so. I mean, I know it was his choice, but... I just keep thinking, what could I have done differently? Where did I fuck it up? And I think letting other people into his bed was a big mistake."

"Okay. So you're learning that about yourself. That not drawing that line makes you feel nervous. That's good. You can't expect to know that without having to learn it. I mean, you're seventeen, for godsake. You've got a lot figured out already."

"I'm almost eighteen."

"Oh yeah, when's your birthday?"

"Next week."

"No shit! Mine's in two weeks. We should do something cool. Okay, but anyway, I think you're taking on too much responsibility. Here you are, a high school kid just new to everything, and he's older and letting you in on this whole new world. It should be him that's looking out for you. Him that's making sure you're okay. It's not your job to keep him faithful."

"Lisa says I'm being hard on myself."

"Maybe. But you're also letting him off and not treating him like an adult. And he's older than you. What if, in a few years, you're in that position, living on your own, working, and you meet some younger high school guy? Would you push him into stuff before he was ready? I know you wouldn't treat him the way Jeremy treated you."

"How do you know that? I mean, I guess that's true, but we haven't hung out for that long."

"Skyler, we've been at the same school forever. I've never heard about you being a dick to anyone, and I can just tell. You've got a kind face."

Skyler looked away. *Was a kind face attractive? Or babyish?*

"Jeremy wanted you for himself, but he wasn't willing to return the favor. That's greedy and childish. And if you get called out for crossing a line, you should be down on your knees begging for forgiveness, not brushing it off and trying to pretend it's no big deal. If it was no big deal, then why did he need to lie?"

"Because I'm oversensitive?"

"Fuck!" Ryan stood up and kicked a tree with his ski boots. Snow fell all over him, but he didn't seem to care. His fury was quite impressive. Finally he came back and sat down. "Sorry. I know it's not helping for me to get mad. It's just...." Ryan leaned forward and put his hands out in front of him like he was holding an imaginary ball. "Being sensitive and feeling things like you do, it's not... weak. It's like you think that's the gay part of you, the soft spot that can get kicked in, but it's not. Not all gay people are sensitive. Not all gay people care and love like you do. That's just racist."

"Racist?" Skyler tried to smile but it was a little shaky.

"Bigoted, prejudiced, whatever. I'm sure there are plenty of gay guys who want to fall in love and settle down and be exclusive. But there's lots of straight guys like that too. That's what I want. And there's lots of straight slut guys who want to bang the world."

"I guess I'm one of the gay sluts."

"No. You're not. I'm not talking about how many people you sleep with or what kinky positions you do it in. I'm talking about how much it impacts you. You care about people. Did you ever try to trick anybody to get what you want?" He put an arm around Skyler. "I'd hate to see you get less sensitive. All cold and jaded? That would be terrible." He pulled Skyler closer, their puffy jackets compacting until Skyler could feel solid body underneath, and suddenly the tears that had been threatening just popped out of his eyes and raced down his face.

"Aw, come 'ere." Ryan's other arm came around him, and Skyler let go of the stiffness he'd been clinging to since the car ride up here and just sank into Ryan's arms. Their helmets clunked together and his goggles sprang loose and hung off the back, but Skyler had bigger problems. His nose was running and sobs were choking up his throat in a painful logjam as his body convulsed with each one. He squeezed his eyes shut, clamped his jaw, and didn't let any sound out of his mouth. Ryan's arms were tight and seemed to wrap all the way around him. He couldn't quite dare to wrap his own around Ryan and so they folded up awkwardly between their bodies. Skyler cried about the pain of Jeremy for a minute and then cried about how heartbreaking it was that Ryan was straight. *He's like the perfect guy. Shit.*

Ryan didn't try to say that everything was okay or that Skyler was overreacting, he just relaxed and held on, rubbing Skyler's back now and then. The tightness of his embrace seemed to speak for him, saying that he wasn't uncomfortable or embarrassed and he wasn't hesitating in any way. Finally, Skyler was able to get himself back under control, and then there was the awkward problem of pulling away with a blotchy face and a runny nose. He wiped it on his glove as he withdrew and then realized it was Ryan's glove and muttered, "Sorry."

Ryan dug out a crumpled Kleenex, handed it over, and then put one arm back around Skyler's shoulders. "I'm taking you to lunch today, by the way."

"What? No, I can pay."

"Consider it a you've-had-a-shit-month present. Are you cold?"

Skyler gave a shaky laugh and nodded. The cold was seeping into him, actually, and Ryan's arm around him felt like the only warm thing in the world. Ryan rubbed his hand up and down Skyler's arm hard, warming him up. "We'll get moving in a bit. Here." Ryan put his palm against Skyler's cheek, but the hand was freezing and Skyler's face was actually flushed. "Oh, that's not helping, is it?"

Skyler took Ryan's hand and warmed it with his breath. "You're cold too. Let's go."

"You sure? I'm alright."

"I'm pulling my shit together here." He sniffed hard and shot Ryan a tight smile. "You must be the most non-freaked-out-by-crying guy in the world."

"Hey, I have two sisters and a mom who forces me to talk about my feelings. She's a counselor."

"Oh! I should have asked her." Skyler frowned, feeling like a self-involved teenager. Again. God, finding out that Ryan HAD an older sister had been a real wakeup call. What other things had he not found out yet? Important things. He resolved to pull his head out of his ass more and pay attention.

They skied a few more runs and then came out down in the village. There was a bar and grill called Santé that took minors, and they clomped in in their loosened ski boots.

"Order something big," said Ryan, looking at the menu. "You'd be surprised how much more you can eat after skiing, and you need feeding up as it is."

The comment stung. Sure, he knew he was underweight before and now he looked like a bean pole without his clothes on, but it hurt to hear it from Ryan. *It doesn't matter, asshole. Remember?* Ryan looked up to ask him something and stopped. "What?"

"Nothing. What are you having?"

"A burger, I think. You liked those yam fries, right?"

"Yeah. Maybe I'll get those." Food was free at the restaurant where he worked, but most of the time he was just too run off his feet to take advantage of it until he was way past hungry. When he ate out and had to pay, he always ordered something small, no drink. It kept costs down.

"Only that?! Dude, you're going to waste away. You want an iced tea?"

"Water's fine."

"What, are you on a diet or something?"

Ouch. "Look, I know I'm scrawny, okay? You don't have to rub it in, and you don't have to pay for me." Skyler kept his voice low. They were in the back corner of the restaurant, but he was embarrassed enough to not want anyone else to overhear.

"Whoa! Scrawny? What the fuck? You think I'm saying that you're... like, unattractive?!" Ryan's voice was not at all quiet.

"Whatever."

The lady at the next table looked up at them.

"Skyler, you're like the hottest guy I know! You could go to a concentration camp and get super skinny and you'd still be hot. I'm just saying I want you healthy. And happy."

Skyler took off his helmet and set it on the table. "I'm going to the bathroom."

As he started his slow ski-boot thumping walk away, Ryan raised his voice. "He's the hottest guy, right? I'm trying to tell him."

"Oh, for sure. Beautiful bone structure." It was a woman's voice, no doubt from the next table, but Skyler just walked away and pretended not to hear.

He came out of a bathroom stall a few minutes later to the view of Ryan at a urinal with his pants undone. He averted his eyes quickly and washed his hands. God, this morning's bedroom adventure kept bouncing back into his head like a super-bounce ball in outer space. It felt like it might never lose momentum enough to stop boinging up at the wrong moment. It had been terrifying. He kept picturing Ryan waking up properly and freaking out and pushing away in disgust. Or worse, blaming him and thinking that Skyler had somehow tricked him or rubbed the gay off on him. The fact was that he'd spent most of the night trying to move away from Ryan's ultrawarm body and casual touch, but Ryan wouldn't know that. He had completely not expected Ryan's gentle surprise and then proverbial shrug. That just didn't happen. He didn't even seem to feel awkward about it. How was that possible?

He glanced into the mirror in dismay at his hair and started trying to move it around with his wet hands. He tried very hard not to let his eyes flick over to where Ryan was zipping up his pants. Suddenly Ryan was bonking hips with him and smiling at him in the mirror.

"Did you just bypass the urinal because you're gay?"

"Yup."

"Huh."

Ryan washed his hands too. "Your hair is perfect as usual, Romeo. Leave it alone."

"It's totally messy!"

Ryan shrugged. "I like it messy. Here, like this...." Ryan leaned in and used his wet fingers to twirl bits of hair straight up.

A guy came out of a cubicle toward the sinks and then stopped dead in his tracks. His face took on this pained, disgusted look in the mirror, and he turned toward the door instead. "Fucking fags," he muttered.

"Fucking rednecks," Ryan called after him in a strangely friendly singsong, never taking his hands out of Skyler's hair. "There, now *that's* how you should wear your hair!" He turned his bright smile to the mirror and their eyes met. Skyler's hair was messy and crazy, but there was an almost style to it that did look somehow good enough.

"Thanks," whispered Skyler, dropping his eyes.

"Any time you need some styling, I'm your man."

"No, for the... guy. I'm sorry you got that aimed at you."

"Man, you're not responsible for that asshole's dumbassness. It's not your fault. Fuck, you're at least doing something about it."

"Oh yeah, like what? Standing here?"

"Like being out. I can see that now. Being out is really cool. It's fucking balls-of-adamantium cool."

"Thanks."

"No, thank you"—Ryan swept his hand out and bowed slightly at the waist—"for doing your part to educate the dumb fucks of the world. Please, after you, sir." He swept his hand toward the door, and Skyler just shook his head and laughed.

As they were edging back into their seats, Skyler noticed an exit door next to them and read the words "No Admittance, Spa Area." Curious, he retraced a few steps and peeked over the frosted pane of glass. There was an outdoor hot tub with a good-looking couple drinking champagne. The woman sitting on the edge was a beautiful blonde in a bikini. Ryan was at his side peering out before he could turn away.

"Seems like some kind of lifetime achievement, doesn't it?" said Skyler. "Drinking champagne in a hot tub in some place like this."

"You think?"

Skyler sat down and they argued again about food. He finally ordered a chicken Caesar, and Ryan ordered him an iced tea as well and a poutine "to share." Skyler really was hungry when the food arrived, and Ryan was so funny that the meal seemed to rush by, and suddenly his straw was sucking air instead of iced tea and there was no food left. Ryan had somehow signaled the waitress without him noticing and was punching in numbers on the little Visa machine before Skyler could stop him.

The next few runs took them to a different part of the mountain, and Ryan gave him a new tip each time they got to the top of a chairlift. Once it was a note about the distance between his skis, and once it was a demo on how having one leg slightly forward instead of side by side would improve his control when he turned. Skyler tried to cram it all into his brain, but at a certain point, his legs just stopped obeying commands. He hit a softer pile of snow and couldn't quite compensate, and suddenly he was sprawling ass over helmet.

He lay still for a moment, waiting to see what hurt, and then slowly tried to get himself sorted out. One ski had popped off and was a little above him on the slope, and Ryan was herringboning up the slope toward him at a very fast pace. His ski prints looked like giant bird tracks. *Pterodactyl.* Skyler laughed. It was kind of a relief to have his first wipeout over with.

"You okay?" called Ryan.

"I think so."

"That was quite the rag doll. At least it wasn't a full yard sale, though, that's good."

"Yard sale?" said Skyler. Ryan was getting his lost ski.

"You know, when your gloves fly this way and your goggles fly that way and both your skis go sliding in different directions. This was a, let's say, medium-sized wipeout. Come on, there's a spot we can take a break at soon."

Skyler did have to hold onto Ryan's offered arm to get the ski back on, and then he skied after Ryan, glad for the greatly reduced speed. The run forked and the V in the middle was Ryan's rest stop. Skyler thumped down on his ass gratefully, clouds of steam huffing out of his mouth. God, he was tired. Ryan popped his own skis off and sunk them butt end down into the snow so they stood up like sucked-thin candy canes. He sank to his knees and slowly began piling snow over Skyler's legs.

"Ah, what are you doing?"

"Burying you."

"Do I look that dead?"

"I'd say you're almost done."

"Almost? My legs are no longer attached to my nervous system. Is that going to get better?"

"Well, we have to ski out of Serwa's, which means we have to finish this one and then take the chair up again to get there. But don't worry. We'll rest a bit." He worked steadily, and Skyler was too exhausted to bother stopping him. He lay back in the snow and closed his eyes. After a while, Ryan said, "Hey, you got the camera?" and Skyler dug for it and handed it over, realizing that his whole lower body was now submerged in snow.

"Okay, make like you're dead." Ryan pointed the camera at him. Skyler flopped back down and let his tongue hang out. Ryan laughed, took a couple pictures, and then lay down next to him and held the phone above them. "Take off your goggles and say 'cheese!'" He took off his own and took a picture and then turned and planted a big wet kiss on Skyler's cheek just as the flash went off again. Ryan leapt up, howling with laughter and looking at the phone.

"Oh MAN, you've gotta see your face! HA! That was awesome! You look like you just wet your pants." Skyler was floundering on his back like an overturned turtle, trying to kick his way out of his snow pack. "I'm putting it on Facebook. What should I call it?"

"What? You are not! Ryan, you better not be!"

"Maybe 'Big Gay and White?' Ha! Or 'My big fat gay wedding.' No, no wait, it should be, 'Ryan finds out the hard way that not all gay men like him.' Oh, that's good."

Skyler had wrestled free of the snow but was still wearing his skis, which were not cooperating in the least. Ryan easily dodged his frantic grabs. "RYAN. Stop right now!" Skyler shouted. "You don't know what you're doing! Stop! Please."

Ryan's thumbs stopped dancing over the screen for a moment. "Dude, relax. It's just a funny picture."

"NO. It's not! Don't you get what it would do to you if people at school thought we were together? Or your parents? Just think about it for a second! Please."

"I post funny pics all the time."

"Yeah, with STRAIGHT guys!"

"Okay, so you're worried that people will be mean to me if they think I'm into you." Ryan lowered the phone a bit.

"YES!"

"Any other objections?"

"Isn't that enough?"

"Nope." Ryan lifted the phone up again.

"Wait! Ryan, that's basically public. It doesn't mean anything to you, but it will to other people. What about your work?"

"Blah, blah about HOW mean people might be to me, but there's nothing else bothering you? I mean you're not, like, mortified to be seen with me or something?"

"Of course not! That's not the...."

Ryan pressed something on the phone and put it in his pocket. "Done. It's done. Cool your jets, Brad Pitt. We are now like... online dating!" Ryan's grin was so wicked it was twirled on both sides.

Skyler sank down on his butt in the snow and just stared straight ahead. *He just risked so much and he doesn't even get it. God, what have I done to him?*

Ryan sat down, too, and handed over his bottle of Fireball. Skyler took a long swig and looked down at the bottle. The label had a red demon with the muscled naked body of a man. Skyler choked a laugh. "Oh look. It's you."

"You think I'm that ripped?" Ryan flexed.

"Ryan, can you be serious for one second? You have no idea what you just did."

Ryan shrugged. "I think I have a small clue. I got called a 'fucking fag' today, remember?" Suddenly Ryan's sunny smile was gone and his eyes were gleaming in anger. "It doesn't matter that we're not together. No one should talk to you like that no matter who you're with. And if you have to deal with shit like that, then I'd rather be swatting them back than watching them eat into you."

Skyler sighed. It really was amazingly sweet. Here was Ryan wanting to stand up for him not just from the outside, but willing to step over the line and get picked on too. It was crazy. Maybe it was also very Ryan. There was no controlling him. God, that was frustrating. *Well, there's nothing you can do about it now. Except maybe... give him a taste of his own medicine.*

"That was the stupidest thing anyone's ever done for me. But maybe the nicest too."

Ryan hadn't shaved since they'd arrived. He had a fine smattering of stubble along his jaw, shining gold in the sun. Skyler leaned over and kissed Ryan slowly on the cheek, letting the tip of his tongue swirl over Ryan's stubble. "But if you want to kiss me, do it right." He got up and cocked an eyebrow at Ryan's openmouthed stare. "Now let's get out of here before the gay police show up." A wicked grin of his own twizzled the corner of his mouth.

"Those guys can ski?" Ryan's eyes were twinkling as he looked over his shoulder, like someone might be after him.

"For sure, haven't you seen James Bond? Those guys are always skiing after him like crazy." He sang the theme song and did some whooshing actions with his arms. "Dun-de-de-la, dun-de-de-la...."

"Whatever, James is like the ultimate straight guy! He bangs every hot chick he can." Ryan got up and started getting his skis on.

"Got something to prove, maybe? Didn't you see the new one? He totally admits he's been battin' for both teams. I mean, I'm not complaining. You can't let that kind of talent go to waste."

Ryan laughed out loud. "You know, he never does stay with one girl...."

"Exactly. He's got the itch, and the ladies never quite scratch it."

"Nah, I think he's just a slut and a workaholic. He'll do whatever and whoever if it'll help the mission."

They skied away and the James Bond theme music carried on in Skyler's head, giving his legs back a little responsiveness. By the time they had taken the chair back up and were heading down Serwa's again, however, his legs seemed to be made out of cooked noodles.

They took a small branch off on the right side and suddenly they were on a narrow track that rolled up and down like satin ribbon with forest on either side. They didn't pass one person on this little cut-through track, and there was this lovely sense of peace and beauty with just the two of them to experience it. Ryan really did ski beautifully. He made it seem so effortless and smooth. It looked like dancing. Then suddenly, they were coming out of the woods into an open area.

Ryan stopped and pointed. "There's the house. Come on, let's have a hot tub before dinner."

"Oh, no thanks, I wanna cook tonight."

"You don't have to do that."

"It'll get it off my mind."

Getting all the gear off was a lot easier than getting it on, but Skyler was still wiped out by the effort. "You take the first shower," said Ryan, springing up the stairs two at a time. Skyler followed more slowly, each stair announcing itself in his calves and thighs. He was actually breathing hard when he got up the first two flights. It was weird to feel so tired.

Skyler locked the bathroom door carefully and used his shower time as a preemptive strike against the boner-from-hell. He opened the door to let some of the steam out, and Ryan strolled up in only a towel. "Almost done." Skyler tried to smile and not look at Ryan's arms, but Ryan came right in and started turning on the shower. "I was just going to...."

"Yeah, go ahead," said Ryan, dropping his towel on the floor and sliding open the glass doors of the tub. Skyler felt like his eyes noticeably bulged out at the sight of Ryan's full nudity from the back. He knew he should avert his eyes, but they were laser-beam-welded to Ryan's body, and his brain stopped working entirely. Somehow seeing Ryan's whole form uninterrupted by lines or fabric was entirely different from seeing Ryan in his swim trunks or his boxers this morning. Maybe it was the way all of his muscles flowed into each other, every curve connected to the next. His bum had these little hollows on either side below his hips, and the cheeks looked somehow soft and hard at the same time. The glass doors above the tub shut, but Skyler's view was interrupted only by the drops on the clear panes. Ryan's face was turned right into the water, and so it seemed like there might be one more stealable moment before Skyler really had to tear his eyes away and run for it.

Ryan stood still, one hand on the shower wall, and just let the water flow over him. It seemed to dance down his body, the water turning to ribbons that snaked back and forth over his skin. His hair curved down in locks as he let his head hang forward. Skyler's hair product jar was still in his hand, but he couldn't quite seem to use it. He backed up until he bumped into the half-open door and then—finally— turned and fled.

He was pulling the door shut behind him carefully when Erika spoke and he almost jumped out of his skin. "Ryan showering?" Skyler nodded and blushed. "God, he's got no personal space, does he? Never could get him to shut the door when he goes pee."

Skyler followed her down the stairs. "Yeah?"

"Yeah, totally embarrassing. Our last house only had one bathroom, so my mom blames it on that. It must be double weird for you, though, right?"

Skyler flicked his eyes to hers. She looked… sympathetic, maybe. "Well…."

"I mean, if I had a guy friend and he was all naked all the time, it would be weird."

"Yeah. Okay, yeah, it's a bit weird, but he… doesn't mean it." Erika's eyebrows went up. "I mean, he's not like showing off or something. Is he?"

Erika sat on a stool at the island in the kitchen. "Nah, he's never been much of a show-off. I think he'd rather have people laugh at him. Last year the guys were doing jumps off that ledge out there." She pointed over to the snowy slope next to the house. At the top, there was an overhang. It was a cliff maybe as high as the four-story house and the slope was extremely steep.

"They were jumping that? On skis?"

"Yeah, but Ryan waited until everyone went in. Mom finally yelled at him that it was too dark and he had to stop. He was landing it better than any of the other guys, so I asked him why he didn't do it in front of them. He just shrugged and said that he'd jumped it so many times, it wasn't really a fair advantage." Erika hopped down and put some music on. The sound seemed to get Skyler's nerves under control. He took his yogurt containers of frozen soup out of the freezer and dug out a big pot.

"What are you doing?" asked Erika.

"Making dinner. I made some stuff at home."

"Really? Wow. Mom's going to freak out."

"Well, I just want to do something for them. It's awesome here. And your dad got me a free ski pass today."

"What are we having?"

"I made a carrot soup—it's coconut curry—and an apple and pecan salad, but I wasn't sure if everyone would like that so I made a macaroni and cheese as well."

"Nice! I bet they'll love it."

Skyler smiled back at her. She looked a little like Ryan in her facial structure and her coloring, but she wasn't tall and bulky like he was. "You're in grade nine, right? Who do you have?"

They talked about teachers for a while, Skyler offering sympathy and advice here and there, and then Ryan came down.

"Hey, I love this song!" Ryan ran over to the iPod hookup on the fireplace mantel and started the song over. "Okay, Erika, it's time for a rematch. Whoever has the most hilarious dance move wins."

Skyler recognized the song now: it was "Boredom and Joy," and it had this great opening that made him want to get up and dance. Erika rolled her eyes, but she was smiling too and jumped down. The soup was on the stove, slowly thawing, the mac and cheese was in the oven, and the salad just needed putting together, which was better done right before serving it. Ryan was dancing around, and he had a kind of natural groove. *God, he looks good.* Skyler's knee bobbed up and down to the music, and he hovered at the kitchen counter. He'd done a lot of dancing in clubs and at parties this past year, and it had been incredibly fun to just let loose and move. But this was Ryan. *Do not dance with this guy. Don't do it.*

"This one's called the sprinkler." Ryan spun in a circle and one arm shot out at regular intervals like he was spraying the room. Skyler laughed.

"Don't forget the Worm." Erika was on the floor undulating. It was pretty funny.

"The Rooster." Ryan put both hands on his head in a Mohawk of fingers and started strutting around. Skyler laughed again and Ryan did his herky-jerky move over into the kitchen. In a strange high voice, Ryan said, "The Rooster demands that you play!" He poked Skyler in the ribs with fingers that were still on his head.

"Hey!" Skyler took a step back.

"Do not anger the Rooster! He will peck you to death!" Ryan lunged forward again, and Skyler held up his hands.

"Okay, okay but I don't have any moves!"

"What's the funniest animal you can think of?" shouted Erika over the music.

"Uh, a penguin?"

"Yeah, do the Penguin!"

Before long all three of them were laughing hard, and then Ryan's dad slid in, which seemed awkward at first. Then "Moves Like Jagger" came on and he did some robot moves and jazz hands that were really pretty hilarious.

Dinner went really well. Everyone wanted to try everything and exclaimed over the food. Skyler had run upstairs to throw on some skinny jeans and a button-up shirt, but then wished he hadn't. Luckily, no one seemed to notice that he was trying too hard. Ryan's mom said, "Skyler, you've got to tell where you got these recipes. How did you get that soup so lemony?"

"It's the lemongrass. I just bought a tube of it, though, so it was kind of cheating. Do you know the *Rebar Cookbook*? The soup was something like 'Thai Carrot Coconut Curry Soup' and I think the salad was the 'Gala Apple and Spiced Pecans Salad.'"

"Yes, I do have that book. Delicious, honey. And that was so thoughtful of you to make macaroni as well. I think we'll have leftovers tomorrow."

There was some lovely music on that seemed mellow but also enlivening at the same time. Erin called it Bossa Nova. Everyone was drinking red wine, although Erika was only allowed to have a single small glass. Ryan's dad kept filling up Skyler's glass, and before long he felt a little flushed and floaty. Maybe that was why he didn't hesitate when the conversation came around to him. Ryan's dad ("please call me Dave") was asking about sports, which was an uncomfortable subject for Skyler since he hated most of them.

"No sports at all? But don't your parents want you to have that team experience? I think that's so good for kids."

"Well, my dad's not really around much. My parents are divorced, and he's been a bit odd since I came out. I think he wanted me to play because he never got to, and so it was disappointing to him that I didn't show much talent. I was on some teams when I was younger, but as it got more competitive, I just hated it more and more. I can't really catch or throw or kick or hit anything, so that does limit me." Skyler laughed, but Dave didn't. "It's okay, though. I mean, it would probably be hard now anyway."

"You mean being openly gay on a team." Dave was nodding as though he was thinking this over.

Wow, he actually said the G word! Skyler wasn't sure whether to be impressed or wary. Where was he going with this?

"But isn't it harder in lots of situations for you now? I mean, there's nothing wrong with being gay, but teenagers don't know that. Kids can be so, well, immature. And cruel. It must be really tough to have to deal with their attitudes. Do you think coming out has really helped you?"

"Dave!" Ryan's mom smacked him on the arm lightly.

"No, that's okay. It's a good question really. And I'm not above taking the easy road and just surviving if that's what it takes, but it wasn't really about that. I mean, I know that I should be able to be myself and I do have a little bit of that righteous feeling sometimes that the world needs to learn a thing or two... but that wasn't the deciding factor."

Everyone else at the table was quiet and listening, and Skyler wanted to glance around at them, but he felt like if he looked away from Ryan's dad, he would lose his nerve. He set down his fork. "It's like... imagine that you were born in a gay world and you were you, right? You liked women. And everyone around you thought that liking women was either evil and warped or at least stupid and weak. So you grew up trying really hard to pretend to be like everybody else, to do what all the other guys are doing, but at a certain point, people expect you to start making out with men and trying to get in their pants and you're like, uhhh, no way! And so what do you do? Do you just keep lying and marry a man? If you keep pretending, then all the people around you are going to get lied to. You're never going to have a real friend who gets how freaked out you are all the time or who you can talk to about the amazing girl you met. And you'll never have a hope of meeting the person that you could fall in love with, because they're off limits. Even looking at them the wrong way could get you into trouble. You're not just giving up being loud and proud, you're giving up any real relationships that you might be able to have. Not just with lovers, but with friends as well."

He picked up his fork again and stabbed a piece of apple. "I'm sure it's not the right choice for everyone to come out in high school, but it was right for me. And you know, the straw that broke me was when that kid killed himself, you know the one that came out and got basically hassled to death? I mean, it seems like a good reason NOT to come out, right? But to me it was the opposite. It means there are tons of kids out there just like me who're freaked out about what they might be, and they really need someone who can just step forward and be okay out there in the spotlight. I figured I was lucky enough to have a great mom and an awesome best friend who support me and I could weather it in a way a lot of other kids couldn't."

Skyler cut up his lettuce in the silence that followed, trying to make it into smaller bites. It felt rude to just shove the leaves into his mouth the way he would at home. He and his mom often read while they ate dinner, comparing notes when they felt like it. This was a family with five people and a dog in it. This was a household. It felt like there were rules he should know but didn't.

Dave said, "So you could have kept it hidden but you decided not to. I think that takes a lot of courage. But if you could change it and choose…."

"Dave!" said Ryan's mom.

"I just mean, if you could make yourself like girls, would you?"

Skyler had just taken a bite of salad and it suddenly felt hard to chew. His throat tightened. To never have fallen for Jeremy, to have never fooled around with Jeremy's friends, to not have the boner-from-hell whenever Ryan was being warm and kind? To maybe have a nice safe crush on Lisa or to even be going out with her? God, that sounded easy and just... better.

"Skyler, you don't have to answer that," said Ryan's mom.

Skyler swallowed. "When I came out, I would have said no way. But lately?" He shrugged and looked down at his plate.

Ryan's fist hitting the table made everyone jump. "Dad, that is the most asshole comment! I can't believe you! No one asks you whether you would change being straight or not. You don't even think about it!" He was sitting on Skyler's left, and now all efforts not to stare at Ryan were out the window.

Dave held up his hands. "But nobody's persecuting me because I'm straight. I'm just asking him if he had the choice. Clearly he doesn't have that choice, but if he did...."

"What the fuck is that supposed to mean?" Skyler had never seen Ryan look so angry.

"I'm just saying that I sympathize with how hard it must be. I'd spare him that suffering if I could. Wouldn't you?"

"NO! Fuck no! You're the one who's always saying 'Go travel, find yourself!' God, can you hear what you're saying? Spare him from the pain of being true to himself? Spare him the chance to find someone he loves and to have real friends? Didn't you hear a word that he said? Sure it sucks. Sure the kids at school are assholes. I was one of those assholes myself actually before Sky gave my head a shake. He woke me up! He's already this, like, force to be reckoned with, and he hasn't even gotten to college yet. Think what he'll be like in a few years!"

Ryan's mom laid a hand on Dave's wrist. "Honey, you don't pick who you fall in love with. Remember when we met?"

Dave's furrowed brow relaxed. "What, you didn't pick me?"

She smiled. "And you didn't pick me. We were just drawn together like magnets and there wasn't any way that either of us was going to back out."

He smiled and put a hand over hers. "And I wouldn't change it if I could."

"Neither would I." She leaned in and kissed him. "Now who wants dessert? I think I'm too full."

Skyler wasn't sure whether to leave his mouth hanging open or to shut it and pretend to keep up with the rest of them. *I can't believe Ryan swore at his dad! And his mom didn't even tell him to watch his language.* Skyler couldn't remember his mom or dad getting mad like that, even when they were splitting up. That had been mostly silent anger. *And Ryan was yelling, and nobody seemed to think that was weird....* In fact, everyone was chatting normally and getting ice cream. Maybe the unspoken family rule was that it was okay to argue?

Ryan's knee bumped his under the table, and Ryan motioned with his head and raised his eyebrows in a you-want-to-get-out-of-here question. Skyler shrugged a shoulder. Ryan stood up and started clearing the table and Skyler joined him.

"We'll do that, Skyler. You cooked dinner. Go and relax," called Ryan's mom.

"What do you want to drink?" asked Ryan, peering into the fridge.

"I'll just have another Ribena and soda."

"Did you bring this?" said Ryan, looking at the Ribena syrup.

"Yeah. Did you have it as a kid? Black currant is my favorite. You want one?"

"Sure."

Skyler had brought a box of No Name soda as well. He figured it was cheaper than bringing that much juice and would keep him hydrated without drinking them out of house and home. It now seemed kind of embarrassing, like something an old lady would drink.

"I like it," said Ryan. "Very refreshing." Ryan smiled and Skyler averted his eyes from the warmth of it. "But it definitely needs vodka." Ryan pulled a bottle out of the freezer and topped up both of their glasses.

Erika said, "You guys want to play Settlers of Catan?"

Ryan shook his head, eyes only on Skyler. "You want to set up my laptop and then watch a movie?"

Skyler shrugged. "Whatever you want."

Ryan brought his laptop into the den and copied the photos from his phone onto the computer and used his credit card to buy the video editing software that Skyler recommended. It was tempting to look at Facebook and see what Ryan's photo was stirring up, but Skyler pushed that out of his mind.

"Hey, do you want to play with my helmet cam?" Ryan asked.

"You have one? Yeah, cool! That sounds awesome. Do you have footage from it on here?" Skyler looked over his shoulder.

"Yeah, somewhere." Ryan passed the laptop to him.

"I don't really get your system," said Skyler.

"There's no system, dude. I just dump stuff in and walk away."

"Do you mind if I organize this a bit? You really need some folders."

"Sure. I can never find anything." Ryan pulled out a bunch of different DVDs while Skyler sat intent on the laptop. When Erika put on music in the living room, Ryan leaned back against the door and it shut with a click. "Sorry about my dad. He's normally really nice."

"Oh I don't think he was trying to be mean."

"He didn't have to try. That was pretty awful."

"At least he gets that it's hard, I guess."

Ryan got them more drinks and they watched the first X-Men movie, one of Skyler's favorites. The couch was black leather, kind of cold and slippery, and Ryan turned off the lights and threw a fuzzy blanket over both of them. Before long, Ryan's splayed thigh was resting on Skyler's and Ryan's arm was on the back of the couch behind him. The drinks were gone pretty fast, and Ryan paused the movie to go and get more. Skyler was so thirsty. He for sure hadn't drunk enough water today, and the wine and now the drinks were going to his head. Ryan came back with salty microwave popcorn as well, and soon those drinks were gone too. Ryan's body seemed to slowly mold around his own, and it was easier to just relax against that firm warmth than to try to maintain the tension in his body.

As more of his body touched Ryan's, Skyler thought over the dinner conversation again. *Was that a warning?* Was Dave getting the idea that Skyler's gayness might rub off on Ryan somehow? Was he uncomfortable with Skyler as a friend choice at all, or maybe just with Ryan's affectionate nature around someone on the other team? *But how much of Ryan's affection has he actually witnessed?* There was the car ride, if he was paying attention. Maybe he just knew that Ryan was physical with his friends, and that that would be a problem with a gay kid.

The thought was interrupted by Dave poking his head in the door. Skyler sat up straight and tried to put a little distance between him and Ryan. "We're heading to bed. Night, boys." Was he frowning? He was definitely frowning.

"Night," said Ryan and Skyler together, and the door closed again.

"I don't think your dad approves of me," Skyler whispered.

"Naw, he likes you."

"Yeah, but maybe he thinks gay is contagious. Like I'm going to convert you or something."

"Or maybe you're like Rogue and one touch will suck my life force out and almost kill me."

"I can kind of relate to her, actually. With her gloves on all the time."

"Hey, I was kidding. Who cares what he thinks." Ryan moved his arm off the back of the couch and onto Skyler's shoulders, rubbing his hand up and down Skyler's arm. "You can take your gloves off with me." His smile flashed in the dark and Skyler laughed, letting his head rest on the couch. Ryan moved a bit, sliding Skyler's shoulder onto his chest, so their heads were almost touching. Skyler brought his knees up under the blanket and allowed himself to rest against Ryan. Was there really any harm in it? Maybe Ryan was as starved for physical affection as he was. Was it really wrong to fill up your tank when someone offered a cuddle with no strings attached?

The alcohol seemed to have turned his bones into gummy worms that had been soaked in hot water, and he just felt so good. Part of him knew it was wrong when he nuzzled his head back and forth a bit, but the pleasure of the closeness was too overwhelming to ignore. He felt a moment of fear; had he ruined it? But then Ryan's head leaned against his. Ryan's arm came diagonally across his chest, his hand resting on Skyler's ribs.

Now and then Ryan would mutter something at the movie, usually something funny, and Skyler would laugh. *Is this what it's like to be on a normal date? But without the kissing.* Normal dates had kissing, didn't they? And sure, kissing was great, but wasn't that how he'd gotten into so much trouble? This was safer, provided he could keep his half-hard cock concealed beneath the blanket.

The movie ended and they watched all the credits, neither of them eager to move. Finally the screen went dark and Skyler said, "Want to watch something else?"

"Naw, we shouldn't get to bed too late. We could go for a quick hot tub, though."

"Sure."

"I'll grab the trunks," said Ryan, and then he was up and out of the room before Skyler could even sit up properly. He put the movie away and turned everything off, but Ryan wasn't back. He swept the kitchen floor but couldn't find a dustpan and had to leave this pile of dirt just sitting there. He was wiping the kitchen counters when Ryan came down the stairs. He threw a set of trunks at Skyler and then started taking off his shirt. "I've got a surprise for you."

"You do?" Skyler missed catching the trunks and picked them up off the floor. Ryan just smiled his bright smile and pulled off his socks. Skyler tried not to scurry for the bathroom door like a scared little girl when Ryan started undoing his pants, and resisted the urge to lock it behind him. He tore off his clothes and pulled on the goddam too-big shorts, avoiding looking at himself in the mirror this time. When he came out, Ryan was nowhere to be seen but the door to the deck was ajar.

He stepped out into the cold and sucked in some air. There was solid ice under his bare feet and he grabbed for the side of the tub as he shut the door. Ryan was already in and smiling widely with two champagne flutes beside him. Skyler's shorts bubbled and burped up air as he sat down into the extreme heat.

"Here." Ryan handed him a glass. "It's a new drink. Ribena, vodka, snow, and a splash of soda."

"Wow, snow! It's like a slushy! Thanks!"

"It's not champagne, but hey, at least you have the beautiful blond." Ryan tossed his hair.

Skyler laughed and sipped the drink. "It's delicious."

"The back door opens on a lot of untouched snow, so don't worry about dirt," said Ryan. Skyler grabbed his throat and pretended to choke.

"Very funny, but seriously... you like it? Now you can say you drank a special drink in a Big White hot tub."

"Are you kidding? It's awesome! If you're not careful, you're going to have to work at getting rid of me."

Ryan laughed and told Skyler about where he wanted to show him the next day, which was a great opportunity to study his face. The skin on Ryan's bottom lip was chapped, and he kept nibbling at it. It was very distracting. So was the way the ends of his hair were wet and hanging in little points. It almost brushed his shoulders, and that led to his collarbones and his chest. *Oh man.*

"Ready for bed?"

"What? Oh sure."

They got out and toweled off, and Ryan grabbed them both water glasses for the bedroom.

Skyler remembered the kitchen floor, and asked, "Hey, where's your dustpan?"

Ryan looked confused. "We don't have one. Why?"

"Well I swept the floor, but..." Skyler pointed at the pile of dirt he'd left.

Ryan grabbed the broom, swept the pile over to the sink, used his toe to flip up this panel on the bottom of the cabinet, and the dirt was just sucked away. "It's an internal vacuum thing. Weird, huh?" There was a suction sound until Ryan flipped the panel back down.

"That is seriously fucked. Where does it go?"

"I dunno. Crazy, isn't it?" Ryan messed up Skyler's hair and punched his shoulder.

"Ow! What was that for?" Skyler laughed.

"Don't feel like you have clean shit up. Just have fun, okay? You're here to chillax." He flashed this smile that was so warm and friendly, and then he was loping up the stairs, two at a time.

Ryan showered while Skyler put his clothes back on downstairs. This time it didn't seem as weird when they brushed teeth together in the upstairs bathroom, even though Ryan was only wearing his towel.

When they got up to the bedroom, Ryan said, "Okay, only boxers tonight. Otherwise we're going to be raisins in the morning."

"God, my legs are so weak and tired. The stairs are killing me," said Skyler, tossing his clothes down beside his bag.

"Skiing will do that. We should have drunk more water. It's so freakin' hot up here."

"And the door rattles. I think it's the air trying to get up here."

"Right, here, shove my jeans under the crack. That might keep it still and keep some hot air out." Ryan opened the window a bit wider and then climbed into bed. Skyler turned off the light before stripping down to his boxers and then climbed in as well. He wasn't surprised to feel Ryan's leg touch his.

"How long have you been single?" asked Skyler.

"Since the summer."

"Do you miss... I mean, do you...."

"Get lonely? And horny? Fuck yeah. I'm a guy."

"There are lots of girls that like you."

"Yeah, whatever."

"There are! They talk about you, about how hot you are."

"They do? What are you, like a spy? Ha, this could be really useful."

That hurt really bad, but Skyler couldn't seem to stop his mouth. "Yeah, they talk about what you wear and your body and stuff."

"Seriously?"

"Yeah, you are a gift to women, my friend." *And to gay boys everywhere.*

"Yeah, well, it's not easy being me." Ryan laughed. "I haven't been in too big of a hurry to get involved, and you know how fooling around can get you into trouble. I had an arrangement once with a friend, but that's no longer an option."

"Oh?"

"Yeah, I think that's why my parents are kinda weird to you, actually. There was a guy, a friend, and we got goofing around and talking about how horny we were and how often we jack off, and then he just whips it out and starts showing me how he does it. Well, I didn't care. It was kinda interesting, actually, and so we'd do it together sometimes. But then this one time, my mom came in and caught us and she was cool. I mean she didn't say anything, just like 'Oh!' or whatever, but the guy freaked and booked it. And then later my mom wanted to have this heart-to-heart about how it's okay to be gay. And fuck, I know it's okay to be gay, but it wasn't like that. I mean it wasn't like I had a crush on him or something, and then after him, I really was in love with Chloe. I wasn't faking that. And this guy, it was just fooling around, like...."

"Playing," Skyler said.

"Yeah, exactly. I didn't love him and he didn't love me. We were just guys being guys and mixing it up a bit, you know?"

"I don't know. I mean, there's no way I could do that with Lisa. Uh, god, just thinking about it makes me want to hurl."

"She's got a nice body, though," Ryan said.

"Uh, okay, that's just creepy. I mean, I guess I can look at her and say yeah she's a pretty girl, but her body, like thinking about her body naked or something... maybe you would feel that way about Erika."

"Oh god! Gross! That's just disturbing."

"Yeah, right! Exactly. Disturbing. She's like my sister."

"Yeah, I get that. But what if it was a girl that you didn't feel like that about?"

"I don't think so. I'm just not wired that way. To me boobs are like hanging sacks of fat. I mean, ew." Skyler shuddered.

Ryan laughed. "Seriously? Wow! That's just crazy."

"But that's just me. I'm sure there are lots of people who don't have that kind of, I don't know, like, aversion to one gender. So you're into girls, but you don't mind guys."

"Well no, I mean, I'm straight, but I'm just open-minded, I guess. I wouldn't do that kind of thing with just anybody, but this guy and me, we knew each other super well, we were like cousins kind of, because our parents are so close, and it just didn't seem wrong."

"It sounds hot to me."

"Yeah, it was kinda hot. I mean, all guys must wonder what other guys do, right? And this guy had some great techniques. And we didn't have to worry about all that other stuff like we do with girls. It was just friends getting off."

"So what happened after he booked it?" Skyler said.

"We're not, like, enemies or anything, but I hardly ever see him. He tries to act like he's all normal, but it's awkward." Ryan sighed. "I never told anybody about that."

"I won't say anything."

"Thanks. I mean it's not like I watch gay porn or something. Guys are just horny all the time, right?" Ryan said.

"Yup."

"I mean, I have to jack off just to get to sleep at night. It's a natural thing. Like, like maintenance. I don't see that it's so different if I do that alone or with a buddy. If everybody does it, why does it have to be this big secret?"

"So you think that's why your mom gave me permission to... ah...."

"Yeah, I think so. God, she totally thinks I'm gay, doesn't she? And you know, she said she wasn't going to tell my dad that time, but I think she did. Maybe when I invited you to come on the trip. I mean, what else was he on about tonight? That made no sense."

"So he thinks you're into both, then? Like, bi?" Skyler tried not to whisper it, but his voice did get softer.

"I guess. Yeah, that makes sense. He's given me those talks about sex and protection and stuff, and I think he knows I'm into girls. So I guess he sees it as a choice for me and why would I get off with a guy when it's so dangerous?"

"Right."

"But it's less dangerous in so many other ways. It's straightforward," Ryan said.

"And you don't think this other guy was starting to have feelings for you?"

"What? No way."

"Huh."

"I mean, don't you feel like you know how guys' bodies work way better than any girl our age? I mean some girls have a clue, but you HAVE a male body. You just get how it works."

"I like to think I give a better blow job than a girl could."

"Huh."

"Well, I know the equipment." Skyler kept his eyes on the ceiling.

"Exactly."

"So, you're... looking to replace this guy?"

"What?"

"Your AWOL friend. Your fuck buddy."

"No! Hey, I didn't mean it like some kind of come-on. I was just trying to explain my parents' insanity. And I don't want you to feel weird if you get a hard-on or something. I mean, man, I get them all the time. You don't have to worry that I'm going to freak out or something. You can just tell me."

"So if I had a hard-on right now, you'd want to know about it?"

"Sure. Why not? Is that wrong?" Ryan said.

"I guess not."

"God, I'm so glad you get it. I thought you would." Ryan moved closer and touched Skyler's hair in the dark. "You want a massage?" Skyler shook his head. "You sure? I don't mind."

"Nah, I'm too tired."

"Okay, well... sleep well."

"You too." Skyler rolled away on his side and bent his knees around his rock-hard erection. Ryan was restless for a while, but gradually his breathing evened out and he edged up against Skyler's back. His body curled slowly around Skyler's, and his cock took up residence in Skyler's butt crack.

Finally, around 2:00 a.m., Skyler couldn't take it anymore. He threw back the covers and sat up.

"Wuh?" Ryan said.

"You're humping me."

"I am?"

"Yeah."

"Sorry. I guess I was having a good dream." Skyler squeezed his eyes shut, unable to answer. "Are you mad?" whispered Ryan.

"No. But you've gotta defuse that bomb. I can't sleep with that thing."

"Yeah, okay. You want me to go down to the bathroom?"

"Whatever."

The movement of the sheets took on rhythmic movement for a minute and then there was stillness. "Sky?"

"Yeah."

"You're hard, too, aren't you?"

Skyler sighed. "Maybe."

"You come, too, then. It'll make me feel like less of a perv. Come on, I'll race ya."

Skyler laughed and sank back onto the bed. He was so tired he could feel his blood pumping in his eyes. "Fine." He dug his hand into his shorts and his dick was so sensitive it almost hurt to grab it.

"You want some oil?"

"No."

There was only the sound of their breathing then and the rapid movements of the sheets. Ryan grunted and came first about twenty seconds later. "We have a winner," he whispered.

"Yeah, well, you cheated with my ass crack."

Ryan laughed. "Yeah, Mr. Stupid does have a thing about ass cracks." There was some more silence as Skyler fought the anxiety and arousal that were warring for his attention. He pumped harder and harder, but he couldn't seem to get there. It was torture and the friction was starting to burn.

Ryan rolled away for a moment and then sat up. "Hey, I can help."

"NO!"

"Sky, it's okay. It's just me. Let me see, okay?" He took the comforter and peeled it back. Skyler's hand was down inside his soft white boxers. "Well first of all, the poor guy doesn't need to feel shy about it." Ryan pulled Skyler's shorts down until the elastic snugged up under his balls. They were shaved and his cock was uncut, and Ryan looked but didn't mention it. "And second of all, it looks like you're not being very nice to him. Try this." He moved Skyler's hand and dripped a little oil on the shaft, rubbing it in with his palm. His hands were big and warm and gentle.

"Check out this stroke my friend showed me." He took hold at the bottom and worked his way slowly up to the top, corkscrewing his fist, and then he rubbed the pad of his thumb along the underside of the head. Skyler shivered and groaned. Ryan smiled. "Good, eh? I think it's important to get off when things are shitty. It keeps your spirits up. It keeps anxiety down. My mom said she knows a doctor who uses a masturbation schedule to treat depression."

His hand continued on with its magic movements, his eyes roaming over Skyler's body. Skyler turned his head away. Ryan's voice was soft. "You can move into my hand. I don't mind." Slowly Skyler started to thrust, and Ryan matched him perfectly. He added a little more oil and picked up the pace until Skyler was bucking and gasping and fisting his hands into the sheet.

"Come on, now!" whispered Ryan, adding his other hand under Skyler's balls, massaging the deep root of the muscle. Skyler came hard, squirting up his belly and onto his chest. He made small, agonized sounds, his head thrashing back and forth, as the spurts came out, and Ryan's hands stayed firm on him until he lay still and gasping for air.

The little towel appeared and Ryan wiped him off. "Wow. I'd say you had MSB. Massive sperm buildup. Very dangerous. Feel better?"

Skyler felt naked and raw. He shrugged and curled up on his side away from Ryan, pulling his boxers back up. It wasn't wrong, was it? He just wasn't sure anymore what was okay and what wasn't. There was a tightness in his chest; what was that?

"Sky?" Ryan's hand was warm on his bare back, and then Ryan's chin perched on his shoulder. "Hey, I just wanted to make you feel better. Okay? Didn't you like it? Did I fuck up somehow?"

Skyler rolled onto his back and looked at Ryan's face in the darkness. His brow was all knotted up and his eyes were shining. He wanted more than ever to kiss Ryan's sweet mouth. He wanted to grab him and bury his face in Ryan's chest and tell him that this wasn't playing around at all. This was deadly serious. There wasn't any way that coming in Ryan's hand was maintenance on anything. Not even in the same galaxy…. But the fact that Ryan could confuse the two spoke volumes. It just wasn't the same thing for him. And there was no way to explain that. You either felt it along every nerve ending in your whole body, or you didn't.

Skyler lifted an arm, and Ryan's eyebrows went up. "You wanna hug?" Skyler nodded and Ryan sank slowly and carefully into his arms. The sweaty skin on Skyler's chest stuck to Ryan's and pulled a little as Ryan changed position, and then the embrace was warm and tight and lovely. Ryan sure did know how to give a hug. One arm was around Skyler's neck and the other hand was running up and down his side. He leaned his head against Skyler's and asked, "You okay?"

Skyler swallowed a lump of tears and nodded. It was a lie but better than having to confess how he really felt.

"You thinking about Jeremy?"

Wow, for once I am so NOT thinking about Jeremy. But he nodded again anyway. That was an easy explanation. He tightened his arms around Ryan and allowed himself to run a hand over Ryan's hair. It was so silky. He stroked it again, promising that it was the last time, but it felt so good that his palm went back for more, his fingers digging in and sliding through. What did it matter? Maybe Ryan couldn't feel the difference between a loving caress and a little slap and tickle?

"He was a fool to lose you, Sky. You can do so much better than him. I mean, what kind of asshole wants someone else when he's got you?" Skyler's breath huffed out. It was somewhere between a laugh and a sob, and it shook his body. "I'm going to take care of you, buddy. I'm going to get you back on your feet, okay? Lots of exercise and time outside, make sure you eat lots of good food, and get you on some kind of schedule. You'll feel better, I promise. Okay?"

Skyler nodded again and then let Ryan roll him into a spoon position and wrap around him. One of Ryan's legs was between his own, and Ryan clasped his chest and held him.

"You can lean on me while you get over him," whispered Ryan into the back of his neck. "I want to be there for you."

Skyler relaxed a little and just felt Ryan's strong body cradling his. No matter how stupid it was to love that, he couldn't help it. Jeremy had never offered to cuddle or hold him, and it always felt somehow awkward to ask. He just wanted to sink into that embrace and rest for a while. He closed his eyes and a single tear slid from one eye, over the bridge of his nose, and down into the other eye. Maybe there were important things wrong here, but he was just so tired and Ryan was so warm and lovely.

He slept then, straight until morning, and woke with morning wood. It took a moment to figure out what was going on, and then he woke up a little more and realized that he was lying mostly on Ryan's bare chest with his head against Ryan's neck and his pecker pressed up against Ryan's hipbone. He lifted his head a little and Ryan shuffled him a bit, and then there was Ryan's hard-on right under his own hip. He groaned as Ryan pressed up into him.

"What are you doing?" Skyler murmured.

"Good morning, sunshine. We aim to please. Don't you like it?"

"So your plan is to get me off every day so that I feel better?" he whispered.

"My plan is to make you happy."

He fought the terrible urge to grind against Ryan's body, but it was so good to feel Ryan's obvious arousal. Ryan slid his hands down Skyler's sides and hooked his thumbs on the waistband of Skyler's boxers. He tugged them down a little, and then they were rubbing against each other, hard. Ryan reached for his oil and wriggled his own boxers down. Their cocks slid together in Ryan's well-oiled hand and Skyler gasped. It was so slick and so smooth and so hot. He gave in to it then and let his hips go, ramming down again and again. He lifted his face from Ryan's neck and risked a peek at Ryan's face. His eyes were closed, his eyebrows up, his lips parted. His face was wide open. Skyler came first this time, onto Ryan's stomach, and then had a moment to worry that the sticky cum-puddle might gross Ryan out. That was settled quite definitively when Ryan smeared it on himself and came hard.

Ryan wiped them both with his somewhat crusty little towel and said, "I think you're going to feel good today. Just a guess."

"And how about you?" Skyler looked at him from under his eyelashes. "How are you going to feel?" Ryan's smile was wide and so bright.

"I already feel awesome. Come on, let's eat."

CHAPTER 6—SKYLER

THE MORNING was strange, mostly because it wasn't different. Ryan chatted away and made them eggs, and Skyler watched everyone and felt completely freaked out. He went hot and cold and couldn't seem to speak properly. *Can they tell? Maybe not if I could get myself under fucking control and act normal!* Ryan's parents didn't seem to be paying any attention, thank god, although he did get one long look from Ryan's mom before she started ignoring him. She must know something was going on. *Fuck. Did we make noise this morning?*

Ryan still touched him all the time, but now those twinges of shame about how much he liked it were more twinges of confusion. Did Ryan know that he was turned-on? And if he did, would he mind or would he just smile and shrug and say, "Cool." Skyler didn't know what to think about it aside from the fact that he was sure he didn't want to think about it. He could have a part of Ryan that he never dreamed he could have. Wasn't that good?

They decided to go for an afternoon-only pass, which was cheaper, and Ryan organized the morning suit-up anyway so they could build up a toboggan run next to the house. He frowned at Skyler's rubber boots, but there were no extra winter boots that would fit him, and so Ryan brought down some extra wool socks and conceded the point. Skyler was glad he'd splurged at Mountain Equipment Co-op and bought a nice winter hat. The sun was out and über-blinding as they stepped out of the carport, their breath clouding in the cold air. Ryan ran back in for sunglasses, and Skyler had a moment to just stare around him.

The cat track that they had skied down to get home yesterday curved up into the forest like a miniature extension of the real road, which ended out front of Ryan's place in a large open turnaround area. The house opposite them was almost as crazy-awesome, with its raw wood and big windows, but they hadn't run into anyone staying there. The end of the cul-de-sac wasn't wooded for a little ways, and the area was a large blanket of white interrupted only by the track cut down into its chest-high bank. Next to the house, the empty space was a very steep slope that ended in a bowl. The top of the slope had a rocky point jutting out in the middle, where Erika had said the guys used to jump from.

Ryan handed him some beautiful Ray-Bans and started tromping his way up between the little cliff jump and the house, his legs sinking down into the snow as he went. Icicles hung down from the roof like decorations, and Skyler was looking up at them when one leg sank down to midthigh. Ryan laughed. "Want a hand?"

Skyler shook his head and ended up crawling out. He was sweating and puffing by the time he'd freed himself and followed Ryan to the top.

With the trees at their backs, the house on their lefts, and the snowy view spreading out before them, it was truly breathtaking.

"You like it?" Ryan looked at him shyly.

"I love it. I can't imagine how anything could be more beautiful."

Ryan smiled. "I love it too. It's special. Here, you wanna take some pictures?" Ryan dug in a pocket.

"I brought my camera. Thanks, though." Skyler's camera was an older digital. It took a decent picture, but he couldn't control the lens much. Ryan made his way back down while Skyler played with the lighting and tried to capture the texture of the snow. He came back up with a snow shovel and a couple of toboggans that looked like short, fat surfboards.

"It'll take a while to pack the run down enough to make it fast." He set to work shoveling out a flat spot at the top of the slope and whacking the snow down with the back of the shovel. Then he got on the toboggan and scooted himself forward using his heels and slid about halfway down. He sat in the snow and smiled up at Skyler. His sunglasses really were cute.

God, he looks good. Skyler sat on the board, feeling a little foolish and a little nervous, and then slid down right into Ryan, who managed to lurch a little out of the way.

"Sorry! I have no idea how to aim this thing. Oh god, I've got snow up my back already."

Ryan lifted the back of Skyler's jacket up and dusted off what he could. "You need to tuck in this layer." He plucked at Skyler's shirt. "Come on, I wanna make the path up into stairs."

The more they slid down, the more the run compacted. Soon Skyler was carving out the slow spots with the shovel and smoothing them down with his own ass and the toboggan. The run got longer and longer until they were ending up in the bottom of the bowl and sometimes even sliding up the rim a bit. Every time they gained ground, the tromp back to the path meant sinking down past their knees again and almost swimming in snow. Erika and her friend Emma from next door came out and loved the run, shrieking and whooping as they came flying down it. Emma swore a lot and made fun of everything, but Ryan just laughed and bugged her about it. Before long she couldn't help but just smile and enjoy herself.

"Let's make an igloo," said Ryan.

It took a long time to pack down a mound of snow big enough to satisfy Ryan, even with both of them shoveling. It was nice to work next to Ryan. He always had something funny to say, but it was more than that. He had a way of being clear about how to do something without it sounding bossy or condescending, and he worked really hard. It seemed like he'd never get tired. Carving out the inside of the mound took time too, but soon the girls joined them and they had a space big enough to climb inside.

Erika's friend was watching Ryan and finally she said, "I remember when you guys used to jump that." She pointed up at the overhang.

Ryan shrugged and then looked at Skyler. "You want to see me jump it?" His smile had that little curl that lifted his cheek up into a little plum of flesh. All Skyler could think about was wanting to make him smile like that in the bedroom and then taking that flesh between his teeth. It looked so succulent.

"No!" he said when he realized that Ryan was already turning to walk back to the house.

Ryan turned back and his smile just fell off his face like a little kid's when their ice cream came off the cone. "Why not?"

"Ryan, that's really high. How high is that?"

Ryan's smile was low volume, but at least it was back. "It's way smaller than a lot of the jumps I do. No problem." He trudged through the deep snow and disappeared into the house. Skyler looked at Erika, his expression worried.

"Don't worry. He's really good."

"I know he's really good. That's not the point."

"It's what he does," Erika shrugged. "Guess he wants to show you." Her friend frowned.

Before long, Ryan was back with his skis over his shoulder and climbing up the path they'd made. "I put my helmet cam on. It should get a cool shot of this."

The girls stood at the bottom close to the house and waited. "Tell us when you're ready!" shouted Erika. She pulled a phone out of her pocket and started setting up a shot, and Skyler took out his camera and turned on the video.

"Okay!" shouted Ryan from out of sight in the trees at the top, and then he appeared for a second before launching into the air. He seemed to fall for a long time, his legs and arms controlled and curving into a slow-motion crouch as he landed in the deep snow and disappeared for a moment in the spray of powder.

Jesus. That was fucking beautiful. Skyler was moving before he realized he'd decided to, because hard on the awe of that jump was a heart-stopping fear. *He could be hurt.* He tried to hurry, shoving his camera into his coat pocket without even turning it off, but the snow was so deep, he kept losing one leg or the other thigh-deep into it.

"You okay?" called Skyler. Ryan was undoing his skis and looked fine.

"Yeah, princess. I'm fine. That wasn't a big jump, okay?"

"Well, then I guess I don't need to drown myself in this shit to make sure." Skyler lay down on his stomach and tried to crawl forward to pull his leg out of the hole that seemed to only be getting wider and deeper the more he thrashed around. Ryan laughed and started toward him.

"Didn't think I could make it?" Ryan sat down next to him.

"Would you quit being a macho ass and help me out of this hole? I'm not doubting the size of your balls, okay?" Skyler blushed. *Nice choice of metaphors, fucktard.*

Ryan laughed, though, and muttered, "No, I guess you know more about them than most people," but made no move to drag him out of the hole he was making. Skyler lay still for a moment and just rested.

"Your sister said you weren't a show-off."

"I'm not really."

"So what was that?"

Ryan shrugged and looked uncomfortable. "What, you didn't like it?" He'd taken off his sunglasses and hadn't bothered with goggles, and his face had this look. Kind of lost. And suddenly Skyler couldn't tell him not to be a showboat ass.

Skyler sighed. He hated the idea of Ryan hurting, and here he was, unharmed and yet still looking like he was in pain. *This is what he can do. Don't shit on it.*

"It was beautiful."

"Yeah?" Ryan's smile unfurled again. "I know it's not the greatest life skill in the world, but…."

"But it's still amazing."

"Yeah?"

"It looks like flying."

"Or falling with style."

Skyler laughed. "Okay, Buzz. You wanna let me film you properly?" *God knows that last shot is probably jerky and jumbled.* He'd followed Ryan all the way down, though. There was no losing track of Ryan, was there?

"Seriously?"

"Yeah, but if you hurt yourself, I'm going to kill you. I'm serious."

"Got it."

Ryan made his way back over to the path, and unfortunately, Skyler saw the perfect spot to shoot from. Ryan's landing spot was in the middle of the little bowl at the base of the overhang, and the primo spot was farther still. He tucked his camera safely in a zip-up pocket and floundered some more. Ryan had to wait for a while at the top until he got himself over there and up the curve of this bank and set up. The house was in the background and it was going to be great. Skyler sat and used his bent knees as a tripod. "OKAY!" he shouted.

Ryan whooped and a few moments later came flying between the trees and sailed up into the air. He pulled his knees up and his arms were up like some kind of martial arts movie where they freeze-frame the guy hanging in the air, and then swoosh, he landed and carved hard to the right, away from the house and toward Skyler. The girls wooed, and Skyler used the lens to try to get a look at Ryan's face. Was he okay? As the shower of snow cleared, he could see Ryan again, his whole body turned and focused on Skyler. Skyler held one hand up and Ryan waved and smiled from ear to ear.

Ryan jumped a few more times, and Skyler had to pull his fingers inside his gloves and squeeze them against his palms to try to get them warm in between shots. Ryan called, "C'mon, you're going to freeze your balls off over there," and Skyler started the trudge back, which was a lot easier now that he'd squashed and smashed the snow down so much.

The girls went in to warm up, and Ryan disappeared inside the snow cave on his belly.

"Come on, come inside," he called. It was a tight fit, and they ended up half leaning back against the wall, unable to really sit up. Skyler took his sunglasses off in the dim light. Ryan said, "What do you think? It's a little small, I guess."

"Small?! You built a snow cave, man. It's amazing! I love it!" Skyler smiled and was surprised to see Ryan look shyly away.

"WE built it. How are your hands? Getting cold?" said Ryan.

"A bit," said Skyler, but he couldn't help taking out the camera to take some pictures.

"Hey, take some of us together," said Ryan. They wiggled around in the tight space to try to get both their heads in the shot and ended up lying down side by side so that Skyler could get the cave opening behind their heads. It needed a flash and Skyler was adjusting the camera to try to get it to look the way he thought it should. "You really love that, don't you?"

"Sorry, this is really boring, isn't it?"

"No, take your time. It's nice to see you into something. You get this look on your face."

"I do?" Skyler turned and Ryan's face was so close to his own. Ryan's hair stuck out from under his hat at a funny angle.

"Yeah, it's like this." Ryan furrowed his brow and made his eyes really big. Skyler laughed.

"I guess I have the opposite of ADD, more obsessive-compulsive. Once I find something that I love, I just want to do it all the time."

"I used to feel that way about soccer."

"But not anymore?"

"Nah, I quit the team."

"What? Seriously?" Skyler lowered the camera and stared at him. "When?"

"Just before we started hanging out. That's what the guys were bugging me about that day I was such a dick to you. I was trying to lighten the mood or something dumb like that, I guess. Maybe I just didn't want to talk to them anymore and there you were, so easy to joke with."

"Ryan, what the hell? How long have you played with those guys?"

"Oh, forever. A lot of us started when we were three or four."

"Jesus."

"I know, it's kind of a soccer neighborhood, isn't it?"

"No, I mean I had no idea. I never asked you about it. I feel like a jerk for not noticing you weren't going to practices or anything. I've just been so caught up in my head lately. And you did say you weren't feeling it anymore."

"Yeah, I just couldn't figure out what it was for."

"Maybe it was for fun. Aren't you always telling me to have more fun?"

Ryan shrugged.

"Are they mad? Your team?"

"Yeah, some of them are. I don't get why."

"Well what did you say to them?"

"I just said I was too busy and I wasn't into it anymore. But they were really bugging me about it. I started just leaving my headphones on all the time and pretending I didn't hear when they yelled after me down the hall."

Skyler thought of that 'Headphones' song Ryan had said was his theme song. He did wear his headphones all the time at school, didn't he? Sometimes just one earbud, but they were always there. *I thought he was just kinda tuned out and not caring, but it's not like that, is it?* Ryan was isolated, or maybe isolating himself.

"Maybe they think you're ditching them."

"More like them ditching me. Most of them I don't see any more now that I'm not at practices and games."

"Well, hanging out with me isn't helping."

"Whatever."

"Seriously, Ryan. It probably seems weird to them."

"So what!" Ryan looked really pissed.

"Whoa, I'm just saying…."

"I don't want to hear it. You're like my best friend right now. How would you like to hear Lisa say that you shouldn't hang out with her? It's bullshit."

"Hey, don't get mad."

"Well don't insult my friend."

Skyler took his picture, the flash lighting up the walls of the dome, and then turned the view screen toward him. "You think I make funny faces. Talk about grumpy."

Ryan laughed, his face transforming into its usual sunny expression. He grabbed the camera and started tickling with one hand and taking pictures with the other. Soon there were arms and legs everywhere, and Ryan was pinning him. Skyler kicked one of Ryan's feet out, and Ryan landed heavily on Skyler's chest, knocking some air out of him.

"Holy shit, you're heavy!"

"What, don't you like being squashed?"

"That's the problem. Get off."

"What, you like it?"

"Ryan, get off."

"I don't think so. I'm quite comfortable here." He propped his head up on his fist. "Are you blushing?" The corner of Ryan's mouth curled. "I like it when you blush."

"Ryan, this is going to get really awkward very soon."

"It's not awkward for me. I'm fine, thanks." Ryan's wicked smile was showing teeth now.

"Well I'm not. What if your sister comes back out here? Or your parents come home?"

"I thought you liked being alone with me."

"I do."

"Do you?"

Skyler looked into his eyes and something changed. All the teasing and playing were gone from his mind, and all he wanted to do was to lift up ever so slightly and kiss Ryan's mouth. He swallowed hard. *What would happen? Would he kiss me back? Would he finally get what it means that I'm gay and get really grossed out?* He wasn't sure where the line was between straight guys messing around and actual gayness, but kissing was for sure crossing that line. *Wasn't it? I mean there had been those funny kisses on the cheek before, but that was just joking around.* This would feel nothing like that, and Ryan would have to be dead not to feel the difference this time. Ryan's smile fell away. *Oh god, he can tell. Shit! Do something!*

Skyler jammed his freezing fingers under Ryan's jacket and managed to find some bare skin. Ryan yelped in surprise, and then Skyler was out from underneath him and crawling out of the cave followed by Ryan, who was laughing again.

"Hey, want to slide down the cat track?"

The trail was just wide enough to get groomed but not steep enough to really pick up speed. To make it more fun, they ran up the slow curves and slid down on their bellies, and then Ryan had the idea to double up. Skyler was just sitting down when Ryan dropped down behind him on the toboggan. It was far too small for the two of them and Ryan's bent legs were pressed into Skyler's. They were coming around a curve and it was hard to think and suddenly Ryan was shouting, "Lean, lean!" and he couldn't react fast enough. They slid off course and ground up against the snowbank on the side of the trail.

They tumbled off, but the snow was soft enough not to hurt. Skyler lay on the ground, breathing hard and looking up at the sky.

"Hey, are you okay?" Ryan crawled over.

"Yeah, look at the clouds!"

Ryan lay down next to him and watched. The clouds were so low it looked like you could touch them if you could just jump high enough. The wisps were sailing by unbelievably fast.

"I've never seen clouds that close. Jesus. Or moving that fast. It's crazy that they are just silently flying by right there."

"Yeah and it doesn't even feel windy." They lay there for a while just watching the tattered gauze of the clouds unroll and unravel as it raced by across the deep blue of the sky. It was startling how beautiful it was, and they were the only people to witness this moment. Ryan was looking at him, but it took a minute to be able to look away from that. "I guess the air currents are different up against a mountain."

From Ryan's face, Skyler could see that it affected him too. He looked overcome and said, "Like we're in the sky."

"Exactly."

They looked back up at the sky and just lay there for a while. It was so nice to get to share something like this with Ryan. Neither of them belonged to a church or anything, but this moment had a kind of sacred feeling to it. There were things here that were special, that were awe-inspiring, and it meant something that Ryan could appreciate them too. But did sharing something like this make the morning's casual encounter better? Or worse? Could you be close to someone and still use them to satisfy your body's urges? Was that friendship with a side of convenience or just more of the dangerous ground he'd just gotten out of with Jeremy and his friends? Was Skyler an idiot for letting last night happen? And what about that almost-kiss moment?

Maybe the lightbulb moment that he'd been so afraid Ryan would have in the car wasn't about boners for Ryan. Arousal and the male body just didn't freak him out. Maybe his line would be when he realized that Skyler had stopped seeing him as a friend on that car trip, and that touching him back wasn't just friendly affection or some physical resetting of hormone levels. Ryan moved a little and their shoulders touched. Clearly Ryan needed a friend more than Skyler had realized. Quitting the soccer team was a major thing, and maybe

Skyler's clear lack of ability in sports had made him so much less threatening than the other guys Ryan knew.

Ryan was the one to break the spell, worrying that Skyler would get too cold lying in the snow. He couldn't really argue since he was starting to feel the cold seep into his bones. They had a quick lunch and skied down to the ticket window for afternoon lift passes.

They were on the chairlift when Ryan got quiet. Without thinking, Skyler asked, "What are you thinking about?" *Oh god, what if he's realizing that this was a big mistake?* But Ryan just smiled a little sadly and swallowed.

"I was just thinking about Chloe. You know, before things went to shit. She was so... great."

"Yeah? What was she like?" *Oh god, now he's going to talk about how much he loves women.* Skyler pushed the thought away. It was great that Ryan wanted to share things with him. The least he could do was listen, right?

"Well she was pretty and fun and everybody liked her, but I don't know, she had this sort of awesome pigheaded sneakiness about her too. Like she wouldn't bother arguing with people, but she sure as hell wasn't going to do what they thought she should. God, I loved that about her."

"You guys were in love?"

"I was."

"What about her?"

"Well, I thought we were both in love, but now I don't know. I think I just started not really paying attention. We'd been together for over a year, and I mean, I wanted her all the time, but I wasn't... looking at her right, you know?"

"Listening?"

"Yeah, I wasn't listening. I should have seen it coming. She would smile but not like she was really happy, and I'd just bug her about it. Telling her to lighten up and have some fun. But I wasn't making sure, you know? That she was okay. She had a fight with one of her friends and she got really mad that I didn't get it. I think that was the beginning of the end. Maybe I thought she was being a drama queen. And you know, when I found out about the other guy, that's what she said. 'He cares. He listens.' God, it was my own fault. I was so into going to parties and practices and games, and sure, I wanted her to come along, but I didn't like hold her and tell her how much I loved her and ask her how her day was, and pay a-fucking-ttention! God, I was so stupid."

"I think that's called being a teenager. It's pretty normal to be caught up in your own head," Skyler said.

"Yeah, but she wasn't. She was always checking on me and asking me about stuff and doing things for me. She let me know. Every day she let me know. She was always texting me and I got so that I wouldn't even bother to text her back."

Skyler took the strap of one pole off over his glove and put his freed arm around Ryan. Ryan hung his head and then peeked sideways at Skyler. His smile was fleeting and shy. "Thanks."

"Hey, you've been hugging me. The least I could do." Skyler smiled.

"Well, this wasn't exactly part of the Make Sky Happy Plan."

"Hey, you can't MAKE someone happy. You can just be there and do what you can. And this does make me feel better, actually. I mean, it sucks that you feel all that stuff, but if you can talk about it, then it makes me feel like less of a mess when I talk about my shit. You're not all Prodigal Son who can do no wrong."

"Yeah, as if." Ryan laughed.

"Seriously, any mom wants a son like you. Good-looking, strong, good at sports, lots of friends. You look pretty perfect most of the time."

"You think I'm good-looking?"

Oh, this was dangerous. Skyler was a for-shit liar, but he had to keep it light. Maybe if he could say it right, Ryan would get it figured out and just pull back a little.

"Ryan, please. You're like some kind of Norse god. Jesus, with the hair and the eyes and the…. God, stop smiling like that. Gay over here, okay? I can't even look at you." Skyler shook his head in mock-disgust.

Ryan laughed and Skyler rubbed his hand up and down Ryan's arm. "And you know, I think you've really taken some time and thought about what happened with Chloe. That's pretty rare. You've been so the opposite of that oblivious guy with me. I'm like your practice girl."

"What?"

"Well, maybe I get what girls want. I'd give you an A for attentiveness."

"Thanks."

"And I think it would have been a lot easier for you to just blame her and call her a bitch and get together with the next girl."

"Well, I did do that actually. That didn't go well either. But after that, I just didn't want sex for a while. I mean, I wanted it, but it just felt too... dangerous or something."

"She really broke your heart."

"Chloe? Yeah." Ryan swallowed and looked away.

"Well, I know how that feels. It really, really sucks."

"Yeah. It totally does. And I know that you get it, and god, that's nice, you know? I thought I had lots of friends, but this fall I realized that I just can't talk to them about shit. None of them want to hear how fucked up I'm feeling. Sure, they'll get me drunk and take me out, but they don't...."

"They don't hold you when you cry."

Ryan looked at him in surprise.

"Oh sorry. Did I say that out loud?" Skyler smiled. "Hey, I'm gay. I'm allowed to talk about crying. God, how many times have I cried in front of you now? Pathetic." Skyler shook his head.

"But not all gay guys are like that, are they? I mean, what about Jeremy and those guys?"

"Yeah, that's true. He didn't like me to get too serious. He'd tease me about being a little old lady, always responsible and kind of boring, I guess."

"See, that's not exactly Mr. Sensitive talking, and I'm pretty sure he was 100 percent gay."

"Yeah, fair enough. Hey, I don't mean to make him sound like a total douchebag all the time, though. There were things about him that were great."

"Like what?"

"I dunno, he had this feeling about him. Like he was... enthusiastic about living. He once got down on his knees on the street and wouldn't get up until I kissed him. He was just kind of dazzling. Embarrassing but dazzling."

The wind picked up as they crested the top of the hill, and Skyler took his arm back, getting his poles sorted out well ahead of the end of the line. There was nothing more embarrassing than splatting out on the ground as you got off.

They got off the chairlift without incident, and Skyler turned and smiled at him. "I'm glad we got you your corduroy yesterday."

"Yeah, thanks for letting me rush you all the time. There's nothing like a freshly groomed run before anyone's tracked it out."

The snow was still nice in the middle of the day, but not so smooth under his skis. They skied the first run, Ryan doing little side trails that ended in small jumps back onto the run. It was fun to watch him and getting easier to look around more and not lose it and bail. There weren't very many people, and there was lots of uninterrupted space around them as they wove back and forth between the snowy forest on either side. The mountain was just as glorious today, a thousand shades of white, and the sky a brilliant blue overhead.

Skyler felt light. And, he hated to admit it, good. Sure, the sexual thing with Ryan was totally confusing, but there was something about it that was also a weight off his shoulders. The fear of Ryan finally figuring out that he was turned-on or noticing his boner-from-hell... those weren't the end of the world now. Maybe he could keep it on a kind of friend level, and it wouldn't feel dirty or wrong. Wasn't this time with Ryan worth some tightrope walking? Just being with someone who paid that much sweet, kind attention... God, it was lovely. *Maybe if I can just play along that it's just getting off to me too?* Would that be so bad?

C HAPTER 7—R YAN

R YAN'S PARENTS and Erika were invited next door for dinner, but Ryan didn't want to go. *How awkward would it be to bring Skyler over there?* Luckily his mom didn't argue about it. There were plenty of leftovers, so they had some time before they had to heat anything up. Ryan gave Skyler the Wi-Fi password, put out some chips, opened some beers, and turned on the gas fireplace.

"Hey, check out this picture of brain coral." Skyler had his laptop set up at the dining room table. Ryan was surprised he remembered the coral, which was super cool, and went and got his laptop too.

"I've been meaning to send you this," said Ryan, opening up his browser. "I keep hearing all these breakup songs on the radio and thinking about you, so I put them together onto my YouTube account. Grooveshark is good, but this way you get the lyrics too. I'm e-mailing you a link to it."

"Like a playlist?"

"Yeah. Is that depressing? Maybe you shouldn't be listening to crap like that." Ryan's hands had frozen on the keyboard, and he looked intently at Skyler.

"No. Ryan, that's great. It's like your mom said, songs mean a lot."

"Yeah, I had that when Chloe and I broke up this summer. I put some funny ones in, too, though, so it's not all a big bummer. Here, look." Ryan's smile was back, and he pressed play on a video and angled the screen so they could both see it. It was the video for the "Fuck You" song by CeeLo Green, which was really hilarious. By the end of it, they were both smiling, and Ryan was tapping his leg up and down and grooving his head back and forth.

Skyler said, "Have you seen the sign language video of this? You know that girl?" Ryan hadn't, and so Skyler brought it up on his laptop, and Ryan laughed and laughed.

"That was AWEsome!"

"I know, right? I love how she just goes for it. She just puts herself out there. I think that's why it's gotten so popular."

"And her cute hair. Kinda like your flop top." Ryan tugged on Skyler's long over-to-the-side bangs. Skyler blushed. God, he was cute when he blushed. Ryan ran the backs of his fingers over Skyler's cheek, and those big brown eyes flashed over to his. "You're blushing."

Skyler frowned. "Well, don't bug me if you don't want to make me uncomfortable."

"Hey, I like your hair. I wasn't bugging."

"Show me the rest of the videos."

"Nah, I'll make another set. Fun songs that make you want to get up and dance." Ryan pushed the laptop away a little.

"You don't have to do that."

"I'm not doing it because I have to."

"Well, ah, thanks."

"Hot tub?" Ryan said.

They went up to change, and Skyler walked into the bathroom first to get the trunks from the top of the sliding shower doors. Ryan shut the door behind them and started stripping off his clothes. *Sky needs to lighten up. Changing is so not a big deal. I mean, they'd seen each other naked, right? And had touched more than that. But that was the problem, wasn't it?* The more clothes Ryan took off, the more Skyler blushed. *Maybe if I just pretend I don't notice?*

Ryan was naked now, and he was hopping on one foot, getting his trunks on. Skyler leaned back against the door and crossed his arms, so Ryan risked a look at his face. He was blotchy red and frowning and no longer trying to pretend he wasn't staring. He looked right at Ryan's eyes, and Ryan tried a smile. Skyler didn't smile back. He pulled up his trunks. *If he's turned on, why does he look pissed? Maybe he thinks I don't want to?* There must be some way make that clear. Hadn't Skyler said that he knew what girls liked? Maybe it was just like flirting with a girl.

"Hellooo," Ryan said, walking toward Skyler until their bodies were almost touching. Skyler shook his head.

"Out," he said, opening the door.

"What? There's no one home."

"And if there were, they would all shit themselves about what you want to do in here."

"Oh yeah? And what is it I want to do?" Ryan let his smile grow wider and let their thighs brush ever so slightly.

"If you don't know, I'm not going to tell you." Skyler opened the door, pushed him out, and shut it.

Ryan frowned for a second. Was he mad? Maybe it was only okay in the bedroom? *Goddammit, I guess I have to wait some more.* It was nice seeing Sky pushy, though, somehow. Ryan laughed as he thumped down the stairs. Skyler was hot when he was pushy.

He made some special drinks in glass glasses this time and got into the hot tub to wait. God, Skyler looked good when he came out. Those shorts were going to be his from now on. That stomach and that bit of hair he had leading down under the waistband, with those divots on either side. Damn, he was easy on the eyes. And the way his skin goose bumped up when he came outside and his small pecs seemed to stand up; why couldn't they just go to bed now? *Oh yeah, dinner.* That was maybe important.

Sky was shivering as he climbed into the scalding water, but the view of the landscape stopped him. Ryan followed his gaze out over the balcony. The sun was just going down and coloring the sky in a hundred reds. Sky whispered, "Oh man, I wish I had my camera."

"Too hard. Take a picture with your eyes," said Ryan. He put his fingers up and made a little *zztt* noise like he was taking a picture. Sky smiled, so maybe it was the right thing to say. He sank down into the water and knelt on the seats, looking at the sunset. Ryan was relieved Sky didn't try to move away when he edged closer, and they knelt side by side with their elbows on the edge.

"Sometimes the camera does separate you from the world. You're right, it's good to put it away sometimes," said Skyler.

"Live in the moment."

"Yeah." Skyler turned and looked at him, and it was wonderful just being next to him. Ryan couldn't help but smile, but then Sky's eyes locked with his and Ryan's smile fell away again. What was that? Sky's eyes were so big and dark and serious, it was hard not to get lost in there. But then Sky turned away and the moment was over.

"I made you a drink." Ryan handed one to Skyler.

"My favorite!" Sky smiled and Ryan perked up. "Thanks, but um, isn't this glass?"

"My parents aren't here. It's fine. We're not going to knock them over. And I wanted to show you something. Later." He waved it away and took a measured swallow of the slushy drink. "So how are your legs? Sore?"

"Only when I walk." Skyler smiled.

"The hot tub will help." He put a hand on Skyler's knee and ignored the flinch under his hand. He put his other hand on Skyler's calf and pulled the leg gently up until Sky's foot was in his lap. Sky looked like he might protest, so Ryan went in quick for the calf muscle, pressing his fingers just so. Skyler melted.

"Ohhh. You ARE good at that."

"Yup." Ryan beamed at him. "Lots of sore legs around here. Lots of practice."

Skyler lost his words for a while then and closed his eyes.

It was interesting to touch a man's leg like this. *I guess it's always been my mom, my sisters, and my girlfriends.* The leg hair was different, but so were the muscles, and the muscles felt very good. He took another measured sip of his drink with one hand, holding Sky's foot firmly with the other so he wouldn't try to escape. Skyler wasn't built up or anything, but he had these long, lean muscles that were somehow hot in their slenderness. Sky would look good heavier too. God, it was true. Sky would look good any way, and feel good too.

"I don't know why the guys are so scared of touching you." Ryan shrugged. "I love touching you."

"I noticed."

"You don't mind, do you?" He stopped moving his hands.

"You stop doing that and I might die, okay?"

Ryan laughed and pressed his thumbs in circling motions until Sky groaned softly and let his head flop back. "Wait, I might actually die FROM it." Skyler sighed slowly and sank a little into the water.

God it was nice to see him unwind. It was gratifying, satisfying in some special way. *We can go to bed early maybe. Right after dinner.*

Ryan thought about what he might say to get that to happen. Maybe music? He wanted to play Sky something special. He thought about what songs would be perfect for tonight and kept taking measured sips of his drink until it was empty.

"Okay, it's ready. Here." He passed the empty glass to Skyler, whose eyes snapped open.

"What?" Skyler took the glass and looked down inside it. Each time Ryan had let it sit for a few minutes, the surface of the drink had started to freeze, and each time a ring of ice had formed with jagged crystals reaching toward the center of the glass. He'd spaced the sips out and measured them by eye so that the rings would be evenly spaced down the inside of the glass. The outside of the glass had frosted over as well, so the whole thing looked like its own strange sculpture. Skyler's jaw dropped open and his eyes got round.

"That's what you wanted to show me before? You made this for me?" he said, and Ryan nodded. "Ryan, that's... so...."

"Silly?"

"Sweet. Beautiful. Amazing." Skyler grabbed his bicep and slid toward him. His eyes looked shiny and wet.

It wasn't that big of a present. It seemed wrong that he was so impressed by it. *Didn't anyone ever give you anything nice?* And then Skyler's face was suddenly really close to his and looking at him with those big eyes and his heart started beating faster.

Ryan didn't know what to say and so shrugged. "It's just a glass."

That was obviously the wrong thing. Skyler's face fell and his hand slid away into the water. *Shit. What did I say this time?* He was filled with the desire to do something better than just a glass filled with crystals. Something cool.

Skyler was turning away.

"Hey, I got something better. Watch this." Ryan pushed himself up out of the water, climbed from the edge of tub, and in a flash was standing on the rounded beam of the balcony. They were on the second floor, but the snow bank below wasn't that far down. He let out a whoop and then jumped. He whooped again when his hot body hit the snow and his legs sank down into it. It was a surprisingly soft landing really, but the snow was so cold it felt like it was burning his skin.

He looked over his shoulder and laughed. Skyler was hanging over with his hand on the railing and his mouth open super wide. A wave of happiness rose up from his burning feet, and he did a backflip into the snow behind him for good measure. Then he struggled up, floundered for a second, and hotfooted it to the front door.

When he got back upstairs, Skyler was standing in the hot tub with his mouth still open. Ryan laughed again and shivered his way back into the water. The heat was crazy on his skin, and he sucked in some air and winced.

"Are you okay?" said Skyler. He looked really freaked. Ryan laughed and grabbed his hand.

"Sit down, you're going to get cold." He tugged on the hand until Skyler sat next to him. "I'm fine." He'd lost that hand in the water somehow, but that was okay. Skyler was close again. *Did he like that?*

"That seriously scared the shit out of me. You could have killed yourself!"

"Nah, I've done that lots of times. The snow is really deep."

Skyler shook his head. "Yeah, but…."

"You just have to not slip on the railing."

"Okay there you go. Totally dangerous! Don't do that, okay? You just about gave me a heart attack." Skyler let out a huge breath. "Are you hungry?"

"Always."

"Let's make some food."

After Ryan's super-fast shower, they warmed food up in silence together. Ryan put some music on. It did lighten the mood. He always wanted to play Sky something cool.

"You have great taste in music," said Skyler.

"Thanks. What do you like?"

"Oh I don't know, lots of stuff." They sat down with their soup at the kitchen island.

"Like what? What's a song that you like?" Skyler couldn't seem to think of one out of the blue for some reason, so Ryan started naming bands and asking him about them.

"You'll probably think this is lame, but I love that Katy Perry 'Firework' video," said Skyler.

Ryan hopped down from his stool and brought over his laptop and started fiddling with it. "Let's watch it."

"Now? No, that's okay." Skyler looked embarrassed.

What, does he think I'll laugh at him? "Hey, I like everything."

It took a second to find it on YouTube, then the video started and they watched in silence. Ryan smiled at the part where fireworks came shooting out of Katy Perry's chest. She was belting it out about igniting and letting yourself shine. It was hopeful, empowering. And then there was a part near the end where these two guys kissed, and he glanced at Skyler, who looked away.

"It's not just that part. It's the whole idea."

"Of breaking free."

Skyler's eyes snapped up to his. "Yeah." He smiled.

"I like it. Anything else by her?"

"I like that one." Skyler pointed to the video thumbnail for 'Wide Awake.' "I see it as an apology for all that 'California Gurls' bullshit." They watched that too.

Skyler said, "I love it when her younger self stamps her foot and blows all the bad guys away."

"That's her younger self? Huh. The punching Prince Charming in the face was pretty sweet. That's actually a good breakup song. Balls out. You mind if I add that to your playlist?"

"Sure. Did you e-mail me the link to that?"

"Nah, you don't want that right now."

"Yes I do."

"I'll make a better one."

"If you do, then you can send that later. Please?"

It stopped him. When had Ryan ever heard Skyler ask for anything? It was quite a compliment. Or maybe he was planning on getting really sad soon and needing some breakup tunes. Either way, Ryan couldn't say no to a "please" from Skyler. *God, I'd give him my left nut if he said "please."*

"Okay, it's yours, but no binge wallowing."

Skyler's phone chimed that he had a text, and he checked it and then stood up.

"What?"

"Nothing."

"Sky, you look like your dog died. Who was that?"

"Jeremy."

"No shit! What did he say?"

"It just says, 'I miss you.'"

"Huh. And you haven't heard from him until now?"

"Nope."

"Are you going to answer?"

"I have no idea." Skyler grabbed his beer and took a long drink. "I mean, what would I even say? 'Thanks for fucking me up?'"

"Well, you don't have to answer."

"What does he even mean? That he wants to get back together or that he wants to get laid?"

"You could ask him."

"Yeah, I could. But I don't think I'd believe whatever he said. I wonder now whether we were ever really together in his mind. Did he EVER take me seriously?" Skyler grabbed his bowl and washed the rest of his soup down the sink.

"What are you doing? You haven't even finished!"

"I feel like I'm going to throw up. It happens every time I think about him."

Ryan stood up and turned Skyler's shoulders toward him. "Hey, when Chloe left me I had the same thing. I kept trying to figure out if she'd ever loved me. But it doesn't matter whether he really loved you or not. Maybe he's too fucked up right now to be there for you or appreciate how awesome you are. Whatever. That's his shit to sort out. What matters is that you didn't deserve it."

"Oh yeah, 'cuz I'm so great."

"You are great. You're strong and you care and you want to do the right thing. You were even brave enough to trust him and try his kinky sex shit. If you asked him if he loved you, I bet he wouldn't even be able to answer you. He doesn't even know. But if he doesn't see it now, he probably will later. He'll probably wake up one day and get how big of an ass he was and wish he hadn't fucked up such a sweet deal." *God, wait, is that what's happening now?* Would Skyler go back to him? The thought of Sky walking back into Jeremy's life was awful. It was an actual physical pain that ran through Ryan's body. *Why didn't I even consider that this might happen?*

Some couples at school broke up over and over again, but kept getting back together. *Who am I to tell him what to do? I have to let him find love wherever he can. Oh god.*

"Would you? Take him back?" Ryan held his breath.

Skyler shook his head and wouldn't meet his eyes. "Not after one text. It's too little too late. Right?"

Ryan could see the doubt in Skyler's face. *Oh fuck.* How far would Jeremy take this? Would he show up at Skyler's place when they got back? Would he apologize? Ryan could picture Jeremy saying all the right things, getting down on his knees or some romantic shit, and Skyler starting to cave. Jeremy would touch him just right, kiss him all slow, and Skyler wouldn't be able to say no. He could see Skyler's eyes closing and his mouth opening as he eased back into Jeremy's arms.

"I don't want him to hurt you again," said Ryan. But that wasn't quite the whole truth, was it? He wasn't just afraid for Skyler's sake. *Oh god, am I jealous?* But that couldn't be right. Maybe it was that Skyler wouldn't have time to hang out anymore if he was back with Jeremy. That was kind of selfish, wasn't it? All he wanted to do was to rant about what a jerk Jeremy was and how Skyler shouldn't respond in any way, but part of him knew if Skyler wanted to talk to Jeremy, there was nothing he could say that would change that. And Ryan's ranting would just make Skyler do it secretly instead of talking about it.

It almost killed him to ask, but he said it anyway. "What do you want? Do you want to talk to him?" *It's time to not be a selfish prick. Forget about what you want. He deserves to be happy. He deserves to have friends that don't push him around.*

"I don't know."

"Okay, so partly yes and partly no. What's on the 'yes' side?"

"Well, I'd love to tell him off. I'd love to hear that he gets that he crossed the line and that he's sorry."

"Okay and what's on the 'no' side?"

"What if he doesn't get it? What if he can tell how fucked up I am over him and all he wants is to just fuck me again, and I'm too weak to say no to him? Or too blind and stupid to see the truth."

Oh god, that is a real possibility, isn't it? Shit. "You're not weak, Sky. You're the strongest guy I know. It's like what you said to my dad, you came out because you could take it. It's fuckin' hard, but you can deal."

"That's not because I'm strong, that's because I have backup. I have people telling me I'm great every day, people I respect. This is different. God, I wanted a boyfriend so bad that I just let it all go down, whatever he wanted. That was so stupid. I can't do that anymore."

"Maybe you didn't know what you wanted. Specifically, I mean. But what about now?"

"I want to not get used again."

"Okay. And?"

"I want to be with someone that I trust. Someone that cares about me. I'd rather not be on my own. I can do it, but having someone was really nice, you know? Even though it sucked sometimes."

"You're a hot guy, man. A guy that's doing well and making great plans. You're smart and brave and kind to people. You won't be on your own for long if you don't want to be."

"Ryan, how many guys do you think have asked me out at school?"

"I dunno. A few?"

"None."

"What? Well, that's just because they're scared."

"So? It still means I'm on my own."

"But that's just high school. In a few months, everything's going to change. And for now, you've got me."

"Yeah, but you don't...."

"What?"

"Whatever. You're a really awesome friend, Ryan."

Ryan searched Skyler's face. *I don't what? I don't get how hard it is? I don't understand things? I'm not smart enough?*

Skyler closed the space between them, tucking his chin over Ryan's shoulder and wrapping his arms around him. It was so new for Skyler to initiate a hug, and Ryan's heart swelled. There had been that time in bed when he'd lifted an arm up, but that was more like an invitation to hug. And there was that time on the chairlift, but that was a pity hug, not really like this. Skyler's arms were tight around his body, and he could feel the desperation. It was wonderful but awful, too, to feel him so upset.

"I just want you to be happy," he said softly into Skyler's hair. "It kills me when you're sad." Skyler's arms tightened a little.

"Thanks," he said and pulled away.

"You know what you need? Let's go for a snowshoe! Get your blood moving, get outside."

"Thanks, but I think I know what I have to do. You mind if I work on the computer for a while?"

"Sure. You okay?"

"Yeah, I just want to do some stuff."

Oh god, he wants to e-mail Jeremy, doesn't he?

Skyler put his phone in his jeans and moved his computer over to the couch, propping it on his lap. Ryan tried to play Hill Climb Racing on the iPad, but his eyes kept flicking back over to Skyler. He looked so tense and unhappy, typing away like crazy. If he was writing to Jeremy, could Jeremy have written back already? Maybe they had some kind of online chat thing and they were talking right now. Skyler took out his phone and started playing with it. *He's texting him back. Fuck.*

A couple of minutes later, Skyler's phone chimed that he'd gotten a new text. A feeling of dread washed over Ryan, and he turned the iPad off. He needed a distraction. He'd downloaded the day's pictures when they came in and now looked through them. God, Sky was a good photographer. He saw the beauty in things, and it was so cool to see things the way he did. Ryan wanted so badly to go over to him and stop what Skyler was doing. To show him the pictures and tell him how special he was. To show him that he deserved better, or maybe to just distract him and satisfy him until he wasn't so lonely anymore.

He fought the urge to go to Sky. If he wanted time to sort this out, a friend should give him that. But it was hard. Everything inside him wanted to get up and walk over to the couch. *God, am I losing him right now? This very second?* Suddenly he couldn't stand it and he got up.

"Hey, I'm going to snowshoe for a bit, okay?"

"What?" Skyler stopped typing.

"I won't be long."

Skyler got up and went over to the glass deck door to look at the thermometer. "Ryan, it's fourteen below and dark out. You can't go by yourself."

"Whatever, I go all the time. I'm just going to go up the cat track and back. I'll be like fifteen minutes or something. No problem. I've got my headlamp."

"Are you sure? Aren't there like cougars or something?"

"Naw, it's fine. People use these trails all the time. I know this place really well, okay?"

"Well, take your phone." Skyler unplugged it from the dock. "Then if you twist your ankle or something, you can call me." He held it out. "Take it and I won't worry as much."

"Alright, fine."

The air outside was cold. It went right up his nose and almost burned its way down his throat. He didn't actually bother with snowshoes, just put on his headphones and put iTunes on shuffle. The cat track was packed enough to walk on, and so he ran the first bit, the beam of his headlamp bobbing along the empty track in front of him. He'd needed to move, but he slowed to a fast walk once he'd warmed up a bit. Exercise always helped when his head got too crowded. He just focused on his breathing for a while, watching it puff into the cold air again and again, but the sparkle of the snow and the trees he was passing held no thrill for him. He wasn't even listening to the music.

Something was wrong. *No shit something's wrong.*

He didn't want to think about it, and that was when he could tell that he had to. There was a spot in his mind that he'd been skirting around, something he was avoiding. He tried to relax and look at it. *I thought we were going to fool around more. Is that what it is? I just assumed we'd get to tonight, tomorrow night, Sunday night.* Three more nights had felt like forever, but that was ridiculous, wasn't it?

A song came on called "Suddenly I See," and the words sunk in. Could he see why the hell it meant so much to him? A very small light started to glow inside Ryan's mind. He stopped walking and closed his eyes. Skyler was right there behind his eyelids, his big eyes focused on the computer as he typed like a demon. There was this scary stillness inside Ryan, as if he were listening, waiting to hear a sound that had been outside of his notice until now. It was like hearing water dripping all night long and opening your eyes to suddenly realize your roof was leaking.

All that longing to go to Skyler wasn't just wanting to comfort him, was it? It wasn't just that he could relate to someone who was going through a hard breakup. And it wasn't just that Ryan was floundering and needed a friend right now either.

There was something that he was missing. Something obvious. He waited, hardly breathing, and took a closer look around the inside of his head. Skyler's face was really beautiful. He had amazing eyelashes, but Ryan could still picture how Sky's brow was pulled down in concentration and there, there it was, the desire to walk over there and erase that furrow from his face. He wanted to make Skyler smile that slow tentative smile, to see his face get pink from a compliment, to run his fingers over that warm blush. That was part of this... unnamed thing, wasn't it? A large part of him was pulling away from thinking about this, but then there was Skyler, typing away on this laptop. Was he drifting away? *I have to figure this out now. I've got to turn and look at it instead of just keeping my back to it.*

And what about Jeremy? What if they were getting back together right now? What if Jeremy was begging for forgiveness online? Ryan wanted to rip that computer out of Skyler's hands. Oh, he WAS jealous, all right. Or maybe more than jealous. Maybe scared. And sure, it was scary to think of Sky getting treated badly and getting hurt even more than he already was. But it was also the fear that what they had right now was already over. Being away from school and friends, it was like a little bubble of time up here. And it was ticking down. It had been ticking down the whole time and Ryan hadn't wanted to think about it.

All they had was a weekend left, and then it was back to the old life of putting in time and hoping that Skyler might be able and willing to come over after school every few days. And then to hope that they might get some time alone together.

That was another part of it: time alone. He'd been craving that and only that for weeks now. Time alone with Skyler. And maybe some situation where he could put an arm around him. Wanting to touch him was like starving but never getting full. The more he got the chance to touch Skyler, the more he wanted to. It was wonderful and satisfying, but it just made the wanting worse. Except for that time when he'd rubbed Skyler's back, when he'd felt Skyler's body give up the last of its resistance and relax in his hands. That had been perfect. And when....

Oh god. That was it, wasn't it? He wanted to rip Skyler's clothes off! Heat flooded Ryan's face and ran down his chest.

Could that be right? Ryan looked at Skyler in his head and tried to clear his mind. *If I could do anything, what would it be?* He could see himself sitting down next to Skyler, that desire was obvious. The whole room separating them had been painful. And of course, he'd want to put an arm around Skyler's shoulders, just to have some physical contact with him. But that wouldn't be enough, would it? He'd want Skyler to look at him and tell him everything, to feel the tension and the secrets leaving him, and have the sharing of those things bring them closer together.

A wave of fear washed over Ryan, and he had to start moving again. He opened his eyes and started jogging down the trail. Nobody came out here at night, and the stillness and quiet and movement seemed to drain away enough of the fear to think again.

Okay, what else? If it could be anything?

He could picture Skyler looking at him the way he had in the snow cave. Lying there underneath him with his eyes wide and his mouth slightly open, his face had changed and it hadn't been funny anymore. Ryan wanted that moment back but instead of Skyler wriggling free, he'd want to lower himself down and....

Oh my god, I want to kiss him! Jesus! Like full-on french kissing? He pictured Skyler melting in his arms, their tongues meeting and sliding, his fingers slipping around the back of Sky's neck pulling him closer. His cock picked that moment to wake up and stand to attention.

Oh yeah, it was not just a peck on the cheek that he wanted. This was serious intense make-out material, and just the thought of it made him rock hard.

What the hell did that mean? Messing around jacking off with a buddy wasn't the same at all. *Kissing?* He'd never wanted to kiss another guy before. That was completely different. He wanted another drink suddenly. *I've been drinking more, too, since we started hanging out. Is this why?* It was easier to pretend, wasn't it, when you were drinking? Easier to just say that what you were feeling and doing didn't mean anything.

A tremor ran down Ryan's body, and he picked up the pace. His snow boots sank a little with each step, which was great because it made it harder, and the harder his body worked, the less freaked out he felt.

The question remained, how had he confused the two things? He'd swallowed the lie whole, and worse, he'd lied to Sky. He didn't want to fool around now and then because they were both single horny guys. That wasn't it at all. *Why do I always have to figure things out too late? Goddammit!*

He turned back then, back toward the warmth of the house and back toward Sky.

He peeled off his gear and tried to wave casually as he came up the stairs. "Hey," he said.

"Hey!" Skyler's mad typing stopped. "You okay?"

"Yup, I'll be upstairs, okay?"

"Okay, I'll just be a minute."

Ryan took his laptop up to the bedroom and looked through his iTunes. *What would Sky like?* Whatever happened tonight, at least he still had some time with Sky. He could still give him something, and the new playlist should be perfect. Something Sky could listen to with headphones, not just on YouTube. But then, Sky's crappy cell didn't hold music, did it? He never wore headphones. *Maybe I could get him an MP3 player for his birthday.* But would they still be hanging out when they got back to school? Would Skyler be spending his birthday with Jeremy?

And what about that moment in the snow cave? Skyler always got things faster than he did. Sky'd said something, hadn't he? That it was going to get really uncomfortable? He'd known. He'd known even though Ryan didn't, that the moment was over-the-line hot. And he'd stopped it. He didn't want to cross that line then, did he? Maybe fooling around was okay, but kissing was just too weird with a straight guy? Or just not what he wanted with Ryan. He'd said that thing in the bathroom too: "If you don't know, I'm not going to tell you." After all he'd gone through in being gay, some guy coming on to you and calling himself straight must be really aggravating. *And let's face it, even if I called myself gay, he could do so much better than me.*

He started two playlists, one called "Clear Sky," which was the cheer-up one he'd offered earlier, full of fun songs with good dance beats, and another called "The Truth," which he resolved to never share with Sky or anyone else. This one started with the song "Suddenly I See," but there were other songs coming to mind now that he'd opened it up. And those were all love songs.

CHAPTER 8—SKYLER

HE HAD to talk to Lisa. Right now. He opened his e-mail for the first time in days and skipped over all the new messages in his inbox. When he hit Compose, everything he'd put off telling her came spilling out in the e-mail about how he'd stupidly thanked Ryan for being affectionate with him on the way up here, about the turn-on factor and the amazing time together and the bedroom encounters. Then he texted her, painstakingly on his crap phone with no keyboard, to tell her to check her e-mail. He was looking through the texts he had completely missed over the last couple days when Lisa opened up a Gmail chat window about a minute later that started with…

Lisa: What the hell?! I thot he was straight!

Skyler: He IS straight! That's the problem!

Lisa: WTF?! How is THAT straight?! And what's with that FB pic?

Skyler: I don't know! I'm the gay guy ok? To him it's just messing around. It doesn't mean anything

Lisa: But it does to u right?

Skyler: Of course it does!!

Lisa: Shit

Skyler: Yeah

Lisa: I'm going to kill him

Skyler: What?! No! I thought you'd be mad at ME!

Lisa: Whatever. U can't dangle a hotdog in front of a starving dog and expect him not to gobble it

Skyler: Thanks. I'm a dog now?

Lisa: U know what I mean

Skyler: So you don't think I'm an idiot? For letting this happen?

Lisa: Hell, I think anyone would be hard pressed to say no to Ryan. He's fucking hot

Skyler: True

Lisa: And ur all mashed up right now. Ur entitled to do stupid shit if u want to

Skyler: Great. Is that like a free Stupid Pass or something?

Lisa: Yup. But u know this is going to bite u in the ass, rite?

Skyler: Fuck

Lisa: Yup

Skyler: Jeremy just texted that he missed me

Lisa: What!?

Skyler: Yeah, and I had this moment where I actually considered going back to him

Lisa: Shit. The pass doesn't cover that kind of UBER Dumb Shit, ok?

Skyler: I said it was a moment. It's over. But you know why?

Lisa: Y?

Skyler: Because then maybe I could stand this thing with Ryan for longer. Maybe I could hang out with him all the time and fall for him more and more and never get to kiss him or tell him how I feel if I could go over to Jeremy's every week or two and get nailed into the fucking wall

Lisa: Wow

Skyler: I know. So fucking disturbing

Lisa: Aw honey! :(

Skyler: That's when I knew I had to call you, but my fucking phone has no long distance. Thanks for this, by the way. It's a huge relief just to tell someone what a freak I am. Fuck, I feel like a fucking bomb about to go off

Lisa: No wonder! And ur not a freak. Ur an amazing sweet wonderful guy. Ryan is so lucky to get u on a vulnerable day when u might be tempted to give him more than a moment of ur time

Skyler: He's been wonderful actually. God, Lisa. I'm so fucked. I think I'm totally falling for him. What am I gonna do?

Lisa: Where is he right now?

Skyler: He's out snowshoeing and it's minus fucking 14

Lisa: Well u probably don't want to hear this, but it sounds like ur on the rebound. If he's paying u all this attention the way that Jeremy never did, well then the part of u that needs that just can't say no

Skyler: Maybe

Lisa: But is that enuf? I mean is he going to talk about hot girls with u? If he thinks that u guys are just having a little fun, he's not going to like, hold hands or make out with u or be faithful, rite?

Skyler: *Groan* I know

Lisa: And are u ok with that?

Skyler: I don't know

Lisa: U could just tell him the truth

Skyler: I think that would be the end of us hanging out

Lisa: Maybe. Yeah, probably. That would be pretty awkward

Skyler: And I'm basically trapped here with his family until Monday. We've been spending every second together. Oh shit, he just came home! Jussec

Lisa: So wait until u get back to tell him. Take what u can get now and enjoy it. Stop beating yourself up and feeling guilty. If he's offering, u don't have to be all noble and turn him down

Skyler: Yeah?

Lisa: Hell yeah! I think he's getting some great adventures out of it. If he wants to experiment with guys, who better than u? I don't pity him

Skyler: Thanks. And thanks so much for this. Freak-out averted

Lisa: No problem

Skyler: I love you

Lisa: I love u too sweets. Take care of yourself. More than u take care of him, ok?

Skyler: Ok night

Lisa: Night XXXOOO

Skyler shut the laptop and went upstairs to find Ryan. He was sitting on the bed, on top of the covers, working on his laptop.

"Hey." Ryan smiled tightly and moved his computer to the floor.

"Hey. Did you want some time? I can do something else if you're busy."

"No, I'm good. I was just fiddling. So what did he say?"

It took a moment for Skyler to figure out what Ryan meant. "Oh, Jeremy? I wasn't talking to him. I was talking to Lisa."

"Oh!" Ryan's face lit up.

"Yeah, no. I'll text Jeremy back tomorrow maybe. Something like, 'Kiss my ass, motherfucker.'"

"Wow! I think I like Lisa a lot more now. What did you guys talk about?" Ryan's smile was almost blinding.

"Oh, lots of stuff. Yeah, she's pretty awesome." Skyler sat down on the unmade bed.

"You want to hear a song from your new playlist?" Ryan said, grabbing his computer.

"Yeah!"

"Do you know the Flaming Lips?"

"I've heard of them."

"The guy's voice is weird, but it kinda grew on me." Ryan queued it up and said, "It's, like, drift away kinda music," and then he turned off the bedside lamp. "You just have to relax and let it float you along. This whole album is pretty awesome, so I put the whole thing on there."

They shifted around until they were both lying on their backs looking up at the raw wood of the dark peaked ceiling and letting the music move into them. There was this line about being a man and facing things even when you weren't prepared to face them that really sank into Skyler's mind. *Not yet. I'll face it soon. But not tonight.*

They listened to a couple songs in silence, and then Ryan said, "This one's called 'Yoshimi Battles the Pink Robots.' It's pretty hilarious."

It was, and they ended up smiling at each other, and Ryan rolled onto his side and moved closer. Skyler rolled toward him and propped himself up on his elbow. Ryan's hand landed on his shoulder and squeezed. "You okay?"

"I'll live."

The song changed and Ryan said, "Oh hang on, I always skip this song. I'll take it off the list, too much screaming." He rolled away and pressed some buttons, and his shirt rode up, exposing a patch of smooth, firm flesh.

The sound unraveled into the air again, and Skyler sank back into his pillow and listened. There was a line that talked about waiting for a moment but the moment never coming. He thought of what Lisa had said about just enjoying this. It would be over soon, one way or another.

"Ryan?"

"Yeah?"

"What did you do with your friend? You know, the guy?"

"The guy I fooled around with?"

"Yeah. I mean did you ever kiss?"

"No."

"Have you ever kissed a guy?"

"No."

"Have you ever wanted to?"

"No. Not until recently." There was a silence that stretched out and then stretched out again.

Skyler whispered, "Would you like to now?"

Ryan propped himself up on an elbow. "You offering?"

"Maybe."

Ryan edged closer and looked at Skyler for a while, then ran a slow, gentle hand up his arm. Skyler's breath came faster and his cock went from hyperalert to rock hard, but he lay very still. This was up to Ryan. The hand moved from his arm to his shoulder and then up behind his neck and then to his ear. He stroked Skyler's hair off his face. Ryan's fingertips brushed his cheek and down along his jaw. Ryan lowered his face very slowly and his lips were so soft, pressing down onto Skyler's.

Ryan pulled away and looked at him again. His eyes shone in the dark, and this close, Skyler could hear Ryan's breath was coming fast too. Ryan leaned down again, and this time, the kiss changed. It started out soft, but Ryan's tongue came out and licked the spot where Skyler's lips joined, and he was letting Ryan in before he'd even thought about it. *Okay, I won't lead, but following is okay, right?* He opened his mouth a little more and let Ryan's slow, wonderful tongue in to caress his own. It was like a slow-motion kiss. Ryan took his time, and soon their mouths were joining and sliding and Ryan's tongue was moving slowly in and out of his mouth, caressing his bottom lip, teasing, making him want more and more. But Ryan wouldn't speed up. The kiss just went on and on, Ryan's hands moving slowly as well, in his hair, on his neck, thumbing tiny circles on the edges of his ears. Skyler kept his own arms pinned to the bed, but god, it was hard when Ryan was so tender and so, so sweet.

Several songs slid by, but Ryan hadn't moved any closer. Their bodies and legs were still just barely touching. A song came on and the words drifted by, about how all we have is now. The part that said, "You and me were never meant to be part of the future" sounded so much like he and Ryan. They were never meant to have a future together. It was true, all they had was right now, this little moment in time.

Ryan pulled away and looked at him. "You're going to meet some great guy in college. He's going to adore everything about you and you guys are going to fuck like bunnies every day."

"Whatever. You're going to meet some pretty girl soon and get married and have kids. I guess you may as well experiment now before you miss your chance. You'll probably get snapped up in, like, a week."

They kissed again, but this time it was faster and more urgent, and Ryan's body edged closer until it was fully pressed on top of Skyler's. He could feel Ryan's erection against his own, but Ryan didn't rub or thrust up against him. He just pressed and held it there and quivered all over. Skyler'd left his arms lying on the bed for so long he just couldn't stand it anymore. His hands couldn't help but reach up and touch. Ryan's ribs and chest felt unbelievably good. Soft and hard and warm. Skyler's hands were shaking, but Ryan's quivering heat seemed to steady him somehow, and he slid his hands under Ryan's arms and around his back and pressed him closer, closer. *God, he's so heavy. So solid.*

Skyler could feel his head tilting back, his body opening involuntarily, the tender flesh of his neck exposed. Ryan broke the kiss for a moment and whispered, "Tell me. Tell me what you like."

Jeremy had taken charge and at the time that had been really exciting and hot, but in the end, Jeremy hadn't been really paying attention. Had he? He'd done what he wanted, not seeming to really care what turned Skyler on. God, those hickeys? How many of those had he squirmed his way through, too nervous to push away for fear of pissing Jeremy off? It was so nice to have someone start slow like this and ask questions. Sure, questions were hard to answer and kind of embarrassing, but it was better, wasn't it? They made it a conversation.

"I like this," Ryan whispered back.

"Yeah?" Skyler could see the flash of Ryan's teeth as he smiled in the dim light. "Thank god for that. Can I take off your shirt?"

Skyler lifted up a bit and so did Ryan, although it was harder to do than it needed to be, since neither of them wanted any space to come between their pressed bodies. There was some tugging and struggling and laughing, and then Skyler fell back onto the pillow again with his arms above his head, and Ryan looked down at his body and moaned and covered an eye with the heel of his hand. *Is he freaked?!* But Ryan's cock pressed down hard against his own again, and Ryan's body arched like he was struggling hard to master something, and Skyler decided he didn't mind waiting it out. If Ryan needed time, he could have some time.

That didn't mean he couldn't touch Ryan's hair, though, right? God, his hair was like satin pajamas. *Does he slip off his own pillow on this stuff?* It was crazy soft and there was never any product in it, was there? It just curved this way and that way and did its own thing, and it was so, so, so amazing to explore with his fingertips and his thumbs and his palms. Skyler could drown in that hair, pulling it gently off Ryan's face and lifting it up off the hot base of his neck. Oh god. He could just lay there and pant and touch Ryan's hair and be good for about ten years. It was fucking enough, and if that was pathetic Skyler didn't fucking care.

Jeremy had been all about moving through the bases, hurrying things along, switching it up, keeping it fresh. *Fuck that.* Who needed fresh? Ryan was like someone else's pecan pie, and if you got to smell it and pick bits of pastry off the edge of the crust, you should just take that moment to let that gold melt on your tongue and be grateful, right? It was precious and you just got a particular number of minutes before the real owner showed up, snatched it, and gorged her bitch face on the whole thing. But he wasn't going to think about her. He was going to think about letting the skin of HIS hands gorge on Ryan's hair silk.

"Hey, you like my hair or something?" Ryan was smiling down at him.

"Ryan, I LOVE your hair." Skyler didn't stop moving his hands, slow and gentle, until Ryan's head relaxed in his hands and his neck arched a little. "You dye it, right?"

"Nope."

"Seriously?"

"I'm way too lazy. I never even get it cut."

"You cut this and I'm going to kill you," he whispered.

Ryan laughed. "Do nothing. Check. That should be easy. You're pretty demanding."

"Don't get me started."

"You haven't started yet? What do you call this?" Ryan's cute curly smile was back, and Skyler couldn't help but lift up and grab his mouth with his own. That smile had been tempting him too long now. The softness of Ryan's lips was so delicious. There was something about licking across his lips and feeling the edge of his teeth as well that was just so… god! Just so fucking amazing. So soft and hard at the same time. So Ryan. So male.

Ryan pulled back a bit and looked down at him. "Can I touch them? Your rings?"

"Yeah." Skyler's breath caught.

The pad of Ryan's thumb hovered over his nipple and he said, "It won't get them dirty or something?" Having Ryan's hand so close like that was torture. Sure they'd been touching, but this was somehow another level. It was Ryan wanting him to the point of reaching out to explore his body. He wanted to arch up into Ryan's hand, but this was important. Ryan had to make the choices.

"I think they're fully healed now. I should have been more careful with them when they were new."

Ryan's thumb came down, and then the pad of his index finger touched the tip of his nipple as well, and Skyler's shoulders bucked a little. Ryan looked at him, concern on his face.

"It feels good," Skyler whispered. Ryan's fingers came back, stroking the nipple back and forth, circling around it, and Skyler's breathing gasped in again and again. It was amazing how little stimulation had him so close to coming. It was crazy.

"These are pretty fun to play with," whispered Ryan. He leaned his head down and said, "Can I?" sticking his tongue out a bit.

"Oh god, yeah. But I might come in my pants."

Ryan laughed. "Try not to, okay?" His tongue came down so smooth it was almost hard to feel it, and Skyler held his breath. He was so filled with anticipation that his shoulder blades were the only part of his back actually touching the bed.

Ryan's tongue seemed uncertain at first, flicking the nipple and then pulling away, sliding along the ring and then stopping again.

Maybe he doesn't like it. Maybe it's nothing compared to girl boobs. Skyler could hardly get a breath in at all, it was winding him so tight. Then Ryan's whole mouth descended, swirling around and around with his tongue while he held the ring in place with his lower lip. *Wow.* Maybe Ryan wasn't uncertain. Maybe he was a tease. The best kind of tease there was. Over and over his mouth came down, never for long enough, focusing on one nipple and then the other, experimenting with motion and speed and pressure, until Skyler couldn't keep his pitiful sounds to himself when Ryan's mouth left him.

Ryan smiled wickedly down at him and then went for the waistband of Skyler's pants. There was something scary about that. Skyler couldn't think. It was good, right? It was what he wanted, more of Ryan touching him. But.... And then he could see it, how dangerously aroused he was, how he was going to come apart in Ryan's hand any time now. He was going to come so hard, it might make him cry, and that was... that wasn't.... Oh god, if Ryan decided he didn't like it while he was letting go like that, it might kill him.

Skyler sat up and captured Ryan's mouth before he could get too far with the pants. He kissed him harder this time, fisting his hand in Ryan's hair, trying to grab on to some kind of control. He didn't want Ryan to see him like that. So undone, so vulnerable. He wriggled out from underneath Ryan and pulled Ryan's shirt over his head. They kissed again, and then Skyler pushed Ryan gently down onto the bed, kissing his way down Ryan's soft, warm neck and chest. He started working on his nipples and he didn't hold back—this guy was straight. He probably needed every trick in the book to make it work for him. Ryan lay still under him as he sucked, swirled, pulled, teased, nibbled, and Ryan smiled at him but didn't really look overcome. *Shit, he doesn't feel anything close to what I did, does he? Maybe this isn't going to work at all.* But Ryan had liked the kissing, right? No one quivered like that unless they were seriously turned-on. Or maybe scared? *Shit. Is he just scared?*

"Do you like that?" he whispered, hoping the fear wasn't obvious in his voice.

"Sure," Ryan lifted a shoulder. "They're not that sensitive. Not like yours. God, that was awesome." He put a hand between them, circling Skyler's still wet nipple with his thumb. Skyler shuddered and a little sound escaped his lips.

"You seem to have me at a disadvantage," said Skyler.

"I do?"

"I want to make you feel good."

"You do!"

"I mean really good."

"Well this is weird, but it's actually my ears and my neck that... oh!" Skyler's tongue ran down the shell of his ear, and then Ryan's large hands were grabbing him hard around the ribs and air got sucked in between Ryan's teeth. "Oh god!" Ryan whispered as his earlobe disappeared between Skyler's lips, and then his hot breath panted fast and desperate against Skyler's cheek and temple as he worked his way down to Ryan's neck.

Skyler had never really enjoyed the neck attention that Jeremy had lavished on him. It just didn't feel that great, but Ryan clearly loved it. He kissed and licked and sucked and bit until Ryan's breath was ragged and little *Mmm-mmm*s were coming out of his mouth. *It's working!*

He sat up and pulled off Ryan's pants and boxers. Ryan gave up both without hesitating, and then there it was, his large circumcised penis, standing up and lifting up off his belly in eagerness. Ryan was propped up on his elbows, and Skyler looked into his face. His mouth was slightly ajar, his lower lip full and almost pouting, and his eyes, oh his eyes were on fire. *He wants this. Oh, thank god, he wants it!* Skyler stroked his hand up Ryan's bare leg, enjoying the soft bristle of brushing leg hair the wrong way, and then caressed up Ryan's ribs as he lowered his head down and kissed the head of Ryan's cock. Ryan gasped a little and then held his breath, keeping very still.

Skyler brought the hand back down now and ran the backs of his fingers over Ryan's furry balls, loving how tight and drawn up they were. He took the head into his mouth and pressed a thumb at the top of the sac to lift the shaft up to the right angle and traced a slow circle with his tongue along the crease where it joined onto the shaft. He kept his tongue in slow and constant smooth motion, caressing the glans and sliding to invite the whole thing into his mouth. The little banjo string of flesh on the underside was pulled tight under the strumming tip of his tongue, and then he stopped and looked up at Ryan again.

"You like that?" Ryan nodded very hard and fast and Skyler smiled. This might be the one and only blow job he ever gave Ryan. This might be the last sexual thing they did together. *I want it to be the best. I want him to remember it forever.* "You want the whole treatment?" he whispered.

Ryan swallowed and nodded again. Skyler got up and found Ryan's sex kit. The towel was somewhere on the floor, but that was fine.

He found lube instead of the massage oil Ryan had used and coated two of his fingers. Ryan leaned forward to watch. "What's that for?"

Skyler held his eyes for a moment. It was only fair that Ryan should know, right? He hadn't known much of anything when it had started with Jeremy and that had made things harder. He remembered what Ryan had said about expecting him to treat someone inexperienced with kindness. It would be easier to just smirk and do what he wanted, but that wasn't how it should go down. But that didn't mean explaining had to be all doctorly, though, did it? He leaned close to Ryan's face and licked Ryan's lips and then pulled away when he opened up for a deeper kiss.

Then he whispered, "I'm going to put you in my mouth, as far as I can, and then I'm going to swirl this around your asshole while I suck you." Ryan's eyes got bigger and his lip hung down farther. "It's gonna feel really good. Even better is this g-spot inside there. If you want me to slip a finger in and show you, just bend your knees up and spread for me. I promise it won't hurt. Okay?" Ryan nodded, and Skyler kissed him slowly until he felt sure Ryan was still super turned-on and then shifted down again and took Ryan in his mouth. Ryan's cock was hot to the touch, thick and hard, and he hissed as it disappeared into Skyler's mouth. After a moment, Skyler pulled up and said, "Oh and don't grab my head and pump my face too hard or it might make me gag."

He went back to it, letting his eyes flick back to Ryan's face where they were always drawn. Ryan didn't lie back and close his eyes as he'd expected. He stayed propped up and watched and bit his lips and *mmm*ed and panted. Skyler watched his face carefully as he worked his slippery fingers up Ryan's ass crack and then rubbed up and down, back and forth. Ryan squeezed his eyes shut for a moment, his mouth opening wider. Skyler didn't stop. He circled the entrance now and pressed a little on it. Ryan's hips bucked and he opened his eyes in surprise. "UH!"

Skyler smiled and *mmm*ed around the cock in his mouth as he pulled it in and out. Ryan whispered, "That's…. Oh, you were right!" and arched his back and then groaned and slammed forward. "Sorry."

Skyler lifted his head free and smiled. "Go ahead and move. I can move around you, and I want to see you like it." Ryan's eyes were large and round as he slowly let himself go. Skyler made little encouraging noises and soon Ryan was bucking away, and Skyler was riding that up and down, keeping rhythm. Ryan lifted a knee and then the other, and Skyler corkscrewed a finger ever so slightly inside. Ryan's every breath had sound now, keening in and out. Skyler pressed his finger into that hot, tight space slowly, never stopping with his mouth, until he found that little nerve bundle on the front wall and rubbed it. Ryan jolted.

"Oh god, man, I'm going to come! Right now!"

Skyler tried to nod and make encouraging sounds to say that he didn't mind and slid his other finger inside. Ryan came hard. He sat right up and moaned so loud Skyler wondered if his parents could hear it next door. He grabbed Skyler's shoulders and slid his hands down Skyler's back and rammed and rammed as the cum pumped out of him, and Skyler swallowed.

It was beautiful. But more than that, it left Ryan stripped raw. He was still quivering, his whole body spasming as Skyler let him slide free and sat up to look at his face. He curled his dirty fingers into a fist and let his other hand stroke Ryan's damp chest. Ryan was making this little sound each time he breathed, almost whimpering, and looking at him with lost eyes. Skyler couldn't help but kiss him, his tongue swirling into Ryan's panting mouth. *Wait, does this gross him out?*

"Oh, does that taste sick to you?"

Ryan just grabbed his head with both hands and kissed him again, not hesitating to dive in and taste.

Skyler's erection was painful at this point. He'd almost come when Ryan did, but somehow it hadn't quite happened while he was focusing hard to make each movement just right so Ryan's mind would be blown out his ears. It seemed to have worked. Ryan snaked his arms around Skyler and pressed their sweating bodies together. Skyler was still wearing pants, and Ryan cupped his ass, pressing their cocks together.

"Just give me a minute," he breathed in Skyler's ear.

Skyler pulled his hips back reluctantly. Was there any way to come now? If Ryan wasn't turned on anymore, wouldn't any gay moans out of Skyler's mouth seem even creepier than before? He couldn't shake this image of Ryan cringing away in disgust. "It's okay, I'm good." Skyler rolled over and Ryan spooned up against the back of him.

"Are you shitting me?" Ryan whispered, kissing his neck.

Skyler shook his head and squeezed his eyes shut.

Ryan's voice changed. "What, you don't think I can make you feel good?"

"Oh, that's not a problem."

"What then? Tell me. Wait, did you want to fuck me?"

"What!"

"Is that it? I mean, I'd be a little worried that it would hurt, but...."

Skyler sat up and whipped around. "What the hell? I'm not going to fuck you!"

"Okaaay. It's not that crazy of a question. We are having sex here, aren't we?"

"Are we? Ryan, I'm a guy. I keep waiting for you to notice that and freak out."

"Oh, I noticed. The weird thing is, I like it. I mean, I never wanted a guy like this, but I want you. Really bad." Ryan reached for his hand, but Skyler pulled away.

"That's the dirty one."

Ryan laughed and looked a little embarrassed. "Sorry about that."

"I'm not. I almost came in my pants it was so hot."

"Yeah?"

"Oh yeah."

"Come on, let's go wash your hand and brush our teeth and stuff. I don't want to get up again."

Ryan grabbed some towels and headed down the stairs naked. God, his body was amazing, all smooth golden muscle. Skyler followed because he couldn't seem to do anything else. Had Ryan just offered to bottom for him? His mind was already blown and he hadn't even come.

Ryan was turning on the shower when Skyler walked in. "Come on, get in with me."

"I only need to wash my hands. And your parents might come home."

"They'll probably be late and they so don't care." Ryan shut the door and locked it. "Okay?" He hooked his thumbs in Skyler's waistband and pulled the zipper apart, peeling his jeans off him.

The water was hot as they stepped under it, and then Ryan was kissing him and Skyler's arms were sliding around Ryan's neck and their bodies were pressing together. Ryan's hair was getting wet and Skyler ran his fingers through it. It caught and pulled.

"Ow."

"Sorry." Skyler pulled back, but Ryan's eyes held his. There was something in there. It looked like desire, but more than that. Maybe it was need.

Skyler kissed Ryan's hair. "Sorry." He kissed Ryan's ear— "Sorry."—and then ran his tongue along the curve of his ear. Ryan's shiver was such a lovely reward. *This is probably our one and only shower together.* The chances of this happening again were pretty much nil, but maybe if it was hot enough, Ryan might think about it sometimes when he was having sex with his next girlfriend. That was a nice thought. Maybe he could sneak into Ryan's mind, so that when he went to bed and couldn't sleep, it would be his face and his hands that Ryan pictured as he touched himself. He sucked on Ryan's earlobe until he shivered again.

Skyler reached for the soap. There were these little hotel soaps, Jergens, and he rolled it around in his hands, rinsed them clean, and then slid his hands up Ryan's chest. He didn't have much chest hair, just a little on either pec, and it was nice to rub under his palms.

Ryan washed him, too, his face serious one moment, then shy, then smiling warmly at him, and then his eyes burning hotter into Skyler's. There were these crystalline lines of color in Ryan's eyes that were so beautiful, Skyler had to kiss him long and slow as Ryan's hands slid over his skin.

"Let me wash your back," said Ryan, and Skyler turned around. Ryan's soapy hands worked over his shoulders, pressing into his muscles and bringing back the lovely echo of that massage. This time his hands moved down to his hips, though, and then one slid down the crack of his ass, a finger pressing and rubbing tentatively. Skyler put his hands on the cold tile and tilted his hips back. Ryan nestled his hard cock length-wise along the crack of Skyler's ass and slid it up and down between their bodies, his hands on Skyler's waist.

The friction was a little jerky between them, and Skyler grabbed a bottle of shampoo. "This works better than soap," he said, handing it to Ryan. "It lasts longer."

Ryan paused for long enough to make Skyler worry that he'd said the wrong thing and sounded like a complete shower slut, and then there was shampoo dripping down his ass crack and Ryan's cock rubbing it in and nothing else could enter into his overly full brain.

Ryan's shampoo-slick hands came around front and slid around Skyler's cock and balls, stroking, lifting, caressing. A great gust of air escaped his mouth, and he pressed back against Ryan as he felt every inch of his own cock sliding up and down in time to Ryan's as the lather built up. Ryan's arms held him while his hands were working, and then there was biting and kissing on his shoulder and he started making sounds he couldn't help.

Without thinking Skyler lifted a foot up and propped it on the edge of the tub. Ryan pulled back a little, grabbing himself and rubbing the end of his cock right there, right on the entrance. Skyler could feel the head of Ryan's cock teasing the hole, widening it just a little. If Ryan pushed into him right now, without a condom, would he stop him? *No, I want him. Now.* He angled his hips as far back as he could in invitation.

And that was something he had never done. Always a condom. Always. Jeremy had drilled that into him, which was the one caring thing he did, maybe. And here that was slipping away. There was no protecting himself against Ryan, was there? Ryan could do whatever he wanted, and Skyler would give it all away, just like he always did.

But Ryan didn't press in like he'd thought he would. He played around, teasing, and then he slid his cock back up the groove of Skyler's crack and held him close again. His hands came back up front and started stroking harder, one hand cupping his balls.

"You're not going to?" Skyler whispered.

Ryan jolted. "No! I would never do that to you!"

Wait, what did that mean? *Never?* Did he think it was gross? Hadn't he offered to bottom before, or had Skyler misunderstood? Was it the condom? Did he think all gay guys had AIDS or something? *But he said 'to you,' not 'with you.'* Did that mean something? All these thoughts whirled in his mind, and then he couldn't think anymore. Ryan's hands were strong and sure on him and that cock in his crack was pressing hard and it was all too much. He came in Ryan's hand while Ryan peered over his shoulder and exclaimed, not in words, but in no uncertain terms that his cum, his bucking hips, and stifled cries were so wonderful that Ryan couldn't help but moan and come again on the small of Skyler's back.

Ryan's whole body curved over his as he thrust, and it was almost hard to stay standing up, Ryan was so strong and heavy. But then Ryan was ungluing himself and turning Skyler around for a shaky kiss, and their arms slid around each other and maybe everything was okay.

That was when they heard talking right outside the bathroom door.

Skyler gasped and grabbed Ryan's biceps, pushing away. Ryan smiled. "Hey, chill out," he whispered. "They don't care, remember?"

Of course Ryan's parents cared! Okay, maybe Erin was cool with her son experimenting, but that didn't mean she wanted to see it happening. And Dave was definitely not going to love seeing them come out of the shower together. *Oh god, did they hear us?* Why had he gotten into this shower with Ryan when they might be coming home? It was ridiculous. He couldn't just pack up and leave this place if things got awkward. Hell, if he MADE them awkward. Wasn't he the one creating this stupid situation?

He tried to get out of the shower, but Ryan stopped him. "Just wait a sec." He rubbed soap on his hands and then rubbed the base of Skyler's spine, then pulled him back against him again, reaching around him to slowly wash his balls and cock, then up to his stomach. More soap and then his nipples and shoulders. Ryan's arms crossed around him. "Arms up," Ryan whispered in his ear. Was there a question of not doing what Ryan told him to? But then Ryan's hands were sliding over the hair in his armpits, which for some reason made him want to lean back into Ryan and weep. He allowed himself a little sagging in his stiff muscles, and then Ryan slid past him without letting go and cradled him in the spray.

Skyler hung his face in the water for a moment. *Fuck, I am so in love with him.*

Straightening up, Skyler rubbed his hands fast over his body to get any last soap off and then climbed out and toweled off like his life depended on it. He'd never brushed his teeth so fast in his life and was listening at the door trying to time his exit when Ryan reached around him and opened the door. He gave Ryan a desperate look, which was just met with one of those damn curvy smiles, and then dashed upstairs.

He was huddled in bed when Ryan slipped in behind him.

"Hey, come here." Ryan edged forward until he was wrapped around Skyler's fetal position. "We haven't done anything wrong."

"You haven't."

"Oh, and you have? Like what?"

Skyler couldn't answer. All he could think about was putting his foot up on the edge of the tub and tilting his hips back. *I would have let him. God, I let Jeremy walk all over me and I never sank this low.* Somehow, as he thought about it, he could feel a dark chasm of loss opening up inside him, and he had to admit that part of it was Ryan's mom's rule about not transmitting any diseases. It had been almost funny when she'd said it. Of course he'd never expected to get the chance to have sex with Ryan, but protection wasn't even a consideration. He'd never had sex without a condom and maybe Ryan hadn't either, but that wasn't the point. It was maybe the only line he had never crossed. The only part of himself he hadn't handed away before.

"Tell me," whispered Ryan.

"Ryan, I can't do this anymore. I thought I could handle it, but I'm not strong enough."

"What do you mean?"

"I mean I'm gay and you're not. I don't want to play around. I just finished letting guys touch me who didn't care, and here I am doing it again. I can't believe I was going to let you...."

"But I wouldn't have."

"Yeah, and why is that? Because it's disgusting and gay?"

"No! Because I don't want to hurt you! God, what guy doesn't fantasize about getting in the back door with a girl? I don't see how this is any different. But I'm not going to just take advantage because you're turned on. Of course I wanted to, but that would just be wrong."

"Okay, but that doesn't change the fact that I want something that you don't. I've known that since we drove up here, and I let it go and tried to ignore it and hoped you wouldn't see it. And you've been really kind trying to make it normal for me, but the fact is, it's NOT normal between us. I mean, it's not just friendship for me. You might be curious about trying something out and playing around experimenting, but I guess I can't do that with you. It makes me want more."

"Really? You mean you'd go out with me?"

"I would if you were gay."

Ryan's voice dropped down to a whisper in his ear. "I don't know what to call this, Sky, but I'm falling really hard for you. It's not just your body. I mean, holy mother shit monkey, your body has some kind of magnetic force around it and I want my skin on your skin like every second, but it's not just that. I think about you all the time. I want so bad to make you feel good. God, it's embarrassing how bad I want you to like me."

Skyler unfolded a little and turned in Ryan's arms. "You mean that?"

"God, it's fucking terrifying to say this stuff. I mean, I know I'm not gay enough for you. Look at Jeremy. He was like the King of Gay Men. I can't give you that at all, but I can love you. I can look out for you and care and listen and touch you all the time and adore the shit out of you. I don't know if that's enough, but I can be good to you."

"Okay, wait a second. Are we talking about the same thing here? You mean like being together but not telling anyone?" Skyler furrowed his brow.

"No! I mean being together and telling everyone."

"You mean like being my boyfriend? Like full-on together. Like having a relationship."

"Yeah."

"That's what you want?"

"Sky, when I thought you were going back to Jeremy earlier tonight it was like a nice slap upside the head. It takes me a while sometimes, okay? I just didn't see what was happening or I lied to myself about what it meant or something, but now I can see how obvious it was all along. Before I wasn't thinking about the future, I was just thinking about right now, but once I had to think about a future where you were with someone else, it just about killed me. I don't want to lose you."

"You don't want to lose my friendship?"

"Yeah, but this too. The sex part is amazing. And the talking. All of it."

"What about your parents?"

"My mom knows already I bet. My dad might be weird at first, but he won't be mean on purpose. We're probably going to have to have some awkward conversations, but that's not your problem. What about your mom?"

"Are you kidding? She'll be so relieved I'm dating someone my own age. I think she might have hated Jeremy even before we split. He never wanted anything to do with her, and there was so much stuff I couldn't tell her and she worried. I think she felt like me seeing him was her fault because she okayed the fake ID."

"Okay, good. But what about you? Do you want to be with me?"

"Ryan, I've never let anyone fuck me without a condom before. I'd say I'm stupid dangerous crazy in love with you."

"Oh thank god," Ryan whispered and then pulled him tight in a bone-crushing hug. Skyler slid his arms around Ryan's body, squeezing him just as hard. Ryan kissed his hair and his ear and his cheek until finally pulling his head back enough to find Skyler's mouth. The kiss was fast and hungry and filled with the ragged sounds of their breath coming hard. Ryan's hands moved over his back and then cupped his ass, pressing their hips together.

"How are you hard again?" whispered Skyler between kisses. "Didn't I do a good enough job?"

"Too good. I can't imagine ever getting enough of you," Ryan breathed into his ear, and a shiver ran through Skyler's body. Ryan said things sometimes that just struck him straight in the heart.

It was strange how Skyler had wanted to feel this way so badly for so long, and now it was overwhelming and terrifying. If Ryan changed his mind or even rolled his eyes, it would hurt so bad and there was no protecting against that. Had it been safer with Jeremy because he'd always felt a little bit wary? It had been easier to withhold his feelings, hadn't it? Because Jeremy wasn't paying attention and asking him? And maybe because he never knew how Jeremy would respond. It wasn't always safe to lay out his fears on Jeremy's table. He might laugh or make some comment about chilling out and not being such an old lady.

Ryan pulled away a little and stroked Skyler's hair back. "And hey, I don't want you to feel bad about the shower, okay? If I'm touching you like that, I'm asking you to get lost in it. I can't ask you to do that and then do something that might hurt you. I want to be worthy of you laying yourself open for me."

"Worthy? Every time I think you're going to throw me out of a car, you end up putting your arm around me. You haven't pushed me away once yet."

"Throw you out of a car?" Ryan's eyebrows shot up.

"Oh god, on the drive up here? I had this boner-from-hell when you snuggled up to me. I was positive I was going to get busted and you were going to freak out and toss me in a snowbank."

"Really?" Ryan laughed. "I had this crazy dream on that ride. I kept losing track of where you were and then grabbing onto you again. It was like I had to be touching you or you'd disappear."

"You kept tightening your fingers around my wrist and making this little humming noise. It was so hot."

"God, I'm such an idiot. How did I not see it? And the snow cave? You knew I wanted to kiss you, didn't you?" Ryan's mouth turned up at one corner and down at the other.

"No! I knew *I* wanted to kiss YOU! I thought if I tried it, you'd lose your mind."

"Oh I would have. I would have kissed the hell out of you and then probably been such a dumbass, like it was fine because we're such good friends or something. God. Please just slap me when I've got my head that far up my ass."

"So you think you're bi?" Skyler stroked Ryan's hair. *It's okay to touch it now, isn't it?*

"Fucked if I know. I guess? I'm thinking this is not a straight man's hard-on."

"I'm not arguing with that." Skyler laughed. "So are we going to go on dates?"

"Maybe we did already? We had a lunch date."

"No. That was before."

"Okay, tomorrow, then. That can be our first date. I want to show you the village, go tubing, skating, maybe? If there's a day not to ski, may as well be on the weekend when it's busier."

"That sounds great." Tubing sounded kinda scary, actually. He could picture inner tubes bouncing and flipping out of control and his face getting cheese-grated against the snow as he rag dolled down the hill at full speed. And skating? He sucked at skating. But whatever. A day out with Ryan as his new boyfriend? Serious pee-your-pants awesome!

"I don't mind if you don't want to….," Skyler said.

"What?"

"Well to, like, hold my hand in public or kiss me or anything. I'm not expecting you to claim me to the world."

"What? Really?"

"I don't want people to treat you badly because you're with me. That would just make me feel shitty. Like at school. We can just act like nothing's changed."

"I don't think I can do that, but hey, let's not worry about it. Okay? I'll talk to my parents in the morning and…."

"No! What if your dad is super upset? Let's wait until we get back home at least. There's no point in rubbing his nose in it when we're all stuck here together."

"I guess. If you want. You make it sound like dog shit or something."

"Well maybe it is to him. Some people feel like it's wrong or twisted. It's disturbing to them."

"To see people in love? That's just stupid. It's okay to brag about having anal sex with your girlfriend, but it's some kind of satanic rite to do the same thing with a guy?"

"Guys brag about that?"

"Sure."

"Did you ever?"

"Brag? No! I did it once with this girl. Remember I said how after Chloe and I broke up I was a mess? Well, I got stupid drunk at this party one night and this chick pulled me into a bedroom and started taking off her clothes. I didn't have a condom so she said to stick it in the back. God, I think I hurt her. It was bad."

"Did she cry out or something?"

"No, she seemed to like it at the time, but there was blood on me the next morning. Not a lot, but it scared the shit out of me. Like I was this out of control animal or something. I mean it was her idea, but no condom? What was I thinking? I didn't go out much after that. I didn't trust myself."

"Was that the last time you had sex?"

"Yeah."

"It doesn't have to hurt. You can work up to it. Stretch the muscles and learn how to relax them."

"I still think I'd be more comfortable catching than pitching if that's okay."

"Really?" Jeremy had always been on top and so Skyler had started thinking of himself as a bottom. Jeremy's friends that they'd fooled around with had wanted him to top sometimes, and that had been kind of exciting, but it was mixed up with the guilt of that whole situation. What had he liked better?

"Does that matter?" said Ryan.

"No. I'm just surprised. Some guys think the guy on top is more... masculine, I guess."

"Huh. Like dominant?"

"I guess."

"And the guy on the bottom is like the girl?" Ryan laughed. "Is that like a put-down? Like women are more submissive or something? Oh man, my mom would trip out on how sexist that is."

"We don't have to worry about that for a long time," said Skyler.

"We don't? Wait, you mean you don't want to have sex?"

"No, I mean I don't want to rush you."

"Whatever, I'm hard for you all the fucking time. You want to use me in some kind of kinky hot sex thing, I'd say I'm in."

"You must really trust me."

"Yeah. I really do." Ryan kissed him slowly and ran his fingers down Skyler's body until his nipples stood up. "Now strip off so I can get my fix on Sky skin." Skyler shucked his clothes off and threw them into the corner. "I want naked," Ryan said, looking at Skyler's soft tight boxers. Those came off as well, and then he was full skin on full skin with Ryan. He slid around, drinking in the sensation of that warm glowing skin and muscle all over him.

"Wow, you feel amazing," whispered Ryan in his ear. Their cocks were both hard again and rubbing up against each other like lonely cats nuzzling up against someone's leg.

"Let me look at you." Ryan leaned away and pulled the blankets back.

Skyler felt a moment of panic. What if Ryan thought he looked ugly? But he just lay there and looked at Ryan's eyes and there was love and desire there. Skyler lifted his arms over his head and just relaxed them on the pillow. *Let him look.* Everything was okay now. Ryan's hands slid over him and yes, everything was wonderful.

CHAPTER 9—RYAN

RYAN FELT like a little kid in the morning. He just grinned from ear to ear and laughed and bounced around getting things ready. They had a lazy morning and a big brunch, and he got the computer more set up for Sky. His mom dropped them and his sister and Emma at the skating rink, and the whole drive, he kept catching her eyes in the rearview mirror. *She totally knows.*

Was that a good thing or a bad thing? Probably good. It would save having to have this big CONVERSATION with her. *Wait, who am I kidding? This is MOM.* There would still be a conversation, but it would just start in the middle instead of at the beginning. His dad would be another story, but with Mom on his side, it would work out. God, she'd seen this coming way before he did. That was just fucking annoying. *It really wasn't the same thing with Logan, though.* Maybe there was no way to get her to believe that now.

Whatever. The day was amazing and he had the whole thing spreading out in front of him just with Sky. They didn't even have to hang out with the girls, who had disappeared before they'd even shut the car doors. Why fight the smile that just wouldn't stop spreading across his face? Life was so good and he was so lucky. It was time to make the most of it.

They rented skates, and he helped tighten Skyler's up properly, which made Sky blush in that adorable way. The rink was outdoors and covered with snow, so it was kinda lumpy in an unpredictable way, and you could really catch an edge pretty easy. It wasn't the best place to learn to skate, but it was still fun because Sky wasn't shy to grab him and cling on, and nobody stared, which was better for Sky. Sky was so uncomfortable on skates it was hilarious, but Ryan stuck his phone in Skyler's hands, and despite the wobbling, Sky relaxed and took pictures of everything. Ryan skated backward and did a few tricks; he'd done some years of hockey as a kid so skating still felt easy. He pulled Skyler by the elbow and they ended up skating around the outer edge a few times arm in arm. Ryan got them going a little faster, and Sky's legs suddenly went out from underneath him and there was this weird slow-mo descent to the ground full of elbows and knees.

Luckily Sky was laughing. They were kind of tangled up, and Ryan found his face suddenly close to Sky's. Their eyes met and held and Ryan moved in for a kiss, but Sky turned away and stood up.

"What?" said Ryan, grabbing the front of Sky's ski jacket and started skating backward and pulling him across the ice. "I can't kiss you on our first date?"

"Ryan, seriously, I am so going to fall on you again."

"Good, then you won't be able to get away."

Skyler laughed. "Hey, look at those horses! What's on their noses?" There were these big frozen lumps on the ends of their noses.

"Yeah, crazy, eh? They're like boogersicles."

"Ha! That's so awesomely gross! Snotsicles?"

"Yeah!"

"Look at them. They look totally embarrassed!"

The horses were big and gorgeous, all decked out in that old-fashioned stuff and hitched up to a carriage. Business was slow, obviously. They'd been standing there the whole time. Would Sky like to do that, or was that too silly?

"Is it too soon to move on to tubing?" said Sky. They returned their skates and sat inside the lodge building for a bit sipping the hot chocolate that Ryan bought and just trying not to smile at each other.

Tubing was always fun. You stuck your bum in this huge hard donut and got pulled up the hill on this tow thing, and if you weren't careful the tow hook would hit you in the head as you got off. Sky was looking a little green at the top. They hadn't worn helmets and he was rubbing his head.

"Hook get ya?"

"Yeah."

"Yeah, you gotta watch that. Let's go. Hold onto mine and I'll hold onto yours." He couldn't help a wicked smile at that one and Skyler turned away. They perched at the top, held onto each other's tube handles, and then Ryan kicked them off. They picked up speed, of course, and all he could do was watch Sky's face go from blank to scared to delighted to thrilled. Sky let out a big whoop at the bottom and Ryan laughed.

"You liked it?"

"Hell yeah! Let's go again!"

They went up a bunch of times and then ran into the girls. Sky seemed not to mind, and they ended up as a four-person chain, which was pretty fun in a roller-coaster kind of way. He couldn't count how many times they went up and down.

He and Sky stood together talking at the bottom as the girls got ready to go again.

"Haven't you done this before?" Ryan asked.

"Nope. I thought we were going to fly off."

"Seriously? Were you freaked?"

"Nah."

"You were!" Ryan grabbed him around the waist and lifted him up over his shoulder, laughing as Skyler shrieked and held onto his back for dear life. He set him down more slowly. Sky was red in the face and wouldn't meet his eyes. Was it weird to touch him now in public? "Hey, you want to see the ice tower? I'm going to climb it."

"Okay."

The girls hadn't hooked onto the tow yet and followed as they walked away. They raced past and called, "We're going to do the snowmobiles!"

Skyler wanted to see that, which was fine, sort of, but it was just this oval where you got to drive a small snowmobile in a circle for a while. It wasn't that exciting and he was surprised his sister wanted to do it again. Sky took some pictures, of course, and then some video, and then Ryan couldn't stand it any longer. He wanted Sky to himself. Alone. With touching. It was getting dark and colder, and Sky was shifting from foot to foot. Those rubber boots must be freezing. Sky wasn't going to be happy out here much longer, and Ryan really wanted to climb that tower with Sky there to see. He slung an arm around Sky's neck and leaned in close. "Hey, you want to do the ice tower with me?"

He pointed at the tower a little ways away. It was a rectangularish monolith around five stories high, the sides rough with huge walls of icicles, like a four-sided frozen waterfall. It looked incredible in the falling light.

"Seriously?! I sorta thought you were joking!" The girls hopped down and headed off to do more tubing. "I'll take some pictures if you want. Climbing cliff faces isn't really my thing. Jesus, that thing is like a chunk of the Wall from the *Game of Thrones*."

"Hey, you watch that? I love that show!"

"The books were better."

Skyler always said that, and it always stung. *When was the last time I read a whole book?* "Okay, book boy, we all know how much you read." Ryan rolled his eyes and headed for the shack to sign up.

The instructor guy told them that there was a hard side and an easy side, but there was a guy just starting on the easy side, so they'd have to wait awhile if they wanted to do that. Ryan took a deep breath and got the gear on. It was strange to wear the climbing crampons, like having evil robot spikes on his feet, but they really did grip right into the ice as he sank the first ice pick in and pulled himself up. The harness sank into the flesh at the top of his legs, but step by dug-in step, pick by pick, he hauled himself up and up. He knew the guy belaying him wouldn't let him fall too far, but if he slipped off, he could easily swing out, and then his whole body could smack against the wall if he weren't facing the right way.

At first Ryan was thinking about Skyler watching and taking pictures, but as his breath came shorter and shorter, his vision narrowed to the next few moves he was going to make. He was sweaty pretty quick, and then all he could do was focus on the one immediate next thing.

The cliff was pretty much vertical, but there was this one spot, maybe two-thirds of the way up, where it had gotten bulged out somehow, so he had to climb out, almost over his own head. He'd been watching from the snow mobile area, and the last guy had gotten stuck there and had quit. It was really fucking hard. Each slam of the pick was a challenge, and each foothold felt like it was going to give way. His heart was pounding so hard it sounded in his ears, and his whole body was coated in sweat.

Finally Ryan was over the bulge, but he just couldn't seem to make it any farther. The pick kept giving way when he tried to pull himself up by it and his arms were on fire. He felt so weak and heavy. The top seemed impossible. Where was it? Ten feet, twenty? He just couldn't do any more.

"That's it!" he called down. "I'm done."

The instructor shouted up. "You can do it! You're almost there! It's like three more feet! Don't let it beat you! Come on!" He could hear Skyler whooping it up at the bottom, and it gave him a little surge. *Just one more push.* One grueling step at a time, Ryan made it, finally, to the top and could look right over the thing! He held up a climbing axe in his hand and roared! God, it felt good!

He managed to smack against the ice only once as he was lowered down, mostly keeping his feet out in front of him to push off with, and then he was on the ground again. Suddenly his arms and legs weren't working right and his vision was not exactly foggy, but somehow not clear either. He got the harness and crampons off and staggered toward the shack, but then it was game over and he had to just kneel down on the ground and put his head down and not move. All the muscles in his arms decided to cramp at once and the pain was blinding. There was a hand on his back and Skyler was there. Ryan was gasping and shaking his head. "You never get anywhere without pushing too hard," Ryan said.

CHAPTER 10—SKYLER

SKYLER'S HANDS were seriously freezing, and the rest of his body wasn't doing too well either. Thick socks and rubber boots just didn't cut it for that long in this cold, but he didn't have any other boots and he certainly wasn't going to shell out a whack of cash for any. It was nice to be able to take some photos of the girls for Ryan's parents, but after standing around, he was seriously in need of a full body warm-up.

The ice tower was insane. He couldn't believe Ryan was seriously going to climb that thing. *God, I hope he's not doing this to impress me.* It looked like torture. Sure, it was an impressive achievement to do something hard, but that didn't mean it made sense. What was the purpose of it? To feel powerful? How did climbing a big thing really make you strong in any real way? Yeah, it was a physical test, and you had to have some kind of mental toughness to force yourself to do something horrid to your body, but that seemed more like pigheaded macho-ness than strength.

Whatever; if Ryan wanted to do it, then the least Skyler could do was stand there freezing his nuts off to film the damn thing. It was hard to watch. He shook out his legs and arms one at a time, trying not to jostle the camera, as Ryan slowly made his way up the thing. It was snowing again, which didn't help. The skin on Skyler's hands was really hurting now, and his finger joints weren't able to bend right anymore. When Ryan gave up right near the top, Skyler was still so proud that he whooped at how far Ryan had gotten. It really was cool that he made it all the way in the end. Maybe it would make him feel good about himself. Maybe that made it worth it.

When Ryan came down, Skyler kept filming. Maybe Ryan would say something to the camera? But Ryan just walked right past Skyler and then folded up on the ground.

Skyler turned the camera off and shoved it in his pocket. "Are you okay?" He put a bright red burning hand on Ryan's back, but Ryan didn't look at him, just started talking about how pushing too hard was the only really important thing. That felt shitty for some reason, but Sky pushed it away. Ryan deserved to puff his chest up if he wanted to. Then the instructor came over and they started talking about how cool it was to do the impossible. *I guess Ryan's pushed himself physically a lot. Skiing, hockey, soccer.* Skyler remembered his injury stories and wondered for the first time how hard Ryan was pushing himself when he got hurt.

The guy turned to Sky and said, "That's right. Fifty-two feet, my man, that's eighteen meters. Life's not a spectator sport. You should be doing cool things, not watching other people do cool things." He patted Skyler on the back. "I like to bug all my nonclimbers like that." He laughed and followed Ryan into the log cabin to put the equipment away.

"Well, we're all good at different things," said Skyler from the doorway, but nobody seemed to hear him. *Is that what I am to them? A spectator?* All those times he'd tried to play on sports teams and his dad had driven him home from another lost game all bummed out, all those moments when the guys were horsing around and he felt like the awkward weak dork. They all came flooding back.

"Hey, Ryan." This huge guy gave Skyler a hard glare and then edged past him into the hut. "How's it going?"

"Hey, Logan."

"You just climbed that thing?"

"Yeah, I'm pretty wrecked."

Skyler hung back. Was Ryan going to introduce them?

"You make it to the top?" Logan was smiling down at Ryan, his hands on his hips.

"Yup."

"Holy shit! Nice work, man! Hey, what are you doing tomorrow? You wanna hit the black diamonds?"

"I'm here with Skyler. Skyler, Logan. Logan, Skyler."

Logan turned away from Ryan and his friendly gaze was suddenly cold as his eyes swept up and down.

"Logan's family owns the place next to ours. The other half of the duplex."

"Oh!" said Skyler. He hadn't realized Ryan had a friend next door. "Nice to meet you."

"Yeah," said Logan, but he'd already turned back to Ryan.

"We should see who can get the best time. I was up on your favorite run earlier. I haven't seen you on Strava yet. What's up with that?"

"I'm showing Sky around this trip. He's just learning."

Logan turned a cool stare at Skyler but kept talking to Ryan. "Yeah, your mom was over yesterday. She said you brought somebody."

Skyler wondered what else she'd said and which was the bigger crime in Logan's eyes, being gay or sucking at skiing.

Skyler said, "I don't mind, Ryan. Seriously. Go if you want."

"I'll check in with you in the morning, see if you wanna make some real tracks," said Logan. "Later." Logan headed back outside.

Ryan had this flat look on his face. "You ready to go? I can call for a ride."

"Yeah, I'm pretty cold, actually."

Ryan grabbed Skyler's leg and lifted, pulling his rubber boot off. "No wonder you're cold. Look at these socks. Can I have my phone?" He held out his hand.

It was weird on the ride back. Ryan didn't look at him or touch him, he just loudly told the girls about the climbing thing and how well he'd done. Skyler just pressed back into the seat and tried to turn invisible.

Back at the house, he slipped away and had a long hot shower, with the door locked, and tried to rewarm his bones. What had gone wrong? The day had started off so great. *I just don't fit in here. That's what's wrong.* He was like a dog dressed up to try to match these people, but the truth was, he never would. He'd never be super athletic and coordinated. He'd never ski the black diamonds with Ryan, kitted out with all that expensive gear. And that's what Ryan loved to do. How often did Ryan get to come up here to this special place and rip down those favorite runs?

He should be doing what he loves. Skyler leaned his head against the cold tiles and closed his eyes. *What the hell am I doing here? Ryan should be up here with a beautiful girl.* Someone his family would actually like. Someone who made him look good. Instead he was sliding along that knife edge of having everyone think he was gay. Ryan didn't get that people never forgot that kind of thing. If they saw you kiss another guy once, they didn't just let it go. When people found out, this would affect him forever.

Maybe Dave was right. Skyler didn't have a choice in who he found attractive, but clearly Ryan did. Why should he ruin his future because he was crushing on Skyler right now? He was lonely and a little lost at this point in his life. He was curious or, like he'd said, open-minded. Did that mean he should have to live with people's judgment forever? Yeah, it shouldn't matter to people, but the truth was, it did.

Skyler didn't say much over dinner, and Ryan was distracted with his phone and computer afterward, downloading pictures and stuff.

Skyler thought about writing to Lisa, but it all sounded stupid when he thought about writing it down. There was nothing to feel upset about really. He was just overreacting. All Ryan had done was climb. He should be impressed and happy for him.

"Is Strava your favorite run?" Skyler asked as they lay in the dark that night.

"It's not a run, it's an app. It tracks your route when you're running or biking, measures distance and elevation and time and stuff. We use it for skiing too, and you can post your results, so some people get really into competing for the best times. Logan likes to beat me."

"Does that bother you?"

"Not really. It makes him feel good, I guess."

"You should go with him tomorrow."

"Nah, it's cool."

"No, seriously. You don't have to spend every second with me." Ryan didn't answer. "I know how much you love to ski. I have the computer to play with. I'll be fine."

Ryan propped his head on his hand and looked at him. "Is that what you want?"

"Sure."

Ryan sighed and lay back down, his hand sliding over until just the tip of his finger was touching Skyler's shoulder. He traced little patterns on Skyler's skin, and it wasn't long before they were kissing and touching. They both came pretty fast, and then Ryan was asleep, cuddled up against him. Skyler lay there and stared into the dark and wondered what the fuck was going on.

Sunday morning he got up early and showered alone. Ryan came down and they ate together as everyone got ready around them. Ryan's mom, Erin, popped her head back up the stairs on her way out and said, "Oh hey, boys, my friend isn't coming up after all. Didn't want to brave the drive. See you later."

Does that mean I should sleep downstairs? Maybe I should have saved everyone the grief and just slept down here to start with. Then Logan showed up at the door.

Skyler said, "Don't worry about it. My legs are all wobbly anyway. Go and ski like the wind."

Ryan smiled but his eyes looked pinched somehow. Logan just ignored Skyler entirely and chatted away to Ryan about all kinds of stuff they clearly had in common, and then the door closed.

Skyler had a moment of self-hatred when the house went silent around him. All this beauty, all this wealth, and he couldn't keep up. He closed his eyes and pushed it away. He wandered into the bathroom and there were those little bars of Jergens soap. He lifted one to his nose and breathed it in. *It smells like him.* Skyler went upstairs and slipped the paper wrapped bar into the bottom of his suitcase. It settled him somehow, knowing he could carry Ryan's scent home with him, no matter what happened.

He set up at the dining room table, picked out a playlist on Songza to keep his spirits up, and got busy looking at the photos. Some of them were good. Looking at the pictures, mostly of Ryan, as the music played got his brain working, and he knew what he wanted to do. He could surprise Ryan with a movie about the trip. It would be nice. He found some tutorials on YouTube about the software and before long was laying out pictures in the video software and picking out music.

CHAPTER 11—RYAN

RYAN PURPOSELY hadn't told Skyler the friend's name, the one that had run for it when his mom had opened the bedroom door a few years ago. There was no point in telling someone else's secrets, especially when it clearly bothered them very much to have anyone know.

It had been strange to see Logan again. He looked like he always did, like the world was irritating to him in some constant way. Ryan had no desire to ski with him again after all this time. God, how many times had they been right next door and Logan hadn't come by to say hi? What did he want now all of a sudden? And making Skyler feel like he was too slow? That was just so rude and so like him. *What an ass.* But now that he'd skirted around talking about Logan at all, it seemed hard to explain why he didn't want to go. He could say that Logan was a dick, but Sky wouldn't just shrug and say okay. He'd want to know what had happened.

And besides, maybe it was too much to expect Skyler to ski the whole time. Maybe it was too much to expect Skyler to want to spend every second with him for a whole week. Wasn't it enough that he was opening up? God, it was so wonderful to feel his muscles softening and see his smile forming on his face, so hesitant. It filled Ryan with this lovely feeling, and how was it even possible that they were together now? Last night… oh god. To see Skyler's body, to give him bone-rattling pleasure like that…. It made seeing Logan again just melt away until all Ryan felt was safe and warm. The thing with Logan had been fooling around. This was a whole other galaxy. He had to not fuck it up somehow, but seeing Logan was seriously weird.

On the chairlifts Logan talked about university and about what a successful businessman he was going to be. He'd asked about Ryan's grad plans, but hadn't really listened when Ryan said he wasn't that into doing anything. Logan just wanted to tell this lame story about how drunk he'd gotten and how many clubs he'd snuck into. Then he wanted to brag about the new mountain bike he'd just bought. Custom everything, of course.

It was a relief to get off the chair, and they skied superfast, like they used to. There was that familiar thrill to the speed at first. After a few runs, though, he was starting to miss Skyler pretty bad. He loved how Skyler saw things up here. He was really moved by the place, something Logan would never be. They were on the chairlift on their way up to Pegasus, and Ryan was starting to just nod at everything and tune him out, when Logan said, "So your mom said Skyler's gay?"

"Yup."

"And you guys are friends? Isn't that a little weird?"

"Skyler is an amazing guy. I really like him."

"Oh yeah?" Logan raised one eyebrow.

"Yeah. He's really smart, he works hard all the time, and he's got this depth to him. I think his life has been tough, and it's just made him this kind of old soul or something."

"What, are you in love with him or something? Ryan, you should hear yourself. The guy's a flamer. You don't want to give him any ideas. And what's with that picture on Facebook? Have you seen all the comments on there?"

I should just tell him. I should just say it. But somehow it didn't feel right to tell Logan anything. Anger rose up in Ryan's chest. This thing with Sky shouldn't be a secret, but Sky kept wanting to protect him from the consequences. Logan being Logan was just making Skyler right, and that was such a piss off.

"Fuck you."

"What?" Logan's white-blond eyebrows shot up.

"You know, you can just ditch our whole friendship because my mom walked in on us. That's fine. Whatever. I told you she wouldn't tell your parents and she didn't, right? She may not get it, but she doesn't actually think we were doing anything wrong. But don't start shitting on my friend, okay?"

"Whoa, Ryan. I don't know what you're talking about."

"Bullshit, asshole! What, did you take some special amnesia pills or something? I don't really care anymore, but you just uninvited my friend on MY holiday and now you want to tell me how to treat him?"

"Calm down, Ryan. God, something crawl up your ass and die? Jesus."

Ryan looked out over the view and ignored Logan for a while as the chair swung in the wind a little. Logan couldn't take the quiet for long.

"Okay, I shouldn't have just walked out back then, okay? It was awkward. I didn't, you know, want you to get the wrong idea." Logan was looking at him sideways.

"What idea?"

"Like that I was into you or something."

"What! Hey, man, things were always totally aboveboard with us. Wasn't that the whole point? We were just guys being guys. You knew I wasn't, I don't know, sniffing after you or something. Didn't you?"

"Well, I just got worried, I guess. With someone knowing about it, I just thought, maybe… you'd take it more serious or something. It was just for fun. Right?"

"Of course! God, I can't believe you have to even ask me."

"Well good." Logan looked out over the forest as well. "So you're not… you know?"

"What?"

"Fooling around with him?"

Ryan turned and took a hard look at him. "Why are you asking me that?" It had felt like a betrayal before, not calling Sky his boyfriend, but now he just smelled a rat.

Logan put his hands up. "Hey, you know I'm not gay, and I never thought you were. I just hear you're bringing this fa—gay guy up here and I started wondering."

"Okay…."

"So are you?"

"I don't see why you care."

"I don't care."

"Really. 'Cuz, you got me up here all alone after what? Two years? Made me ditch my real friend so we could go skiing without him, and now… I don't know. It seems like you fucking care."

"You are, aren't you?"

"It's none of your business!"

"If you weren't, you'd just say it."

"Are you scared that I'm secretly gay and that like, I don't know, rubs off on you or something? What the fuck, man?"

"Whatever. Let's just ski."

"Fine." He had this strong desire to just punch Logan in the face, but luckily they were at the top and they both skied as hard and as fast as they could down the run. It was steep and it took a lot of concentration. That was good. The next chairlift was not so good. They spent most of it in silence, broken only by Logan asking if he was seeing anyone. Logan had entirely missed his relationship with Chloe.

"I was seeing someone for over a year, but we broke up this summer. You?"

"I've got a few girls on the go. Nothing serious."

Logan tried to pick up his chatter again, and then they got off the chair. About halfway down Logan pulled off to the side at one of their favorite old spots and waited for him.

"Mind if we take a break?" said Logan, lifting up his goggles.

They made a bench together like they used to do, and Logan asked if Ryan had any Fireball.

"That's cool you still bring that shit up here. It's like old times." He took a long sip and then said, "I shouldn't have ignored you like that. I just got wigged out."

Ryan didn't look at him. *We did used to be good friends, didn't we?*

"I should have known you were cool. It was nice to have a friend who got it, you know."

Ryan sighed. "Yeah, it was."

"Hey, you got a theme song going these days?" It was nice that Logan knew to ask that. It was something that they used to trade back and forth. Like a code on how they were both really doing.

"'Headphones' by the Mounties."

"Oh yeah, that's a cool song." Logan didn't ask what it meant to him. Had he ever asked? *Did he ever really get that whole thing?*

"So you must be pretty hard up. You been single for a while."

Ryan looked at him.

"I'm just saying guys need to get off, right? It's just natural."

"Uh-huh."

"So you want to? I've got something new to show you." Logan was smiling, but his eyes were weird. Kinda darting around Ryan's face.

"What, here?"

"We did it here before, remember? Yeah, it's freezing, but that just makes it quicker, right?" He laughed and put his hand on Ryan's thigh. "Come on, man, it'll be fun."

Ryan shook his head, and Logan's smile got tighter. "What, are you scared? I dare ya."

"No."

"Why not?"

Ryan's head filled with a seething cloud of why-nots. *Because you haven't even asked me how I've been. Because you just grilled me about Skyler. Because I swear you almost called Sky a faggot. Because I'm not sure that I even like you. Because I certainly don't trust you after two years of you brushing me off. Because I would never do that to Sky. Because touching him is so completely not like touching you.*

But he just shook his head again. "I don't want to."

Logan stood up. He was a big guy and he towered over Ryan. "What, isn't my soul old enough? You've got something going, haven't you? What does he do for you, Ry? Does he deep throat for you? Does he suck it reallll good with his big brown eyes looking up at you like some kinda lovesick puppy?"

Ryan stood up. Suddenly his heart was pounding, and all he wanted to do was knock Logan's teeth out the back of his head. Instead he ground his teeth together. "We. Are. Done."

"I'll say we're done!" Logan stomped his skis on. "Fuck you! You think you're better than me? Well, fuck you and your little faggot fucktoy too! You think you're my only option to fool around with? I don't need to get that dirty."

He disappeared between the trees and was gone. Ryan growled and stomped and kicked some trees as hard as he could and then sat down and texted his sister Stevie in Montreal. They had a system worked out. They used 911 for "someone's in the hospital" and 811 for "I seriously need to talk to you." He put in **811 I might b gay**. And his phone rang about thirty seconds later.

As soon as he said "hey," she said, "Oh thank god, we are finally going to have this conversation."

"What!"

"Okay, don't be mad, but Mom told me about walking in on you and Logan. She figured you might talk to me about it someday and that I should be prepared."

"Oh, for fuck's sake! I think she told Dad, too, you know. Goddammit." Ryan thumped his butt back down on the ski bench.

"Hey, she's just trying to support you."

"Whatever. Did she call you to tell you that I have a gay friend?"

"Yup." Stevie popped the 'p' on 'yup,' like it was no big deal.

"Fucking A. That's just awesome. So everyone thinks I'm gay but me. Whoop-de-do."

"I also liked your latest Facebook post, but hey, I don't think anything. I'm just glad you're ready to spill it already. I've been sitting on this one for years."

He huffed a laugh. "Well you're never going to believe what just happened." He told her a blow by blow of what had happened with Logan, and she seriously couldn't believe it.

"He said you were dirty because you wouldn't let him get you off? What the fuck?"

"Yeah, there's some kind of warped logic in there somewhere." Ryan sighed.

"Okay, I think HE'S gay. That is just so jealous ex! He finds out you're hanging out with someone that might be willing to go farther down the pink brick road than he was, and suddenly he has to know and has to try to get you back again? Seriously gay. Seriously in denial."

"Huh. You think?"

"Totally. Now tell me about Skyler." Stevie's voice was eager, like she couldn't wait to hear this.

It was so easy to talk about Skyler. He was such an amazing person. He could talk about Sky all day. She interrupted, "Okay, hang on. Can you just tell me what it was about Chloe that you really loved?"

"Ahh, okay…?"

"Just humor me," she said.

"You think I never really loved her, right? Because I've been gay all along."

"What? Gimme a break! I was there, remember? She broke your heart, no questions asked. You don't have to try to figure out if you loved her. Of course you did! And I'm sure you had great sex with her. That's not the point."

"But aren't guys that say they're bi just too scared to say they're gay?" Ryan pressed the heel of his hand into his eye socket.

"Bi is not a stop on the road to gay. Except when it is. Sure, some guys are trying to figure out what they like and eventually realize that they like men more or that they're more often attracted to men. But human experience is so diverse, I bet if you can imagine it, someone has experienced it. Plus about 200 percent more that you haven't even thought of yet. And what about girls? There's like this whole other set of unwritten rules for us. It's hot to put on some kind of show and make out with another girl, and no one even calls you bi. You're just adventurous or something. But guys are either straight or gay, no middle ground. It's a really stupid double standard. Now would you just forget about trying to stuff yourself into a labeled box for a second and tell me what it was that you loved about Chloe?"

Ryan took a deep breath and let it out slowly. "Well, she was strong. She was her own person. But she didn't need to boss everyone around either. She had this kind of soft underside, but it wasn't weakness. She was brave about it, about sharing it."

"Okay, so most people have this A or B checkbox in their head when they think about orientation. You're either straight or gay, but there was this study done, this massive sex story collection done by this guy named Kinsey, and he produced this huge report and he broke the data down into eight different orientations, four of which were in the middle. It started this continuum idea, like a gas gauge with straight on one side and gay on the other. The real experiences that people were having showed lots of room in between straight and gay, so there's lots of people who could be calling themselves bi, okay?"

"Four categories? Four in the middle?" Ryan had to stand up and shake out his freezing legs. As nice as it was to have this kind of privacy, it was damn cold.

"I know, crazy, right? At least he took black and white and turned it into that gas gauge, which at least has some range. But it's still ridiculously inadequate because it was based on sexual experience, not on mapping out desire and fantasy. Anyway, it was in the fucking sixties and people still are too uptight to incorporate THAT into the way we think about sexuality. There's a movie about him, though. You should see it. But okay, let's just drop the two-dimensional thinking thing for a second and picture this. The things you like, the things that attract you to someone, are like candies, okay? And everyone has a different candy jar. Maybe your favorite candy is jawbreakers or those old-fashioned black licorice cigars, or maybe you have a thing for cotton candy or something."

"Okay…. Or like those every flavor jelly beans," Ryan could get into this if there were every flavor beans.

"Right, sure. So when you meet someone and you get to know them, some people have your favorite candy inside of them and some don't. Some people do it for you, they light you up like a little kid, and some don't. Some people have a few of your favorites but not enough to keep you happy for long, and some have a big portion of your most favoritest jelly beans ever."

The line was quiet for a minute. "So my favorite jelly beans are…."

"Are integrity, strength, and vulnerability," said Stevie without hesitation.

"Jesus."

"Yeah, and Chloe had them all and so does Skyler."

"Shit."

"And you like having sex with girls but guys don't exactly turn you off."

"But Logan was the only guy I ever... and we didn't even... fuck, it wasn't like that!" Ryan stomped some of the snow down around the mushed down spot he was standing in.

"Does he have your favorite jelly beans? Is he strong and vulnerable and knows who he is?"

Ryan stopped stomping. "Well, no, no, and no."

"So there you go. You didn't have feelings for him because he doesn't have your candy. But you must have enjoyed getting off with him."

"It was just physical. It was like... maintenance."

"And that's how it feels when you have sex with someone you don't care about. It's not emotional. It doesn't touch you or breathe life into your heart. But what if that wasn't how it was for Logan? What if you really do it for him? Or what if girls kinda gross him out but that terrifies him?"

"Skyler was saying that girls turn him off." Ryan stuck his free hand inside his coat and clamped it in his armpit to get it thawed out again.

"Sure, some people get wigged out by one gender. But some people don't really care about that. Some people are all about candy."

"So you think I'm bi." Ryan held very still.

"I think you're Ryan, who is attracted to integrity and chutzpah and naked hearts on sleeves, and you've just met the first guy that really lights up your skin. I think sex and love aren't things you can catalog logically. There're too many factors when you get people involved."

"Like snowflakes. Maybe each one of us forms a little different, and the trick is to see the beauty in that."

"I love how you think you're slow and then you come out with something like that. Yeah, that feels like exactly what I'm saying. Now tell me more about this Skyler." He could practically hear Stevie smiling. "I have a feeling that Facebook pic didn't do him justice. He had a pretty hilarious look on his face. Hey, next time you're on there, tag him in the photo so I can look at his profile. Are his photos friend-only?"

Ryan knew they were public because he'd stalked his way through them before Sky had even had a chance to respond to the friend request. Ryan told her about his eyes and his cheekbones and his hair and his earrings and his nipple rings and his body, although he left some of that out because it felt too private.

"So have you guys done anything?"

"Yeah, but it's not like…. I just thought it would be like it was with Logan."

"But how could it be the same? They aren't the same guy at all. Would you expect it to be the same for me if I made out with one girl or another?"

"I don't know."

"Okay, well, do you find yourself looking at his lips and wanting to get closer and closer to him? Do you look at his skin and just can't wait to touch it? Does your heart beat faster and your cock stand up to attention when you get close to him?"

"Uh, yeah."

"And did that happen with Logan?"

"No! God, you make it sound so obvious." Ryan went back to stomping down the snow, making a compacted circle around him.

"So how are you doing with all this?"

"I don't know. I think I'm a total idiot and I've fucked things up."

"With Skyler?"

Ryan looked up at the sky, ringed with snow-covered trees. "There's just no way he's gonna want… what I want."

"And what do you want?"

Ryan closed his eyes. He wanted to be with Sky right now, putting an arm around him, playing with his hair, asking him questions, telling him secrets, and leaning into him, leaning into his neck, and just smelling his skin. God, just thinking about it made him tingle all over. "I want to be totally with him."

"Maybe he'd love that."

"He's gonna want someone boldly gay, not some guy that's still calling himself straight until this exact minute."

"Well that all depends on what his favorite candy is. Maybe you need to figure out what does it for him."

"He's really smart, Stevie. How can I compete with that? And I doubt that being good at skiing really counts for anything, even though it IS such an important life skill. Maybe soccer. You think he'd like to watch me play?" He rolled his eyes.

"Mom told me you quit."

"Yeah. I just couldn't see the point anymore. The guys are pissed at me."

"Maybe the point was that it made you feel good," Stevie said.

Sky had said that too. "It used to. Lately it just doesn't feel the same. It used to be like being part of something, but now it just doesn't."

"Yeah, group identity is tough. You feel like you belong because you have something in common with people, like you're one of them, but really, you belong because of the relationships you have."

"How many real friends have I got from there? How many of them can I actually talk to?"

"Did you ever tell any of them about Logan and you?" she asked.

"NO!" God, as if Logan needed a reason to hate Ryan more.

"You know, I think him walking out on you made you just not reach out to your guy friends anymore."

"I tried! I tried to talk to them when that shit went down with Chloe, but you were the only one that really helped me."

"I can get that. I'm sure a bad breakup is a hard one for a lot of young guys to know how to deal with. But how many of them have YOU been there for when they were hurting? You can be down on them for not knowing what to say to you or how to help you, but friendship is a two-way street. You've had your heart broken now. You know what a good friend would do and say. You have to build these things between people. The group is just an excuse to try, a starting place."

"Well, they hate me now for quitting."

"Maybe they feel like you're ditching them, like you don't give a shit. Did you even try to explain it to them? There must be a few guys who you respect enough to try."

"Okay, one thing at a time. What do I do about Skyler?" Ryan walked around the edge of his tiny clearing, widening the edges with his ski boot.

"Tell him the truth."

"How? Hey, Sky, I'd like you to wear me like a jacket for the rest of your life."

"Aw, that's really sweet in a kind of creepy-serial-killer kind of way."

"I don't know how to say the right things, Stevie. You know that."

"You do fine, bro. Start with smaller truths if the big ones are too big. Tell him you admire him. Tell him you enjoy his company. Tell him he has beautiful eyes."

"Hey, are you going to tell Mom about all this?" Ryan stopped moving.

"Not if you don't want me to. But what should I say? You know she cares, and she's like a shark at getting information out of people."

He sighed. "Tell her about the candy jar."

"You got it. You okay?"

"Maybe. I still want to kill Logan."

"Hey, he's in a different family from you. Imagine having them as parents. You think they would be okay with him being gay?"

"I really don't think they'd be that bad. And you should have heard what Dad said at dinner." He told her about what Skyler had said about being gay and what his parents had said.

"Poor Skyler! Welcome to our weird family. But you know Dad is wrong, don't you? I mean, that's like saying it's okay to be gay, but it's not okay to be bi. That's ridiculous."

"Or maybe it's go ahead and be bi but don't get emotionally involved with guys."

"Well, maybe that's what Logan's trying to do. Doesn't sound like he's doing very well with that master plan. And it sounds like you've already figured out that impersonal... what did you call it? Maintenance? That's just fucked, by the way. I can't think of a less romantic word. Anyway, impersonal fooling around versus fooling around with Skyler when it means something to you because he means something to you... well, there's no comparison."

"No. No there isn't." Ryan smiled, thinking of that shy look Sky got sometimes.

"And Dad thinks you shouldn't choose the one with love in it? Because of what people might think? Jesus. That's pretty sad."

"Maybe he thinks I'm attracted to everyone, so I can just pick and choose. I think Dad is seriously straight." They laughed and agreed on that. Dave couldn't even figure out which male actors were good-looking. Ryan apologized belatedly for 811ing her, and she admitted she'd bailed out of a lecture when she got the text.

"Ah shit, sorry," he said.

She laughed. "You should call me every time the shit starts hitting the fan. Then I can call you when I'm freaking."

"Hey, I'm here. Slightly clueless, but here."

He was seriously cold by the time he got skiing again and decided to head straight back home. He came in the back door and was just taking his helmet off when Skyler ran toward the stairs. He smiled but the look on Skyler's face was awful.

"Hey, what's wrong?" Ryan said.

Skyler rushed past him and ran up the stairs.

What the fuck? Ryan whipped the rest of his snowy gear onto the floor and ran up after him. Skyler was sitting on the far side of the bed with his knees against his chest, and he startled when Ryan threw open the door. It had been locked but he'd just rattled it and the stupid hook latch had popped up.

"Sky, what's going on?" Ryan sat down and Skyler shook his head, his eyes welling up with tears.

"Hey, are you okay? Whatever it is, you can tell me, okay?"

"Logan was here."

"What? Just now?"

"He went out downstairs when he heard you coming in the back."

"Oh my god." Ryan jumped up. "Did he hurt you? Did he lay one fucking finger on you?"

"He didn't hurt me. He just tried to…." Skyler's eyes overflowed, and he sunk his head down and sobbed.

"Skyler, look at me." Ryan's voice was suddenly very soft. The rage exploding inside him had hit a new level, and suddenly there was this pocket of deadly calm where he felt capable of doing whatever was required to make this right. Including murdering Logan. "He tried to what?"

Skyler lifted his face, and his lips were trembling. "He said that you told him… what we did. And that you thought I would do it with him too. That you didn't mind sharing and were giving him some time with me. He wanted me to give him a blow job. I said no, but he wouldn't leave."

Ryan started to shake. "Holy shit, Sky!" He put his hand on Skyler's shoulder, but Skyler flinched away.

"Don't touch me." The fear in Skyler's voice stopped him, and Ryan softened his voice.

"Hey. I'm going to tell you everything, okay? Everything that really happened, because he is lying his fucking ass off. Okay? Remember how I didn't want to tell you the name of the guy I used to fool around with? Well, it's Logan."

"He's the guy," whispered Skyler.

"Yeah, he's the guy. I don't like telling other people's secrets, but it's not a secret anymore, that's for fucking sure." He told Skyler every detail he could remember, every single detail of his argument with Logan, and then about his call to Stevie. By the end of it, Skyler had stopped crying. "I don't know if you can believe me, but I swear to god, I'm telling you the truth, and I'm so, so sorry. I had no idea he was crazy. I never thought he was capable of something like this."

"I believe you."

"Oh thank god! Can I give you a hug now?" Skyler uncurled a little and Ryan wrapped him in a tight embrace. Ryan rubbed his back and held onto the back of his head. He kissed Skyler's hair and brushed it off his face. "I'm not going to let him hurt you, okay? As soon as you're okay, I'm going to go over there and beat the shit out of him."

"What? Ryan, you can't do that!"

"Like fuck I can't. He's going to need dentures by the time I'm finished with him."

"Ryan, promise me you won't do that! I'm serious. Nothing happened. I'm fine, okay?"

"Nothing happened? How can you say that! He tried to fucking rape you!"

"He... he pressured me. Yeah, I got scared, but he didn't... attack me."

"If he had, he would no longer be breathing."

"Ryan, calm down, okay? I just got freaked out."

"I thought this place would be good for you. I thought I could take care of you properly for a little while and instead you get fucking molested by some ex-friend of mine. Jesus Christ!"

"It's going to be okay. I guess he just wanted to mess with you, right? And it's over now, and he's punished you or whatever. Let's just leave it, okay? But Ryan... do you think you could change the code on the door?"

"Why?"

"Well, that's how he got in. He knows the code."

"He didn't even knock?" Ryan jumped up. "That's it!"

"Ryan, sit down! Ryan!" Skyler jumped up and grabbed Ryan's shirt as he tried to go for the door. "Ryan, I swear, I will never speak to you again if you go over there right now!"

Ryan stopped struggling and sagged a little as he turned back around. He put his arms around Skyler's waist and squeezed hard. "I have to do something, Sky. I can't do nothing. Please don't ask me to do nothing."

"If you go over there and you guys beat on each other, then what? He's a good liar, Ryan. He had me going pretty well there for a while. He's going to lie to his parents about what happened. They might call the police and what do you think they are going to say? You didn't even see him in here. There's no witnesses but me, the gay guy who doesn't have a mark on him. He'll just say that you're gay and trying to hide it or maybe that I came onto him and you found out and got jealous or something. He'll make it look like you're crazy. I'm not letting you get dragged down with me."

"What? This is my mess, not yours!"

"You can't say that. If I wasn't so obviously gay, you probably never would have heard from him again. It was like gasoline on a fire."

"Bullshit. Maybe he should just admit that he's gay, and none of this shit would have happened. He never even hinted that he wanted more than playing around for all that time. He was the one that dropped me after my mom found out, for fuck's sake. He's a goddam sneaky fucking liar. I bet he's got all kinds of lies buried all over the place. I want to just dig it all up and shove it in his face." Ryan stopped short. "You know what? I know what to do."

He pulled out his phone and made a call. It rang for a while, and then he said, "Mom, there's been an emergency. I need you to come back here. I'm at the house. We're okay, nobody's hurt yet, but Logan just broke in here and tried to rape Skyler." His mom's swear words were pretty impressive and pretty loud. "Skyler's talking me out of going next door and turning him into hamburger meat, but this is so not over. I have to do something."

"Stay right there," she said. "We'll be home as soon as we can. Ryan, promise me…. Better yet, put Skyler on the phone."

He handed the phone to Skyler, whose blotchy face went red again and he said, "Yeah, I'm okay." And then tears spilled out of his eyes again. He said *yeah* and *uh-huh* a bunch of times and then, "I will. Thanks, bye," and handed the phone back.

"What did she say?"

"She said that I was right to keep you away from him and that they were on their way. And that you would do anything for me, and I should put you to work so you don't lose it."

Ryan laughed in surprise. "Bitch. You shouldn't be taking care of me right now." He folded Skyler into his arms again. "What do you need?"

"I need you to stay with me."

"Done. What else? The locks? I'll show you how they work, okay?"

It didn't take long before Ryan had both doors reset. Skyler was shivering so Ryan wrapped him in a blanket and made him some hot chocolate.

Ryan's parents had to ring the doorbell to get in, and then Erin was hugging them and Skyler was trying not to cry. Dave brought a bottle of whiskey and four glasses to the kitchen table and asked them to sit.

"Dad," said Ryan, taking a sip and gritting his teeth, "there's something you might know about from a couple years ago." He told them what had happened two years before with Logan, including how often they had gotten together and what they had done. It was awkward as hell, and he blushed from his toenails to his hair, but he couldn't very well ask Skyler to talk about what had happened to him if he wasn't willing to provide the context himself. He tried to explain it to his dad, that guys didn't gross him out in general, but that Logan, specifically, didn't really turn on any love buttons, and that he'd never thought Logan cared much beyond a friendship either. Dave just listened and nodded and drank his whiskey like he wasn't losing his mind.

That led into skiing today and the argument he and Logan had had and then the call to Stevie and everything that she had said, including all the stuff about the candy jar and how each person had different things to offer and different favorites.

"I told her how I'm falling for Sky super hard and how confusing that is, and she, uh, she really helped." He stared at the table and then couldn't help but let his eyes flick to Sky's face.

Skyler wasn't the only one with his eyes bulging out.

"You mind telling them what Logan did while I was on the phone with Stevie?"

Skyler looked away, but he started up his story, leaving nothing out as well. Logan had let himself in, cornered him in the kitchen, and rubbed up against him, and then started following Skyler slowly around the kitchen island, telling him how Ryan had told him to come there and promised him that Skyler would "take care of him."

"I just kept backing up and saying no, and he just kept coming toward me and insisting that no one would have to know, and it wouldn't take long, and that it was what Ryan expected of me. I told him to leave, but he said it wasn't even my house. He had more right to be there than I did, and he could do what he wanted. I thought about running for the bathroom, but he's such a big guy, I wasn't sure I could lock the door before he caught me, and I had this feeling that if I ran, it would make him rush me and do something more… angry."

Dave put a hand on his arm. "You did just fine. You kept him talking until Ryan got home. I'm just glad that the situation didn't blow up into something even worse. Do you want to call the police?"

"No." Skyler sighed. "If he's that good at lying, I'd rather not hear anything else out of his mouth. There's no way to make him confess anyway."

Dave pursed his lips. "Do you mind if we try and handle it from here on? I can think of a method or two that might work."

Ryan's mom said, "This was a desperate move, Dave. Logan is obviously in a dangerous place. I might be able to defuse the situation with him, but I think his parents are in serious denial."

"I knew things were tense, but I had no idea it had gotten that ugly," said Dave. "I think forcing the truth out into the open is long overdue in that household. Skyler might be right about the lying, though. What if we tell him I installed a nanny cam? That we caught him on tape."

"He wouldn't buy that unless he saw the tape himself," said Ryan.

"Not if we offered to show it to him in front of his parents."

"Dave, I think honesty is always the best policy. Lies just complicate things."

"Call it backup, honey. We do things your way and then if that doesn't work, well, we have options." He got up and pulled the SD card out of his camera. "Props make things more believable. Can I see your phone, Ryan? It tracks your calls, right?" Ryan brought up the call log and there was the time of his call to his sister. Dave turned to Skyler. "I think it's important that you see this. In case you start wondering what really happened later. Can you tell me something that he said, Skyler? Can you remember anything word for word? Anything he wouldn't want his parents to hear?"

"Yeah. He said, 'What's the problem? Ryan said you suck guys off all the time. Isn't that why he brought you up here, so we could have a little fun?'"

Ryan pushed his chair back and stood up. "That piece of shit! I can't believe I was ever friends with him!"

Ryan's mom put her hand on Skyler's arm, "Oh, honey. I'm so sorry. That must have been so awful. I hope you know Ryan isn't like that."

Dave said, "Yeah, and he wouldn't have shared all that really personal stuff with us for someone he wanted to use." Dave looked really serious. "I'll admit, I was worried for you, Skyler, when Ry invited you up here. I think Ry's a pretty great catch, and I didn't want you to get hurt if you thought so too." He sighed. "I guess I was scared for him too. For what it would mean for him. But you're a great kid, okay? This isn't in any way your fault." He looked at Erin. "And luckily I have a wonderful wife who can set me straight when I'm being an asshole. You want to go over there now, honey?" She nodded.

Everyone stood up. Ryan's mom hugged Skyler, and Dave wrapped his arms around Ryan and pounded him on the back. "I'm impressed that you boys came to us and were able to lay all of this out on the table. I know that took real balls. It would have been way easier to make this situation way worse."

"Well I was all for caving Logan's face in, but Skyler wouldn't let me. The next-best revenge is to sic Mom on him. Probably cause him more pain anyway, so that's okay by me."

"Gee thanks, honey"—she rolled her eyes—"but you need to recognize that if he's desperate enough to do something like this, he could very well be a suicide risk as well. He's painted himself into a mental corner. Can you boys deal with dinner? Order pizza if you want. I've told Erika to come back here instead of going to their place. She might want to bring Emma"—she looked at Skyler—"Logan's sister.

And if you want us to drive you out of here tonight, we will, okay? Or we can go to a hotel in Kelowna and then come back tomorrow and pack up. That's fine too. You're not trapped here."

"I'm okay. The locks are changed, so it's cool."

She kissed him on the cheek. "The option stays open. Think about it."

After they left, the house was quiet and Ryan looked at him. "Sorry about all that. God, that was embarrassing, but I think it'll be worth it."

"Thanks for telling them all that stuff. It made it a lot easier."

"I think they need to know it now. It's time."

"Yeah?" Skyler held onto the banister at the top of the stairs like he was steadying himself.

"Yeah. Can I hug you?"

They stood in the kitchen for a while, just leaning against each other. "I missed you today," Ryan said into Skyler's hair.

"You weren't gone that long. A couple hours?" Sky shifted in his arms.

"I know. Pathetic, right? But I didn't want to go skiing without you. I know you probably want time by yourself or something, but I don't think I can give you that now that this has happened."

Sky huffed out an attempt at a laugh. "That is so fine by me."

"Hey, I'm trying to say something. I mean, you know that I like taking care of you, but do you get why? God, this isn't going very well."

Ryan put his hands on Skyler's biceps and leaned in slowly for a kiss. He kept his eyes on Skyler's and his breath and heart quickened. He watched Skyler close his eyes just before their lips touched, and then there was skin on skin. He pressed his lips down. Skyler's were so soft under him. He held it for a few seconds and then pulled back, searching Skyler's eyes.

"Help?" said Ryan. "I don't know how to say this."

Skyler swallowed. "You missed me?"

"Skyler, every minute I'm not with you, I'm missing you, and every minute I'm with you, I want to touch you."

"Yeah?"

"Yeah." Ryan closed his eyes. "Do you mind if we go upstairs for a while? I won't do anything. I just need you out of this kitchen and somewhere safer or something."

Skyler nodded and looked away. They headed for the stairs, but Ryan turned back. "Just a sec." He pulled a lasagna out of the freezer, shoved it in the oven, and set a timer.

Ryan put his arm around Skyler's waist as they walked up the first flight of stairs, and then Skyler led the way on the second, more narrow flight. Ryan admired his ass as it moved at face level ahead of him, but casually touching Sky just didn't feel right as he followed him inside. He needed to be careful. He needed to fix this right.

He slid the door shut and locked it, pulled the duvet and sheet back, and climbed in, holding them open for Skyler, who climbed in fully clothed as well.

When Skyler was in his arms again, front to front, Ryan breathed out a long breath. "That's better. God, I needed this." He kissed Skyler's head and squeezed him tighter. *It's time to man up. Don't let this heal over when it's still dirty inside.*

"Sky?"

"Yeah?"

"You believed him, didn't you? When Logan said I'd sent him here."

There was a silence.

"Kinda, yeah," Sky whispered.

Ryan closed his eyes. It was so awful to think of Sky hurt like that. *But have I given him any reason to trust me? How should he know how not-me that kind of thing is?*

"Sorry. I should have known." Skyler's voice was tight.

"Are you kidding? You have nothing to be sorry about! You kept your head when Mr. Manipulation decided to push you up against the wall, and you kept your head when I was going to lose mine. I can't believe you didn't cave in just to get him to leave you alone."

"Thanks." Skyler sounded offended.

"Hey, I did, didn't I? How many times did I buy his shit? 'We're just guys. It's how we are.' God, he had me wrapped around his finger. Or his fingers wrapped around me, I guess. He tends to get what he wants is all I'm saying."

"He didn't get you. Not really."

"No. I'm glad I saved my heart for somebody stronger and braver." Ryan kissed Skyler's ear. "Someone smarter and sweeter." He ran his hands down Skyler's back.

"Ryan?"

"Sorry. I'll be good."

"No, it's just that I want you to know I'm done giving myself away." Skyler pulled away a little.

"You are?" *Oh shit, what does that mean?*

"Yeah, I mean, that was why it was so easy to say no to him. Even if you had wanted me to do it. I'm not going to do that anymore. I didn't even consider it. If I'm with someone now, it's because they're trustworthy. Not because I want to impress someone, or because they know how to make me feel obliged."

Okay, maybe this isn't the end, then, maybe there's a way to fix it. "I hope I can be. Worthy. You know… eventually."

"Whatever! What about when you didn't fuck me, even though I was totally lost in it? And when you didn't go after Logan because you didn't want to risk me holding it against you? And I can't even talk about what you said to your parents yet. Jesus, that was fucking impressive. How many times have you sucked it up and told the truth, no matter how hard and embarrassing it was? That's what trustworthy is."

"Yeah? You know I didn't think there was much chance that you'd even consider me. Who knew that your candy was some guy spilling his guts? I can do that whenever you want." Ryan smiled.

Skyler laughed.

Ryan said, "I'm just worried that… if you could believe what he said, then, well then I haven't explained it right. I just wish I could explain it so that you got it. It's like… we match."

Skyler's breath gusted out of him. "Match? I can't be like you, Ryan. It's not just the straight-gay thing. It's all kinds of stuff!"

"What? Like what?"

Skyler edged out of his arms. "Like this house, for starters. Like this whole frickin' mountain. Dirt gets sucked up into some kind of insane millionaire vacuum hole!"

"We have it like this so we can rent it out."

"Okay, but what about your house back home? You've seen our place."

"I like your house."

"It's not a house, Ryan. It's a basement apartment that we rent in someone else's house."

"So what?"

"So I don't fit here."

"Okay, so fancy shit bugs you." Ryan propped himself up on his arm. "What else."

"Well, I'll never be able to keep up with you. I'm just not coordinated. I can't play soccer worth shit, I can't ski worth shit, I can't...."

"Whoa whoa whoa. So you feel like you can't compete with me physically?"

"Yeah!"

"Who says I want that? You think I only go out with girls who are great skiers? I actually like skiing alone. Well, I did before I got stuck in your tractor beam. Now I just want to crazy glue us together while you're asleep and pretend it was an accident." Ryan smiled but Skyler just scowled back at him.

"But what if this is just how you feel right this minute? What if it wears off and then you're stuck with the whole world thinking you're gay when it was just this one time?"

"Okay, I guess I deserve that because I didn't get it there for a while, but I'm that guy. Fuck. I really need to say this right and I don't know how so I'm just going to spell it out, okay? It's like, I want to tell you everything that goes through my head, and I want you to tell me everything you think and feel about... everything. I want to put my arms around you when you're sad. I want to beat the shit out of people who freak you out. I want you to never look at another guy ever again. I want to curl up around you every night. And... I want to explore your body, god, do I want to make you moan. I never want to be without you, and you know what? That makes me that guy that you hoped to help when you came out. That guy that wonders if it will be okay. It's okay to inspire some stranger, but it's not okay to inspire me to be myself?" Ryan wanted to reach for Skyler so badly but he held back.

Skyler's breath was coming fast, and he leaned in until their foreheads were touching. "Well, if you take out the 'straight' part, it does get a lot clearer. That was pretty hard to get around."

"If feeling this way means that I'm gay, then I'm gay. I'm lucky enough to be wired right to get to love you. How could I not be thankful for that?" Ryan ran his hand gently up and down Skyler's arm. "Get it?"

Skyler blinked a lot and then slid closer until his head was tucked snugly under Ryan's chin. God, it felt good to hold him, to feel the weight of Skyler's head slowly coming to rest on his chest, the tightness of his body starting to uncurl.

"So, what do you think your candy is, Sky?" Ryan whispered.

Skyler went still in his arms, and Ryan had a moment of dread. *What if he thinks it over, and I don't measure up?*

"I've got something for you. I'll be right back." Skyler climbed out of the bed and ran down the stairs. Ryan couldn't wait long and had started heading down the stairs when Sky came racing back up carrying Ryan's laptop.

"Sorry, it's hard to let you out of my sight." Ryan smiled sheepishly.

They climbed back onto the bed, and Skyler balanced the laptop on their pressed-together thighs. There was a video in the editing program Sky had set up, and he pressed full screen and then play.

The video started silently with a shot of snow blowing over the white ground and creating these little wave patterns like on a sandy beach, then the music started softly. Was that a harp? It took Ryan a minute to place the opening as Florence and the Machine's "Dog Days Are Over." As Florence's voice softly began, there was this chairlift shot of Ryan looking out over the white mountains stretching out into the distance and then turning back toward the camera, but you couldn't see his face because of the goggles and scarf. The snow ghosts slid slowly by like stooped robed wizards as the chair rose. The camera whizzed erratically over the ski hill map with all its color-coded runs snaking down, and then swung to Ryan, standing with his back to the sign, just absentmindedly stabbing his ski pole into the snow as he looked out over the mountain.

The music picked up and there was panorama footage of the landscape and view that captured what it felt like to be above the clouds and a close-up of the corduroy of the fresh grooming on the run. Then Ryan skiing, making some wide slow turns, the girls put-putting around on the snowmobiles, and Ryan shoveling like a fiend building the mound for the snow cave.

Florence sang about the dog days being over, and there was the hot tub, empty and steaming into the cold air, Ryan crawling through the snow cave, laughing and bonking the camera as he maneuvered. Then he was lying on his back on a sled, racing down the toboggan run next to the house and burying himself in snow at the bottom. Ryan looked like he was swaying to the beat as he skated backward on the outdoor rink, and then Ryan's and Skyler's arms crossed tight over each other on the tube handles as they whooshed down the tubing runs.

The song had a quiet part in the middle, and there was this beautiful shot of the clouds racing silently across the sky, which of course made Ryan think of lying on the cat track watching the clouds with Skyler, and he reached for Sky's hand and squeezed, never taking his eyes off the screen. *Did he shoot that today?* Sky certainly hadn't taken the camera out at the time.

When the beat came back, it was like the song really picked up speed and momentum, and here Sky had used the shot of Ryan jumping off the little cliff beside the house. He used both shots: the one Sky had taken from his own camera, and the one from Ryan's helmet cam so you got that big leap feeling of hanging in the air. It was timed so the moment he shot off the top, the music went crazy. Florence sang, about happiness hitting someone like a bullet in the back, a line that had never made sense to him, but thinking about Sky, it clicked now. *Blindsided. That's what I am.* And then there was more footage from his helmet cam. It was a bit shaky, but it really gave that feeling of motion and the speed of racing down the runs. It was interspersed with clips of Ryan climbing the ice tower, higher each time. The final shot of the climb, with him punching his ice axe up into the air and shouting, was cut back and forth with shots of him turning toward the camera, super close-up, with tiny star-shaped snowflakes in his hair.

The music went down to just clapping or stomping or whatever that rhythm was. The camera just stayed on that look on his face, wide open, and the smile that grew on his lips wasn't witty or charming, it was huge and filled with overwhelming love.

Ryan thought that was it, but then the song rocked out again, and there was another vista on the chairlift, but this time Sky's hand reached out and tugged the scarf down to see Ryan's face, smiling as he pointed at things. There was Ryan, one foot on top of the other as he leaned a hip on the fireplace and warmed himself.

It ended with a shot of Ryan, thinking he was posing for a photo, holding still at the top of a run with the sky behind him. But the sky wasn't just crazy blue, it also had that wild sparkle that shone and moved all around him like some wild living creature. He looked good. Not just "good-looking," but happy. Solidly, calmly happy with his poles planted firmly in the snow.

Ryan just sat there squeezing Sky's hand and staring at the black screen. It was too beautiful to even comment on. Something settled into his bones. He'd known how great Sky was, sure, but this was different. Sky wasn't just someone special and sweet, he was someone with this hidden superpower who could see what was perfect and beautiful and put those tiny pieces of life together into something so heart-crushingly gorgeous and exhilarating that the life itself shimmered and became something different. Something new. And if he could look at Ryan and do that? Maybe Ryan could become something more whole, or something that was never really broken in the first place.

Sky was just plain good for him.

He thought about climbing that tower and how he'd had a moment of pride and that familiar happy rage. He'd roared even. But it was short-lived. Lately it had felt like those kinds of conquests that had always lifted him up didn't change the big things, not really. But this.

This might change what was possible. The video hadn't ended on that hero shot of him on top of that fucking monolith. It had ended with his eyes and his smile.

Sky turned and put his nose in Ryan's hair. "There's just one kind of candy I'm looking for," whispered Sky. "Love. I think I've always been craving someone who really knows how to."

Ryan put his arms around Skyler, or tried to, and he ended up crushing their joined hands between them as the other arm pulled their bodies tight together. He pulled back to look at Sky, and those warm brown eyes sliding closed and his lips opening ever so slightly for a kiss was such a relief that Ryan actually had this intense pain in his chest at the sweetness of that moment. *Maybe that's my heart bursting.* Their lips touched and Ryan felt like he'd somehow won so much more than just Sky's body. More than even the astounding gift of his friendship.

Or maybe that's just my heart growing to be able to hold this much at once.

It was a pain he hoped would never stop stretching him.

Check out this excerpt from

King of Rain

A West Coast Boys Novel

By Michele Fogal

Being uber-tall and broad made it easy for Logan to hide his sexuality and vulnerability behind armor made of strength, ambition, and emotional detachment. His mask of macho success is shattered when he discovers the friend he's carried a secret torch for has a boyfriend, and everything he's always wanted now belongs to someone else. Logan can't pretend not to care anymore, as his rage erupts in a horrible act of revenge. It's impossible to hide his demons, now that they've broken loose.

Since losing his sweet boyfriend, Jeremy's loud and proud life of sex parties and clubbing feels empty. When he meets the dark and self-destructive Logan, Jeremy recognizes the demons he sees in Logan's eyes. After all, he has plenty of his own.

Logan isn't looking for love, he's looking for punishment and release, but with Jeremy all three seem momentarily possible... until he learns his victim was Jeremy's lost love. Logan doesn't expect forgiveness and knows he doesn't deserve a real life, but after a taste of intimate closeness, finding salvation alone will mean he has to change, or die trying.

Coming soon to
http://www.dreamspinnerpress.com

CHAPTER 1—JEREMY

SURE, HE'D caught me cheating, but I still thought I could charm him back into my bed. That's how much of a prick I was. He was just a soft kid. Or so I thought.

I knew he adored me, and so I waited. I let him suffer some weeks on his own. I mean, really, all the gay friends he'd made in the 'hood were actually my friends. Let him realize that. And let the sting fade a bit, maybe. That never hurt.

We'd broken up over Christmas, so at the end of January, I texted him—early evening, so he'd have all night to think about it. It said, I miss you , and I left it at that. No point in saying I was sorry yet. There'd be time for that later, once I had him within touching distance again.

He didn't reply. I was a little surprised. I thought he'd at least want to tell me off, and any argument was an opening. Silence was harder to work with.

I waited a few days. Still nothing. On the third day, I figured the chance of him answering was getting smaller, so I texted again. Can we go for coffee?

I got an e-mail half an hour later, and all it had in it was a YouTube link of this Lily Allen song called "Fuck You." It was even the version with the lyrics so I wouldn't miss a word. It was pretty hilarious actually. It had this fluffy little melody with those damning words.

This was going to be harder than I'd thought, but it was still an opening, right? And I was the guy that knew how to work an opening. There was a line in the song I thought I could use, so I called him.

There's nothing like a good offense, I always say, so I started in right after he said hello. "What the fuck, Sky? You don't answer my texts, and now you're sending me songs about being a homophobe? I thought you cared about me." That was really low after what I'd done, but my plan would work better if he could blast me a bit to start with. He'd start mad, and then I could work him around with some hard-won words of regret.

I wasn't expecting him to laugh.

But that's what he did. He laughed. I couldn't believe it. Seriously, the kid had been mooning all over me for like six months. I couldn't think of once during all that time he'd ever stood up to me. He'd had these big brown doe eyes for me, and he'd done everything I ever wanted him to do. Well, with the exception of hanging on to the iPhone that I'd given him. I'd wanted him to keep it, but he just walked out without it.

"Excuse me?" I said. "You think I'm kidding?" I really couldn't think of anything less lame than that.

"Jeremy, you are hilarious. Still working an angle. Nice try."

"What? I'm the one calling you after you—"

"Oh, cut the shit." His voice got hard. I'd never heard that before. "I'm so done with your fucking weasel-ass lying."

"I'm not—"

"I said shut it! Now listen up, asshole. You set up the rules about cheating, and you broke them. You know it. I know it. It's done. Over."

"Hey, baby, you're right, okay? I had too much to drink and it just—"

"Save it. I don't even care. And about that song? It totally suits you. You think you're all, like, King-of-the-Gayborhood who knows how the whole thing should be, but you know what? You're not. All I wanted was to love you. You know that? I wanted to give you everything—my body, my future, my family, my heart—and you just looked at that and thought I was weak. You ARE nothing but a fucking homophobe. You fuck and you fuck, but you never let anyone get close, do you? You never let anyone love you. Well, good luck with that. I hope it makes you real fucking happy."

The line was silent for a moment. I literally couldn't think of a thing to say. The kid was still in high school, for fuck's sake. Suddenly, I wanted him back so bad it hurt. It was like something in my chest was crumpling like an empty beer can.

"Sky, please...." What the hell? I never said please. And my voice sounded weird and needy. That wasn't me. "I can try and—"

And then he said it.

"I'm with someone else now."

It was like something crashed into me. I suddenly got it that I didn't have a chance. Why had I thought he would be suffering alone? Just because he'd said it was so hard to meet someone in high school? He was beautiful. Tall, lean—what was I thinking leaving him alone for more than a couple of weeks? I'd played this all wrong, but it just got worse. He kept talking.

"For some reason, my boyfriend thinks I'm amazing and brave and strong. He thinks that me wanting to share myself with someone is, like, the luckiest break he's ever had. So just fucking skip it, okay? Just skip the fucking texts and e-mails and calls trying to work me over for one more lay. You never once came to meet my mom. You never once just held me because I needed it. It was all about sex and what YOU wanted, and you know what? You're a cold lover, and I wouldn't have your hands on me again even if my boyfriend dumps me and I never find anyone else. I never want to feel that alone again."

And then he hung up.

I just sat there on the edge of my bed and blinked. I couldn't think. I had this spooky numb feeling, like when you cut yourself and you don't feel it yet but you can see the blood pouring out and your heart starts to hammer because you know that the pain is coming? Yeah, like that.

I set my phone down on the bed. No, there really was no point in calling him back. All I would get was more of those words, and I really couldn't stand the thought of hearing him say anything else. God, if I could just unhear the things he HAD said. But I couldn't. I looked down, and my hands were shaking. Shit. I was like an accident victim with no CPR and no ambulance to call. I had no clue what to do. I have to get out of here! I stood up and flung open my bedroom door.

MICHELE FOGAL refused to learn to read as a child, but once she got started, she was completely hooked. She did a degree in creative writing straight out of high school and received the Roy Daniell's Scholarship for creative writing and the Norman L. Rothstein Memorial Scholarship for poetry. Then her biological clock went off like an air-raid siren, and she left the starving artist world behind in favor of a corporate job with benefits to help pad the nest. When her kids were born, her passion for stories about hope and love resurged with a vengeance. Now, she is fusing worlds—writing love stories by night and running her online communications business by day, while she lives with her kids and the love of her life in Vancouver, BC. Her home is nestled on a rainy mountainside at the edge of the wilderness, but within the limits of a coastal city. The local overlap between urban technology, wild biosphere and various cultures has given her the opportunity to see how diverse elements can converge into something new, unique and sacred.

Find out more about her and her work here:

Author Site & Blog: http://www.michelefogal.com

Twitter: https://twitter.com/michelefogal

The Books I Love & My Reviews on GoodReads:
http://www.goodreads.com/michelefogal

Facebook: https://www.facebook.com/MicheleFogalAuthor

To you'll always know your way.

SPARK
POSY ROBERTS

NORTH STAR TRILOGY BOOK ONE

http://www.dreamspinnerpress.com

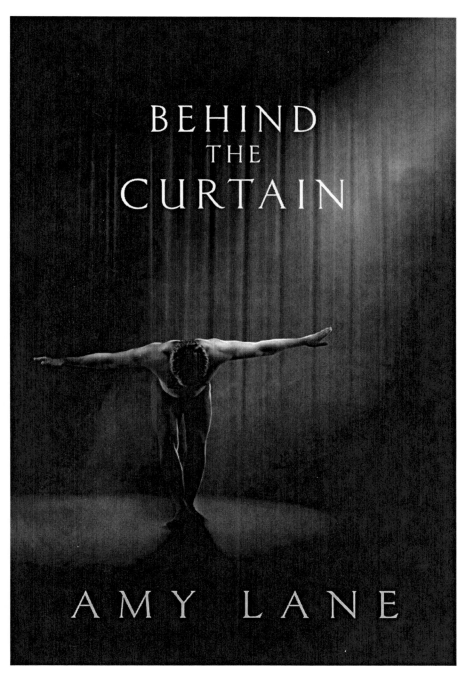

BEHIND
THE
CURTAIN

AMY LANE

http://www.dreamspinnerpress.com

CPSIA information can be obtained at www.ICGtesting.com
Printed in the USA
BVOW05s2109150316

439717BV00007B/13/P

9 781627 989596